AN
EASY
DEATH

Center Point
Large Print

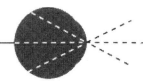

**This Large Print Book carries the
Seal of Approval of N.A.V.H.**

Gunnie Rose:

BOOK 1

AN
EASY
DEATH

CHARLAINE HARRIS

CENTER POINT LARGE PRINT
THORNDIKE, MAINE

This Center Point Large Print edition
is published in the year 2020 by arrangement with
Saga Press, a division of Simon & Schuster, Inc.

Portions of this book were previously published within
the anthology *Unfettered II* published by Grim Oak Press,
in the short story "The Gunnie" copyright © 2016 by
Charlaine Harris Schulz

The text of this Large Print edition is unabridged.
In other aspects, this book may vary
from the original edition.
Printed in the United States of America
on permanent paper.
Set in 16-point Times New Roman type.

ISBN: 978-1-64358-557-4

The Library of Congress has cataloged this record
under Library of Congress Control Number: 2019956938

For my husband of so many years, Hal.
I couldn't have done any of this without you.

ACKNOWLEDGMENTS

My thanks to Taylor Anderson, weapons expert and expert writer, for his advice and time on guns, and to my Patrick, for his gentle corrections, too. Daniel Hale gave me help with the French dialogue—thanks, Dan! As always, my agent, Joshua Bilmes, and the staff of JABberwocky have given me all the support and guidance a literary agency can give, as have Debbie Deuble-Hill, Steve Fisher, and Kyle Loftus at APA, my book-to-TV and movie team, on the West Coast. My assistant and friend, Paula Woldan; my web maven Dawn Fratini; and my Twitter expert, Presley Bumgarner, have been constants in helping me. There are many more people I could and should thank—like Toni LP Kelner, aka Leigh Perry, and Dana Cameron, my friends and beta readers—but I have to leave someone for the next book.

AN
EASY
DEATH

CHAPTER ONE

In the morning I got Chrissie to cut off all my hair. Tarken and Martin would be tinkering with the truck, which was our livelihood. Galilee would be watching Martin, because they had started seeing each other before and after work. Or she would be cleaning her little house, or washing her clothes. I never saw Galilee bored or idle.

But I didn't have to be at Martin's until late that afternoon, so I was doing whatever I pleased. That morning I was pleased to get rid of my hair.

My neighbor Chrissie was not too bright, but I'd watched her trim her husband's hair and beard as he sat on a stool outside their cabin. She'd done a good job. She sang as she worked, in her sweet, high voice, and she told me about her youngest one's adventures with a frog in the creek.

When she was halfway done, she said, "Why you want to cut all this off? It's so pretty."

"It gets all sweaty and sticks to my neck," I said. Which was true. It was only spring now, but it would be the hot season soon.

"You better wear you a hat so your head won't get all red and tender," Chrissie said. "You want it so short I think the sun might get your scalp."

"I'll take care," I said, holding up the only little mirror Chrissie had. I could see part of my head at a time. She'd washed it, so my hair was wet. I thought it was about an inch long. Looked like the curl was gone, but I wouldn't know until it dried.

"You heading out soon? I saw them farmers at Martin's place, when I was coming back from the store." Chrissie's trousers had long tendrils of dark hair all over 'em now. She'd have to brush 'em.

"Yeah, we're leaving as soon as it's near dark."

"Ain't you scared?"

Sure, I was. "Of course not, the only ones should be scared are anyone who tries to get in our way." I smiled.

"You'll kill 'em dead, bang, bang," Chrissie said in a singsong voice.

"Yep. Bang, bang," I agreed.

"Why are they going to New America?"

"The farmers? The part of Texas they live in got swallowed up by Mexico a few years ago. You remember?"

Chrissie looked dim. She shook her head.

"Anyway, the government down there has been telling the Texans that they're not real Mexicans, and their land is forfeit."

Chrissie looked even dimmer.

"Their land is getting taken. So if they've got kin up north or anywhere, even in Dixie, they got to leave Mexico to have a chance."

12

Dixie was so poor and so dangerous you'd have to be desperate to flee there.

Chrissie ran her fingers through the short hair on the left side of my head, and shook her head. "Anyone ever go to the HRE?" she asked.

"Chrissie," I said. She bent around to meet my eyes.

"Oh, sorry, Lizbeth." She began to work on the right side, following her own whim. I tried to remember if I'd ever seen her cut anyone's hair besides Norton's. "I forgot you don't like them grigoris."

No. I did not like magicians.

"Tarken know you're doing this?" she said after a moment. I could tell by the faraway sound of her voice that the question had come from her mouth, not her head.

"No, he doesn't have a say in my hair. Don't you go telling."

"He'll see it this afternoon."

"Yeah, it's a surprise," I said.

Chrissie gave me one of those looks that reminded me she was older than I was. "He ain't gonna like it, Lizbeth."

I raised up my shoulders, very carefully, because I didn't want to jolt her hand. "Not *his* head," I said, and that was the truth. But it was also true that he'd tried to tell me how I should do something one time too many.

When Chrissie had finished, and the little

mirror told me it was cut evenly all over—God knows how—I paid her. She gave me a big smile before she carried the chair inside. She came back out to pump some water to wash her hands, and put some in a bucket to toss around, trying to spread out the long, dark hair that lay in a heap where the chair had stood.

I gave her a hand. When the dirt didn't look like the sky had snowed black ringlets, I went uphill to my place.

Getting ready to leave didn't take long. We should only be gone maybe three nights, at most. And we might even spring for a room in one of the hotels in Corbin . . . providing Tarken was speaking to me by then. We'd get the farmers up to their waiting family, then we'd come right home. It was the most common run we made, and Martin and Tarken had cleared a road to there, mostly on an old paved one. They'd moved all the big rocks and trees, scouted out the likely ambush sites, and so on.

Corbin was over the border in New America, which was where almost all our cargo was bound. It was a bustling town with a number of places to stay, a garage for cars, a stable for horses, a post office, a good general store.

I'd worked for Tarken for two years now, maybe a bit over, and he'd been my man for four months. The first time we went to bed, he told me he'd been waiting until I was old enough.

I hadn't even realized he was looking at me. I'm slow that way. But I'm quick with a gun, that's what counts.

I would never have known I had a talent if my stepfather, Jackson, hadn't taken me hunting with him when I was little. Jackson had seen me snatch a fly out of the air, he told me later, and he'd thought I had the quick hands and the instincts you needed to be a gunnie.

Jackson was right. The first time I held a rifle in my hands, I knew I'd found my calling. My mother didn't like it, of course, but at least I could support myself—and be out in the open—doing something useful. People need protection.

I stuck a pair of pants and a shirt into my small leather bag, a pair of underpants, my toothbrush, and a comb. Packing was done. I'd fill my canteens before I left.

Next I cleaned my old 1873 Winchester, a lever action and a great rifle. It had been my grandfather's. He'd called it Jackhammer, so I did, too. Jackson had given me matched Colt 1911s for close work, and those were already clean after my last target-shooting session out in the empty land around Segundo Mexia. I could fire twenty-seven bullets with all three, had extra magazines ready for the Colts. If I couldn't bring our enemies down with that much firepower, our enemies had an army.

Galilee would bring her rifle, a Krag, since

she was better at long shooting. I'd use the Winchester for the nearer work. She and Martin and Tarken all had pistols, too, though Tarken's was less than a great tool.

Our truck and our firepower had worked for two years. We'd made this same run often.

Winchester in its sling over my back, pistols in their holsters and ready to go, two full canteens on one shoulder, my little leather bag with clothes and extra ammo on another; I was ready. I set off down the path to town.

People were coming home from work, and Chrissie was cooking on a grill outside her cabin, the smoke rising up and the smell of meat giving the air a nice tang. "Good shooting!" she called in her soft voice.

I nodded. I passed Rex Santino. "Easy death," he said in his gruff way.

That's what people wished gunnies. It made me feel good. I nodded back at him.

I didn't want to walk down Main Street. There were too many people. One of them was my mother, who lived with Jackson in a real nice house just off Main. She didn't like to see me leave on a job. That weakened me, too. I took a roundabout way to Martin's house, which situated in a bare dirt lot on the last street north in Segundo Mexia.

Martin's chickens squawked in their pen as I came into the yard. He was strewing feed and

16

smiling, just a little. He sure liked those stupid chickens. His neighbor's kids would come in to feed them while Martin was gone, in exchange for eggs. We do a lot of barter in Segundo Mexia.

The setting sun struck Martin's head with a golden glow. For the first time I noticed that his light hair had a lot of gray sprinkled in. I would pick my time to tease him about it.

Galilee wasn't there yet. Tarken was putting the cans of extra gas on the bed of the truck, and he gave me a sideways smile, which froze when he realized my hair was gone. After a minute he closed his eyes, shook his head, and started back to working.

I'd hear about this later. I smiled. It was going to be fun.

Most of the cargo was sitting on the dirt of the yard or on Martin's front porch. Two of the children were playing a game of hopscotch on the grid they'd drawn in the dirt. I nodded in their direction. I would talk to them when I couldn't dodge it.

The sky went lower, the people on the porch shared out food among themselves, and I went into Martin's kitchen and ate some bread and some dried fruit. I couldn't handle meat before a job.

Galilee came in to sit with me, her Krag under her arm. She had on a gun belt with one pistol, maybe not as fine as my Colts—but the Colts were courtesy of Jackson, so I didn't crow about them . . . much. Her hair stood out from her head like a huge black puff, and she was very skinny and dark. "My friend, you look a sight," she said when she got a good look at me.

"Yeah. Like it?"

"Hell, no. You had the prettiest white-person hair I ever saw. Why'd you do it?"

"Tarken liked it too much."

"So you decided you'd show him what was what."

I shrugged. "More or less."

"Girl. Sometimes I can tell you are so young."

I didn't know what that meant, so I didn't answer. Only, I'd figured since Tarken spent so long running his fingers through my hair, straightening out each ringlet to watch it bounce back into curl, he'd better pay more attention to the girl whose scalp it grew on.

Galilee talked about other stuff. "Freedom built a chair for his little house," she told me. Her son Freedom, who'd been born when Galilee was only fourteen, had moved out of his mom's house when he left school and had gotten a job at the tannery. Now he'd built his own place. (And a chair.)

"He going to find a carpenter to apprentice to?" I couldn't think of anyone around who'd be ready to hire. Bobby Saw already had a girl working for him.

Galilee lost some smile. "You know Freedom.

That boy can't stick with nothing. At least, not that he's found yet."

"That boy" and I were nearly the same age. At least Freedom had stuck with the tannery job. Though he didn't like the work, it was steady money. He kept looking for something else, but nothing had suited him yet. Last time I'd seen him in a bar, he'd groused about it nonstop. He was lucky his girlfriend was sticking with him. Complaining is not attractive.

Martin came in to get a drink, kissed Galilee on the cheek as he went by. My eyebrows tried to climb into my hair, what was left of it. "Well," I said when he'd gone back out. "You're out in the open with it. When did that happen?"

She didn't meet my eyes, but she was smiling again. "Just seemed like it was time. We're getting along good, we want to spend more time together than we are. Ain't no big thing."

"Yet."

"Yet," she agreed.

"Lizbeth," Tarken called from the yard.

"Time to work," Galilee said, and we washed our plates and went to the outhouse and then to the truck. It was spring, days lengthening, and the sun didn't want to give up the sky. There were no clouds, and I stood looking up, seeing the vastness above me, nothing between me and the hereafter. I had my place, standing here on this dirt.

Tarken gave us the nod. He and Martin were taking one last-minute look at the engine.

Galilee and I turned to the cargo. "Time to load up," I called. "Sit in the center, looking out. Her and me, we got to stand up, her at the right side close to the back, me at the left side, closer to the front." I pointed. I had to be clear. They were nervous.

Tarken would cover the straight-ahead from the passenger seat in the cab.

Martin had already arranged their bags against the sides, with two gaps left for me and Galilee just where we wanted them. The cargo had brought too much stuff, but they'd tried to pack it all in. They hated to leave things. This was all they had in the world.

The long, flat bed had sides Martin and Tarken had built, wooden uprights and horizontal planks, to hold everyone and everything in. Provided a little protection, too. And that gave Galilee and me a stable frame to lean on. We would go in last.

The families were standing, milling around, putting it off. "Load up," I called with a little more push to my voice.

They obeyed. One man went in first, to help pull up the wives and the children, while the other remained on the ground to boost 'em up. The younger couple had a baby and a couple of littles, maybe six and four. The older couple had a girl, grown, and another girl about thirteen, and a boy, younger but not a baby. The men were brothers. They'd had farms side by side in south Texas, but when it had become Mexico, they had gradually been pushed out. Their older brother, they'd told Martin, was the one paying for their trip to New America. He was smarter; he'd sold his farm while he still had title to it, and bought land north of Corbin.

It seemed to take a long time, but finally they were all in. Galilee and I scrambled up and took our places. It was Galilee's turn to talk.

"Hear me," she said, and they all turned their faces to her. Dixie people wouldn't have listened to a black woman, but these farmers did. She had the way and voice of someone who knew what she was doing. Her rifle spoke for her, too.

Galilee gave them the usual lecture about staying low and helping us keep watch. They all nodded, even the littles, scared just about shitless. Our prime worry was bandits, who wanted anything they could get: guns, goods, the human cargo. The guns and goods could be used or sold. The humans could be robbed or raped, and then sold to a bordello that wasn't too choosy.

If the New America patrols stopped us, we'd be fine. People were legal cargo, and respectable people like this were even welcome in New America. But if bandits caught us, well, that was why Galilee and I were on duty. That was why the oldest brother had hired us to get the two families through the lawless land along the border between Texoma and New America.

Martin had climbed into the driver's seat, and Tarken had taken the shotgun position, as usual. I stretched forward to rap on the cab roof, letting them know she'd made the speech. The engine began to rumble, and we lurched out of the yard.

As we were leaving Segundo Mexia, I spotted Freedom walking by the side of the road and gave him a yell. At the sight of the truck, he took off his hat and waved it at his mother, who raised her hand in farewell.

"See you soon, son!" she called.

I could feel the farm people's eyes going from the boy to his mother. The two were not exactly the same color. Galilee had gotten pregnant by the son of the landowner her parents worked for. Her parents had sacrificed to help Galilee run away. In Dixie, kids who didn't look like their black mothers were in for a very hard time.

After many adventures, mostly bad, some good, Galilee had ended up in Segundo Mexia. But along the way, she'd learned to shoot. She had a skill. I trusted her with my life.

We were on a good part of the road, one that hadn't been broken. There still stretches around like that. My mother had told me that once almost all the roads were smooth, and that when they cracked, they got repaired. It sounded like a fancy dream. Since we were with the cargo, Galilee caught my eye and raised her rifle just a little. She was asking if I expected trouble.

Kind of to my own surprise, I nodded.

Galilee's eyebrows went up. She was asking me why.

"Full moon," I mouthed, with a tiny point upward.

Galilee shook her head, looking exasperated, her puff of hair flying around her face. She held up three fingers. Nothing had happened for the last three trips.

I held one hand palm up. *Anybody's guess,* I was telling her. I didn't want to jinx us.

Most likely, nothing would happen. We'd done this run dozens of times since I'd joined the crew. We'd had firefights, sure. We'd lost one crew member, an older guy named Solly. He'd taken a bullet to the stomach.

His had been the opposite of an easy death.

But we'd always gotten our cargo where they intended to go, except for two souls. One woman's appendix had ruptured (at least that's what we thought had happened), and she'd died in the middle of nowhere. One boy had been snakebit, and we couldn't control snakes. So we had a good record.

I clamped down hard on my bad feeling and stuffed it away to nowhere. I had to be all in this moment.

"You don't look any older than my seventeen-year-old," said the older farm wife. Her husband had called her Ruth. Ruth glanced at her daughter with pride and fondness.

"I'm older." By barely two years.

Ruth wanted to say more. She was trying to look at my shorn head without making a federal case of it. She decided against comment. Good. I didn't want to talk to them, get to know them. In less than a day, they'd be gone.

I remember running my hand over my short hair. Thinking my skull felt clean and cool as the air whooshed over it. I was pleased with the feeling, though Tarken had given me several more fierce faces while we were loading up.

But Martin had laughed. "You better buy a dress," he'd said, "so we can remember you're a girl."

"You'd never mistake this one for a boy," Galilee had answered. "Now, me . . ." And she'd looked down at her slim body. But Martin had looked as though he liked her just like she was. It was nice.

When we set out, there was enough light that we could make out the landscape—scrubby bushes and cactus, the low, rolling bumps we called hills. Same as everywhere around Segundo Mexia. There were rocky outcrops here and there. Lots of bare dirt.

As Martin usually did, he followed the remains

of the north road. After an hour he had to go slower. We'd reached a section in much worse shape. Might have been laid sometime in the late twenties, never repaired since.

The little kids had been talking to one another or asking their parents questions that couldn't be answered. How long it would take, if Uncle Joshua would be in Corbin when they got there, how long it would be before they got to his farm, if he had children they could play with, how many cattle he had . . .

At first the adults tried to say cheerful things, and act like all was easy and well. But gradually they began to snap a little, and the kids shut up.

Two hours into the run, there was no talking or laughing. The moon was full, but there were some clouds between me and it, and I only caught a peek at it from time to time. I didn't like my view of the sky being blocked. With my left hand I held on to one of the slats; I felt a nailhead, about my waist level, sticking out. I ran my thumb over it. I told myself I'd see to that when we returned.

Because of the clouds, Martin was running with headlights, had to. So even if the engine noise didn't announce we were coming, the headlights did. Galilee and I were paying attention, watching for anything on the ground on either side of the dusty road. That was our job. And we were doing it just as well as usual.

Every other time we'd been attacked, we'd

seen movement, heard yelling, caught a glint of our headlights reflecting off metal. Some clue, some warning.

Tonight the bullets came out of nowhere.

I yelled "Down!" as I fired back, working the lever immediately to chamber another round. I'd marked the flash pretty accurately. The bandit was close. A scream told me I'd gotten him. But there was someone else a bit farther back from the road, out of my range, and I didn't kill him in time. He didn't die before he got a bullet through the cab.

Later I figured the bandit killed Martin with that shot. Because the truck started veering all over and I had to grab the slats to stay in the truck. No way I could fire back. I'd heard the sound of Galilee's Krag, but she was closer to the open rear of the flatbed than I was. I guess she couldn't grab hold in time. One second Galilee was there. The next she was gone, without a sound.

Tarken must have reached over to grab the wheel to try to keep us going, because we straightened out for a few seconds. That was long enough for me to get my balance, fire a shot to let the bandits know we were still putting up a fight. I heard the familiar sound of the driver's door opening, and I glimpsed Martin's body tumbling out of the cab. Tarken had shoved him out to take the driver's seat. When Martin's body hit the road, it kind of bounced and then lay still.

Some excited gunman had shot at the movement of the body, and the bullet ricocheted off the hood of the truck, and I was stung by the tiny fragments that were flung out by the impact.

But I couldn't think about any of this because the headlights raked a figure scrambling through the scrubby trees along the road to keep up. Even as I fired at the bandit, I saw he'd stopped and aimed. The truck lurched, my gun belt caught on the damn nail, and the world came to an end.

CHAPTER TWO

For a while.

When I came to, I was in the middle of a clump of bushes and large rocks. It wasn't dawn, but it was close. A snake was gliding by me. I could just make out that it was a rattlesnake, its tongue flickering out to catch movement. I didn't move. I wasn't sure I could, anyway. I pretended to myself I was choosing not to stir.

The birds were singing, so the gunfire and screaming were long over.

The birds didn't care that I had a bitch of a headache.

I wanted to groan, but I knew I had to make not a scritch nor a screech till I got the lay of the land. When the snake was gone, I looked at myself, as best I could without much movement. I couldn't see a bullet hole; I couldn't see more than a little blood. That was on my hand where it had been under my cheek. My hand was waking up now, and it stung.

Maybe I'd been shot in the head? Because I could tell now that was what really hurt; it throbbed like hell. If I'd taken a bullet to the head, I couldn't imagine why I wasn't dead.

My gun belt was gone. Jackhammer was gone. It was as bad as being naked in public.

I had to get up and find my crew.

I really tried to move, but my head pounded with a terrible pain, and I just couldn't.

Hoping it would ease my head, I even shut my eyes. It was hard to think, I hurt so bad, but I made myself focus out. At first I heard nothing but the damn birds. Then I heard the wind, its quiet, smooth noise moving the grass and tree leaves. Then, it seemed to me, I heard a sigh, a human sigh. Repeated. Repeated.

When I heard nothing more threatening than that, no voices or shots, I figured it was safe to get out from behind the rocks. The first time I made it to my hands and knees, I vomited.

I waited a bit, trembling.

The second time I made the attempt, I managed to crawl out of my little hidden space. Being cautious, watching and listening. I moved real slowly, stopping every few seconds to taste the air like the snake had done. I wanted every clue I could gather about what had happened around me before I made it known I was alive. If there was anyone to tell.

The truck had rolled over onto the driver's side, but it had landed propped up thanks to a boulder with a flat top. The door on the passenger's side was open. The bandits had been in there searching for whatever they could loot. Or maybe someone had crawled out. After I saw the truck, saw the damage, did not see any living person, I threw up again. I felt better after that, but very thirsty. I'd had a drink from my canteen back in Segundo Mexia, before we'd set out. That must have been twelve hours ago now, give or take.

Some people would never be thirsty again.

The almost-grown girl in the older family, the seventeen-year-old, she hadn't made it. There must have been more gunfire after I'd been hit. She'd tried to run. Lots of families taught their girls to run, figuring that a bullet in the back was quicker than what waited for them after capture. My opinion, sometimes they were right.

Sure enough, the wound was in her back. She'd died very quickly. I knew 'cause there wasn't much blood. She was sprawled in the middle of the road, as if she'd been running back the way we'd come when she was hit.

A few yards past her, I could see Martin's body, lying in a heap at the point where Tarken had shoved him out of the truck. Though my vision was fuzzy from the poor light and whatever was wrong with my head, I could see a long, dark line a few yards beyond that; that would be Galilee. From the way Martin and Galilee were lying, it was clear they were dead. I could see blood around them, as extra proof. I did not have the strength to reach them to close their eyes. And I did not have a gun.

I could see something sprawled a ways back, figured it was the bandit I'd shot. There should be another one back in the brush off the road. I didn't have the energy or inclination to find the body.

After five minutes of crawling and collapsing, pushing up to crawl again, I rounded the truck to find Tarken on the other side. It was him making the noise. He'd taken a bullet in the leg and one in the shoulder, small caliber. That's why he was still alive to sigh. I tried to get to my feet so I could move faster, but I got all dizzy. Not possible. In fact, I could not stay up on my knees any longer. I inched along on my belly until I reached him.

"Tarken," I said, just to let him know I was there. I eased onto my side, so I could look at him. We hadn't been together long, not even sharing a roof yet. But this was very hard.

"Lizbeth," he said. "You're alive." He sounded pleased. He sounded like he was dying.

"Yeah. At the moment." My head hurt so bad I wasn't sure that was going to last.

"They said I wasn't . . . worth a bullet. They could tell I wasn't . . . going to make it. They took . . . the clients." He got all this out between the deep breaths. He'd turned his head enough to look me in the eyes. "I climbed out of the . . . truck. Hoped I could follow 'em."

With two bullets in him.

"The oldest girl, she's dead," I told him. "She took one in the back."

"Her mom told her to run." Tarken took a deep breath, let it out. The sigh.

"Her mom was smart."

"She screamed a bit, though. When the girl died." Tarken's mouth turned up a little, almost smiling at the silliness of human nature. I knew him well.

"Yeah. Can't help it sometimes." I had to close my eyes and wait for the nausea to subside. I didn't want to; I wanted to look at him as long as he could look back.

"Galilee and Martin?"

I wasn't sure he was still alive until he'd spoken again. "Yeah. It was quick." Maybe. There was a lot of blood.

"Glad you made it," Tarken said in a fainter voice. "Glad I had you for a while. You're a good gal. You know what you got to do." He said all this in a rush. And then he did die, at what turned out to be the last sigh. He just never drew a breath back in.

So I lay there for a while, planning what to do, in case I lived. I wondered if maybe I hadn't been shot at all. Maybe I'd hit my head on something when the truck had gone over. It was good I didn't have any broken bones. I pondered all this.

My throat was so dry it ached. I needed water. I had to move.

Tarken's water bottle was still in his bag, and his bag was still on his shoulder. He'd hooked it around his neck before he climbed out of the truck, after the bandits had left. He'd taken it for himself—he couldn't have known I was alive—but he hadn't had the strength to drink from it. It was under his body.

I worked it out from under him. That didn't feel good, but I knew he'd be glad for me to have it.

After I drank, I felt better, but I had to rest for a little bit. I guess it was about nine or ten in the morning before I was able to stand and walk. I'd searched around as much as I was able, creeping and crawling to the bodies of the men I'd killed. Their friends had stripped those bodies of anything helpful, but I did find a gold coin they'd missed, tucked in one man's boot. I didn't make it as far as Galilee or Martin. I knew they would have been searched, and I didn't want to see them up close. Though I'd been glad to keep Tarken company in his last moments, those moments had just about done me in.

I'd hoped to find a gun, but no luck. My gun belt had been torn off by the nail, I figured, and who knows where I'd flung Jackhammer when I'd flown from the back of the truck? I must have crawled into the bushes to hide. I guessed the bandits hadn't counted how many of us there were, or maybe they hadn't even asked the farmers. Our attackers had left with all our arms, the two families, the household goods they'd brought with them. Everything.

The bandits must have thought they'd really been lucky. Though they'd lost two of their number, they were probably laughing about how easy it had been. That thought stiffened me up. I was very, very angry.

When I could stand up long enough to search the sideways-tilted cab of the truck, I did find Tarken's handgun, wedged under the seat. In the dark the bandits had missed it. I wondered if Tarken had groped for it, been unable to find it. . . . I made myself quit the thought. This gun was a big, wonderful present from Tarken to me, and I almost wept when I held it. It had seven bullets in it. So seven shots was what I had to work with.

There weren't truck or car tracks anywhere close. The bandits were herding the farm families on foot. The kids wouldn't move fast. I had a chance of catching up. I just had to get going.

I leaned against the truck for a few moments. I hated the way it lay on its side like a helpless bug. The tires were blown, the doors dented, and the glass broken, and I thought an axle would have to be replaced. It looked a sad mess, all broken. I remembered Martin and Tarken working on it the day before. I bit the inside of my cheek.

I knew what I had to do. Martin and Tarken and Galilee would have done the same.

I began tracking. I had Tarken's water, and I had found a sandwich in his bag; that would have to do. I ate it and made myself keep it down. I was slow, because of my head. And my muscles were beginning to hurt from the force of the landing when I'd hit the ground. But I kept moving. There was no one else to do it.

The trail was easy to follow. Lots of people on foot. The two families had taken all their bags and boxes, which was probably the doing of the bandits. They wouldn't have wanted to walk carrying all that stuff, not after the shock of the shooting and the death of the oldest girl.

Early the next morning I found the baby lying by a campfire. It was dead. I don't know why. I didn't unwrap it. Why it died made no difference. Looking at it would only make me angrier. The ashes were still faintly warm at the center. I smiled to myself, maybe. I couldn't tell what my face was doing because my head still hurt fierce. I told myself I was going to catch them in good time.

I put one foot in front of another. I tried not to think about how much I wanted sleep. We'd already lost two of our clients. I didn't want to lose any more.

A couple of hours later I paused under a tree. I let myself sit down, and the relief of it was huge. When I rubbed my face, my hand came away with dried blood speckles. I reached up real careful and felt my scalp. I'd made up my mind I hadn't been shot. I'd just banged my head, and somehow my ear had been cut. That was where the blood had come from. I didn't have the guts to check myself out all over. I didn't want to see all my bruises and scratches. I'd just feel worse if I did.

I had a drink and got to my feet.

Later that afternoon I caught up with the bandits because they couldn't wait to rape the women. They'd started with the younger wife. I thought her name was Martha. Since I could hear them from a far way, it was easy to creep up, hide behind a live oak. The assholes didn't have a watch settled. They thought we were all dead.

I counted four bandits: the redheaded one pumping away on the woman, the one holding a gun on the husband (who was screaming, words I couldn't understand), a bearded man holding Jackhammer, and a short man who was enjoying the rape so much he was holding only his own dick.

The red-haired rapist was intent on his pleasure, so I started out the killing with the ones who might be able to act quick. The bearded man must be first, since he had Jackhammer. When I raised Tarken's pistol, Bearded Man caught the movement out of the corner of his eye and began to swing around. I had to shoot him twice to make sure he was dead, so that left me five bullets.

The armed guard went second, before he could even turn around. I was only worried I'd take out the screaming husband, too. The third man, the one who'd been pleasuring himself, dropped his dick to dive for a rifle. I got him before he could reach it, and he was dead. By then the one who'd been in the saddle had pulled out and was scrambling to his feet. Since he was in midmovement, it wasn't a killing wound, but he was hurt enough. They were all on the ground in a few seconds. Not bad.

I discovered a second later I shouldn't pat myself on the back, because the guard wasn't as hurt as I'd thought. He twisted around to get off a shot in my direction. To my surprise, it came close as a blown kiss. I fired again, and he was out of the picture.

One bullet left, in case the rapist was still breathing.

I spared a glance for the farm people, checking I hadn't shot any of them by accident. None of them were bleeding. They were stuck in the same positions with their mouths hanging open, not yet understanding they were free.

Dammit, the rapist was still moving. I'd wanted to save a bullet. Redhead tried to crawl away, as though he had somewhere to go. I raised the gun again. But I got to keep my last shot.

The husband, with a roar of rage, leaped on top of the rapist with his heavy boots, and then he lifted a large rock and brought it down on the rapist's head, or what was left of it. I waited till his frenzy was through. I figured he needed that. He stood, panting and speckled with blood, and he looked me in the eyes. I nodded toward his wife, who'd turned on her side after pulling her dress down. She was crying, harsh and loud.

The husband helped his wife up and held her to him. The older man went over to the children and his own wife, the motherly Ruth, and gathered them up, trying to reassure them.

Everyone was giving me sideways looks. They were all goggle-eyed at the sight of me. And scared of me. Which I didn't mind. Better than weeping and hanging on me.

"Thank you," said the older man as he hugged the kids.

I liked that. It wasn't necessary, but it made me feel good. "I'll see you safe to Corbin," I said. "I'm the only one left alive."

The man nodded, but he was giving me an appraising glance. "You look pretty rough," he said.

"You paid us to get you there. I will." I wasn't being noble. It was a reputation thing. The Tarken Crew was reliable. That was why we charged a little more. We would never leave clients to die, if we were alive.

The men were disgusted when I told them to take everything the bandits had on them. I had to do a lot of the work myself. I guess their gratitude only went so far.

Martha was still trying to get hold of herself, and Ruth was comforting her; but she had only half her mind on it. The rest of it was back on the road behind us, with her dead daughter. I could tell by the way her eyes fixed on me over Martha's shoulder. She would have questions.

I got my Winchester back, and Galilee's Krag. My Colts, still in their holsters, were stuffed in a sack, with their extra mags. The bandits hadn't taken the time to remove the Colts from the gun belt, which had torn. On that nail, I figured. That nailhead had changed my life somehow.

One of the bandits had a fairly good game rifle, which I was glad to see. I found some ammunition for Tarken's pistol, and I found Galilee's and Martin's handguns. There was even another pistol, so dirty and ill cared for I wondered it hadn't blown up with the firing of it. Another rifle was cheap to begin with, and now it was just about useless. I left that one. I found another handgun and another rifle, cheap but working. I kept hold of those for the moment. The bandits had been short on ammunition, but we got what was there, so we were well set as far as arms went.

We didn't find much food, wasn't much money (which would have been useless in this situation, but always good to have), and none of the bandit clothes were in decent shape. These raggedy men had very little besides what was on their backs, and that was ruined by the blood and bullet holes.

I retrieved the canteens they'd taken from our gear, and I got the kids to fill them all at a nearby stream, which was probably why the bandits had decided to stop at this spot to let their desires out. While the kids did that bit of work, I washed my hands and face and arms downstream. I felt a little better. I tried to rinse off my head, and it hurt so much I had to abandon that.

The younger wife, Martha, the one who'd been raped—whose baby I'd found by the first campfire—was crying again, and her husband was looking at her helplessly. But when her two little ones began to cry along with her, Martha pulled herself together. Ruth helped by finding her sister-in-law a change of clothes, urging her to go wash in the stream. Finally Martha did get clean and put on different clothes, and she looked a little better after she'd washed the man off of her. She stood up straighter.

I liked that. It made me hopeful we could get this done. If I had to drag all of them along, we'd never make it. When Martha began to get her children washed, too, I got the men to help me put the bodies in a heap away from the stream. This was a good campsite. I didn't want to ruin it.

"Time to walk out," I called, and the adults

began to load up with the packs. Even the oldest boy, who couldn't be more than ten, took a little load.

The bandits had made them carry everything this far, which again had helped me catch up with them. But I figured we'd have to find a place to stow this stuff. It would take everything we had to get to Corbin, without being weighed down.

I knew better than to try to persuade them to leave some of the packs, here and now. That would be a useless argument, after they'd lost so much. They'd listen to me after they'd toted their goods a while longer. Already tired in our bodies and minds, we started moving in the right direction. At first no one said a word. They were knocked silent by everything that had happened over the past thirtysomething hours.

That was my grace period. I knew it was over when the men drew ahead of their wives and children to catch up with me.

They began asking questions I couldn't answer, starting with the older brother, Jeremiah. The younger brother, whose name turned out to be Jacob, chimed in soon after. How long would it take us to get to Corbin? What would we eat on the way? Was it likely anyone would come upon us and help us? Or attack us? Where would we sleep?

As Martin had told them when they'd struck the bargain, the trip to Corbin usually took two nights, driving from dusk to dawn while it was cool. One day camping on the road.

This walk would take much longer, of course, and it would have to be in daylight. We'd be able to see whoever or whatever came upon us. Likewise, they could see us—and we were weak.

"Why ain't we following the road?" Jeremiah asked.

I had a hold on my patience, but there wasn't much to grasp. "Because there will most likely be more bandits on the road. And we've only got me for protection. We had to take the road when we had the truck, but we were moving faster and had good gunnies. Now we're cutting across country. It'll be a shorter trip as the crow flies, but we're on foot. We can dodge some trouble, though."

Jeremiah accepted this with ill grace. I could tell he didn't like not being in charge. But the farmer had enough sense to realize I had to lead this expedition.

Jacob just nodded.

I had to get them on my side. Not that they weren't all for our survival, not that they weren't glad I'd saved their lives and freedom, exactly. They were used to being in charge of their worlds, and all the people in those worlds. Especially women. Especially a young woman.

I couldn't put up with argument over everything.

"We have to hunt for food. We have to watch out for dogs. We have to find some kind of protection for tonight. And as for people coming across us? Every now and then the Indians get bold enough to approach. Do *not* shoot at them unless you see them charging at us to kill us."

"Since the president died, the world has gone to hell. God help us all," Jeremiah said, and his brother nodded.

When people said "the president," they meant the last elected president of the United States, Franklin Roosevelt. When he'd been assassinated in some city in Florida, before he could be sworn into office, the government had started down a slope that had gotten slicker and slicker.

After the white government had collapsed, the Indian tribes who could muster up a group of warriors had taken back the land that had been theirs, forcibly if they had to. Now they patrolled it vigorously. Though most tribes were content to let white people pass through as long as they didn't stay, there were some that were not.

And bandits were everywhere, especially in Texoma, New America, and Dixie. I had heard that in Britannia, the area that had knelt to England, there was so much law that bandits were caught and hung quickly. The same for Canada, which had expanded to take in a lot of northern America. Canada had its horseback police, who were supposed to be crackerjack at their jobs. The Holy Russian Empire had a squad of grigoris and militia whose job it was to track highway robbers and kill them on the spot.

But in Texoma and New America, formal justice was scarce on the ground. People were poor, times were hard. That's why the farmers had needed us to get them safe to Corbin.

And look at what had happened.

I was kind of amazed and relieved they accepted my authority now, and I knew it was only because they were so dazed.

As we walked, I had to listen to Jeremiah and Jacob going on at me about all this. It was almost beyond what I could stand, but I had to act like I was listening. Like I cared. They talked about the Deconstruction till I thought I'd scream. I could tell this was all stuff they'd talked about over and over. It was a familiar conversation to them. Comforting.

I hardly needed to say anything at all.

Finally, when they'd run down, and seemed to have settled back within themselves, I handed them each a bandit gun.

"We know how to shoot," Jeremiah assured me, and Jacob nodded with a lot of emphasis.

"Of course you do," I said, and I meant it. Farmers had to shoot wild animals, and their own livestock if the animals were sick. But that was far from being a gunnie. I had to remind them again, "Don't shoot Indians unless they're charging us."

The brothers looked grumpy, as if I was trying to get them to agree to something that was clearly not common sense. "Why?" asked Jeremiah.

"If you do, they'll track us down and kill us all." I knew this. Another gunnie, named Chauncey Donegan, had watched it happen.

The two farmers nodded—after a pause—and this time I believed them. I could move on to another thing I had to make them believe. "But dogs, you got to scare them away with gunfire before they can get in among us. Once they start biting, they go crazy."

"Sure," Jacob said. "We've heard that." He and Jeremiah gave each other a nod. That was settled. Glad to know my word had been confirmed.

While they were so agreeable, I had to tackle the problem I thought would be hardest for them. They were looking tired enough. "We need to be looking for a place to store your stuff. Once we reach Corbin, you can come back with a large party to retrieve it. With mules. And guns. We're too laden down. We've got to move faster."

Jeremiah and Jacob didn't like that so much. Their eyes met in silent consultation. Jeremiah glanced back and saw the women and children struggling with their burdens. "All right," he said after a bit of silence. Jacob nodded, too.

I tried not to look as relieved as I felt.

The two men went back to talk to their wives, reassure their children, and generally act like leaders. They'd had to be given something to do, besides be helpless. They'd both lost a child, and Jacob's wife had been raped in front of him, and they needed to do something besides think of those things. At least until they got to Corbin, after which their thoughts were their own affairs.

I couldn't do anything about the memories in these children's heads. They'd seen things that are bad for kids—for anyone—to see. They'd rallied a bit when I'd set them to filling canteens at the bandit campsite.

So I told the oldest girl and boy to keep their eyes open for some kind of shelter where we could stow their heavy packs. I told the littler ones to start picking up sticks for the fire we'd have that night. I asked them all to keep their eyes open for any sign of life, animal or human.

We took a brief halt while I did all this. I thought if I said one more word, my head was going to fall off my shoulders. I also thought if I didn't start walking again, I'd just crumple to the ground and stay there. I stood straight and called, "Let's move out. Everyone remember their jobs?"

All the kids nodded. "Yes, ma'am," said the oldest girl. "Yes'm," said the youngest. For a second Jacob and Jeremiah and Ruth and Martha looked . . . a little less grim. We started walking, sticking more or less together.

And we kept walking, step after step. I had moments when I wondered if I would die if I ever lay down to sleep, my head hurt that bad.

Finally the sky began to darken. We could stop. In fact, we had to stop. Though it would have been safer to leave the camp black, I let them make a fire. It got chilly at night. They all wrapped up in the blankets from their packs. I had none. Ruth handed me one without a word. I figured it had been her daughter's.

They had some canned food with them, mostly home fixed but some store bought, and we heated it up in their pans. They had some shallow bowls and spoons. They'd been prepared, but not for what had come.

I got as much food in me as I could, but I wasn't able to eat much because of my head. When I asked the farm people to divide up the watches that night, they didn't complain. I might have shot them if they had, and maybe they could see that. I needed to sleep and rest that much.

I did not dream at all, not even of Tarken's eyes as he died.

The next morning it took me five minutes to get to my feet. I was sore and stiff all over, but my head was not quite as painful. It was more like someone was tapping on the inside of my skull, rather than banging.

That was good, because today was going to be harder than yesterday, at least in some ways. I had to get everyone moving, their feet pointed north to Corbin. No one wanted to start out. Everyone wanted to make a wish and be there. Both women and men had cried in the night, for their lost children and other lost things. Their eyes were red and swollen.

After I'd urged them enough, everyone disappeared behind bushes to take care of necessary business, ate a handful of something, drank a little water, and shook themselves awake.

I asked the children to heap dirt on the remains of the fire, and that was a job they could perform with gusto.

We crossed a rail line that morning, but it was all tore up. Maybe it had been abandoned because of this disrepair, or maybe the disrepair had happened after the abandonment. I tried not to spend any time wishing it were in good order. If there'd been a train, we could have stopped it and asked the engineer to send someone from Corbin to escort us, and maybe that would have come about. As it was, we were out in the open with very little protection. Though my vision was clear today, I didn't think I could hit the side of a barn. I hoped I was wrong.

Within an hour the oldest girl, Jael, spotted an overturned wagon. She had great long-sight. No one else had noticed it.

The wagon's axle was broken. I remembered seeing it at a distance on a previous trip. It was mostly whole.

After some palaver Ruth and Martha consolidated what they deemed essential into two packs. Then the two women, Jeremiah's two kids, and I raised the body of the wagon enough for Jeremiah and Jacob to stuff the other packs underneath it. After we eased it down, it looked exactly the same, to my relief.

I looked sharp around us so I could give landmarks to whoever would return. I made them all get branches to sweep away the footprints around the wagon, and I hoped the wind would do the rest of the erasing.

We moved on a lot more briskly, the adults taking turns carrying the two remaining packs. I looked up at the sky to get my bearings, and saw blue so vast it was amazing. Though it might be only spring, the heat had began to climb by midday. We were getting mighty low on water.

Later that day we encountered three Indians on horses. The farmers set up a great clamor, but I told them to shut up. "Remember what I said," I told them, in a voice so stern it was almost like hearing my schoolteacher mother speak through my mouth. Though my vision was beginning to blur a little, I thought I recognized one of the Indians. I walked away from the farmers, toward the horses.

"Are you needing help?" one of them called. His voice was just familiar.

"Standing Still?" I said.

"Gunnie Rose," he said. "Why are you here?"

"We were set upon. I'm taking these people north to Corbin."

"Where is your man?"

"Dead. His friend, too."

"And the dark woman with the big hair?"

Galilee's hair had been very entertaining to the Indians. "Dead."

"I am sorry," he said formally.

"Can you tell me if there is water near here?"

"Yes, at the old settlement. It's north and east of here."

"Thank you. My best wishes to you and your family and your chief."

"Easy death, Gunnie Rose."

"Good hunting, Standing Still."

They turned west and were on their way.

Jeremiah and Jacob were standing tense and ready. It was a good thing I had told them not to shoot before I'd figured out the intentions of our visitors—and it was a better thing that they'd respected my words. I could feel them relax behind me as the Indians vanished.

"What tribe were they?" Jacob asked.

"Comanche," I said. "This area is common ground for the Comanche and the Kiowa."

"How did you know them?"

"I knew one of them. Standing Still helps out my stepfather from time to time."

"Doing what?" Jeremiah said this very suspiciously. Dealing with an Indian made my whole family suspect.

"My stepfather owns a hotel. Standing Still brings in a deer for the table there every now and then."

"I wish he'd brought us one," Jacob muttered.

Sure, because we had the time to skin and butcher and cook a deer, and carry the remains with us. And because we had the money to pay him, which he'd expect, and rightly. I didn't answer. It was a waste of my breath.

I started walking again.

The two men were talking to each other, and Jacob's wife, Martha, moved up to walk beside me. "What did that mean, 'easy death'?" She seemed almost shy with the question.

"He meant . . . he was being polite. That's what gunnies wish each other. An easy death."

Martha was silent for a minute. Just when I hoped it was going to remain quiet, she said, "You have a hard life, Gunnie Rose."

"You do, too. We all do." That was as personal as I wanted to get with Martha. I didn't want to know any of them better.

It was easy to ignore most of the children, because they were scared of me. But the oldest girl, Jael, who was about thirteen, dogged my footsteps. She'd seen me interrupt her aunt's rape and kill the men who'd done that and kidnapped them all, her interest wasn't too surprising. I would have wondered about me, too. But Jael didn't speak, which was fine.

I took a turn at watch this night, since there was no way around it. I didn't think I'd die now, but I wasn't so sure I wanted to live. I daydreamed about a dark room with no sound, no voices. And maybe in one corner, a bathtub and soap. The girl Jael broke into this pleasant picture and sat close to me, cross-legged, staring. I was too tired to mind.

"You shoot a lot of people?" she asked. She had a hoarse little voice.

"That's my job."

"You did good, Gunnie Rose. Thanks."

"Welcome."

"Sorry about your friends."

I nodded. Didn't want to talk about it.

She leaned sideways and hugged me awkwardly. "My name's Jael," she said. "I wasn't sure you knew it. What's yours?"

"Lizbeth," I said.

"Gunnie." She squeezed a little and let go of me to return to her blanket, laid safely by her mom's. I saw Ruth's eyes glint in the firelight. She'd been keeping an eye on her chick. Good. I remembered the girl's name from the Bible. Hadn't Jael killed a man with a tent peg or something? Her parents must have thought she was a pretty fierce kid—or else they wanted her to be.

The next day proved she was.

CHAPTER THREE

A dog pack attacked us in the afternoon, and they got Jael. They'd followed behind us, where we weren't keeping as sharp a watch—I can face in only one direction at a time—and since Jael was lagging behind, they seized her.

I heard the scream and I wheeled. I'd been carrying one of the Colts in my waistband, since my gun belt was broken. I pulled it now, ready to kill. The grown-ups had already waded in, kicking and screaming. They hadn't shot because that wasn't their instinct. If they didn't move, I'd get them as well.

"Stand back!" I yelled with every bit of voice I had, and for a miracle, they did.

Jael was snarling while she struggled, fighting for all she was worth. I ran, took my stance, and shot the lead dog, a large yellow hound with its jaws clamped on her left arm. It dropped dead. Another large dog, which had seized hold of her skirt, let go and backed off a little, growling with bared teeth. The pack was startled, but that would last only a moment. I grabbed Jael up and shot another big dog, this one coming at me. The dogs scattered, but not far enough.

I began backing up, little by little, keeping

my eyes on them. They were bunched together, which made it easier.

"Fire," I shouted when I'd judged Jael and I were well clear.

Both brothers were ready, Jacob with the bandit gun I'd loaned him, Jeremiah with the bandit rifle. Jacob killed a third dog, wounded a fourth. Jeremiah shot three more, which died quickly. Ruth and Martha, and even the children, were pelting the dogs with rocks.

"Move away," I yelled, struggling to hold up the bleeding girl and keep a hand free to shoot. "Keep backing away." I fired into the mass of dogs once more, and a high, keening yelp told me I'd hit another one, maybe more than one.

I could tell the instant the pack decided free food was better than food you had to fight for. They descended on the corpses of their pack buddies. The ones left out of that feast attacked the wounded dogs. It was over pretty quick.

We made haste to get away. Jael's father took her from me. "Don't run," I called. Running prey would be exciting enough to lure some of the dogs away from their meal.

Jael was trying not to make noise, but she was bleeding pretty badly. The pain must have been considerable. She was gulping for air, and her face was streaked with tears and snot and some blood. Her mother was right beside her dad, just waiting to clean up the girl, her own face full of fear.

Finally we were out of sight of the pack. The dogs had not pursued us, at least so far. We had to stop for a moment.

"Do you have any spirits?" I asked the brothers, and Jacob whipped out a flask.

His wife gave him a sharp look. He'd pay for that later. Right now what counted was cleaning the bites, especially the deep one on her arm. Jael's dad put her on the ground and I knelt beside her.

"Pour it over," I said, gripping Jael's wrist and shoulder and extending her arm as if it weren't attached to a girl. Jacob took a deep breath and twisted open the cap. He tilted the flask to pour. He knew full well how painful this would be. Sure enough, despite her best intentions, Jael howled and struggled, without meaning to. Her mother seized her around the body to hold her still. I wanted alcohol to get in every single wound.

Jael had some other bites that had broken the skin, and we took care of those, too. The level in the flask was getting low. Jael reeked of whiskey.

"There's blood running down her leg," Jeremiah said. "Daughter, is your leg hurt?"

"Raise her skirt up," I said, and after a second's hesitation he did so. This revealed a tear in the flesh, bleeding freely. At least it seemed to have been inflicted by one of the smaller dogs.

"Shit," I said, and everyone around me jumped.

"Jael, this is the last one. Brace yourself, girl. I don't want you to lose an arm or a leg or anything else." I used the last of the liquor on this bite. I hoped all the infection had been carried out of her in the flowing blood.

I also hoped none of the dogs were rabid, or we'd lose Jael in a terrible way. Ruth was ready to bandage the leg and the arm with a shirt she'd already torn into rough strips. She did a good job getting the bandages snug enough to stop the bleeding, but not so tight as to cut off the girl's circulation.

Jael was hiccuping by now, making a huge effort to calm herself. The girl was tough.

"We got to walk. The farther away we get, the better," I said, screwing the top back on the flask and returning it to Jacob, though there were only a few drops left inside. "We have to take turns carrying her, because that leg wound is gonna keep bleeding if she walks on it today. Maybe tomorrow, too."

We set off again, moving fast, with no talk.

If we were lucky, the pack would not track us. Maybe they would be full and content. Maybe they'd find easier prey. A few people in Segundo Mexia had dogs as pets, and they seemed good animals. But out in the wild they were killers.

Jeremiah carried Jael first, which was natural. Then he handed the girl over to her mother, who lasted longer than I thought she would. Then her uncle took charge of her, and then Martha.

I had her last. Jael wasn't as big as me, but she wasn't so far from it, either. I'm a short woman. The girl's legs dangled down around mine and banged me. But at least we kept moving, and I could spell someone else so they could rest.

Standing Still had told me there was water in the abandoned town I'd seen before from the west, though never up close. I'd been looking to spy it for the past hour. Finally, about five o'clock, we spotted it in the distance.

Now I knew exactly where we were. We were closer to Corbin than I'd figured. We'd have to stop here for the night. We couldn't keep on carrying Jael. She had to lie down and sleep, and so did we.

The empty town was just as spooky close up as it had been far away. The best shelter was in the old general store, which had three walls up, and half a fourth. Jeremiah, Jacob, and I pulled some boards from other buildings to blockade that gap; it wasn't a very good barrier, but it would slow something down long enough for me to shoot. At least there was plenty of dry wood lying around to fuel a fire on the dirt floor, and I asked Martha to start one right away. It wasn't going to be dark for hours yet, but we needed to eat something hot. I left that in the hands of the adult women.

Jeremiah agreed to leave Jael's side only if

someone sat by her. That turned out to be me. The pump was right outside the general store, and it still worked. I found an old bucket, plugged the hole in it with a rock and some cloth, and brought in water to wash Jael. If she was anything like me, she'd feel better when the dried blood was gone.

Jeremiah had gotten a rabbit earlier in the day, and I'd gotten another. Not much for as many people as we had. Better than nothing. Martha skinned them and cut them up, and she put them in the one pot we'd kept, along with all the canned vegetables we had; again, not much, because we'd left most of that heavy stuff under the wagon. We added some water and put the pot on the little fire, and let everything cook together for a good long while. I checked to make sure the wind was blowing north, so the pack wouldn't catch the cooking smell.

When the pot had cooled enough, the little ones gathered round with their spoons first. I didn't think that was the normal way of things in farm families, where the adults did all the physical work and thus got more food, but tonight that was the way of it here. The five of us got what was left.

Everyone got something to eat; no one got enough.

I watched to make sure Jael took a few bites, but she went back to sleep in the middle of swallowing. We kept a sharper watch that night, fearing the return of the pack.

I hoped we'd reach Corbin in two days. Jael tried to walk, and she managed during the morning, but by noon she was stumbling. After I laid my hand on her forehead, I was careful not to look at her mother. Jael felt warm.

When it was my turn to carry her, Jael wanted to talk. "Have you been outside of Texoma, Lizbeth?"

I couldn't spare a lot of breath, but I was relieved to hear her voice. She'd been silent for a long while. "Yeah. I've been to New America, where we're going. In fact, I think we're in New America now. And I've been in Mexico, on a job."

"What about the HRE?"

"Haven't been in the Holy Russian Empire."

"Do you think the emperor wears a crown all the time? What about his sisters?"

"I don't know. Probably not. Those crowns have to be heavy. They'd give you a headache." Maybe as bad as mine, though it was better than the day before.

"Are they all married?"

"The grand duchesses? I think so." I didn't pay too much attention to stories about the Russian royal family. After all, Tsar Alexei lived all the way west by the ocean, in San Diego, and it wasn't likely I'd ever see him, even if I wanted to. And his sisters were all married and scattered around.

"I bet they had beautiful weddings. I bet they're really pretty."

Truth was, after the exile Alexei's dad, Nicholas, had been so anxious to marry off his daughters to cement their place in the world, the joke was he'd tossed them out of the boat like chum.

I had no opinion of the Russian royal family, and I didn't care that they'd carved their own empire out of part of the former United States. The beef I had with them was that they'd brought the grigoris with them. They were bad and dangerous.

"Why do they call 'em grigoris?" Jael asked, as if she'd read my thoughts.

"Because of their boss, a magician named Grigori Rasputin. He's some kind of priest or holy man, too. Not Catholic."

"Hmmm."

I thought she slept for a minute on my shoulder.

"Are they all bad?" she said, her voice drowsy.

"Some of 'em are." I knew that for certain.

"Lizbeth. I feel better."

"That's good."

This time she really slept. Her mother took over carrying her, and I strode off feeling lighter. We'd all be glad to stop for the night.

I wondered if that was what little girls dreamed

of now. Seeing the Russian grand duchesses, in crowns and long dresses, their diamonds glittering. Had they managed to escape with enough diamonds to glitter? Were they happy, strewn around and married to foreigners?

Was Alexei even strong enough to keep his head up if he wore a crown? When the royal family had escaped the Red Army, the newspapers had reported that Alexei had some real serious disease. Supposedly, that was how the grigoris had gotten their hold on the royals; they'd kept the tsarevitch alive.

I dismissed the royals from my mind. And I never wanted to think about grigoris. I had enough to worry about, right in front of me.

Jael slept through that night. We had to carry her the next day too and ended up making a travois for her out of a blanket and two poles. Dragging it was sure easier than toting her.

We didn't encounter any more dogs or Indians or bandits, but we got really hungry. We'd used up most of the food. Since we'd rationed it, we had some water on hand.

The third day after the dog attack, Jael could walk on her own, and we made better time. That day, early in the afternoon, we walked into Corbin.

CHAPTER FOUR

Corbin was a busy town, better situated than Segundo Mexia. There were maybe three thousand souls. If the oldest brother—the one who'd financed this trip—hadn't given up and gone home, I knew where he'd be staying. Sure enough, when we walked up to Broadhurst's Boardinghouse for Gentlemen and Ladies, there was the eldest brother, Joshua, sitting on the front porch with a glass of tea.

Joshua Beekins was tall and broad and hearty, and he was really, really glad to see his family. He hugged everyone many times, he bellowed all their names, he prayed out loud in gratitude for their deliverance.

After there'd been a lot of greeting and more praying, I had to bring myself to his attention.

"You're . . . ?" He looked at my outstretched hand, puzzled.

"I'm the surviving member of the crew that got them here," I said a little sharply, because I was swaying on my feet with weariness. And I could not push back my grief any longer.

Joshua'd dealt with Martin, so he asked about him first.

"He's dead," I said. I didn't have a lot of energy

to waste, so I couldn't dress it up any. "Bandits. Who also killed the two kids."

Joshua hadn't counted the children present, and he was seriously shocked. But he stayed on track. "Tarken is gone? Galilee?"

"Yes, all gone."

"You lived and got them here." He seemed to think that was marvelous. As in, literally something to marvel at.

"My job. I loaned your brothers two of the bandit guns, but I'm willing to leave them, for protection. And of course, the pay owed."

You could see Joshua thinking of a reason to dispute this, since the other three crew members were dead. But he really couldn't. It was just a habit, looking for a loophole. Joshua was gracious enough about counting out the money owed.

I collected all my firearms from the various places and packs they'd been stowed. I'd have to buy a bag to hold them and the extra canteens. They'd go home with me.

The two families were telling Joshua about the bandit attack, and the dog attack, and the encounter with the Indians, which had gotten much more exciting in the retelling. I was ready for a bed, but I wasn't staying at this boardinghouse. Too much talking.

"You could go back to Wheatlands with us," Joshua said when I told him good-bye. He looked at me with frank appraisal. "There are lots of men there who need a good wife."

"Then I hope they find one," I said. I nodded and drifted away from the group, in which everyone was now all happy . . . and talking and planning. It would be different once the excitement of the reunion eased down. Soon they'd realize that now they had the leisure to mourn for the ones they'd lost.

The farm families had rejoined their lives. After a while this long nightmare of a trip would just be a part of the time they'd stepped outside the boundaries. Except maybe Jael.

A little up the street was Mother Phillips's Boardinghouse. I'd stayed there before, with Tarken on the last trip. I knew it was clean, and I wanted cleanliness more than anything. I reeked. I asked Edna Phillips if she had a room and food. She looked at me and I saw she'd already heard about Tarken. Amazing.

"I have a room, right by the bathroom," she said. "You go up and get in the bathtub. I'll bring you up some food."

"Thanks. Doesn't make any difference what it is."

"Do you want company?" she asked in her neutral voice.

"Not even a little bit," I said. The difference between Broadhurst's Boardinghouse for Gentlemen and Ladies and Mother Phillips's was that

Edna would let whores visit if they were done and out within the hour and they were *quiet*. Otherwise, you never got to stay there again. "I want the bath, and the food, and a bed. And if you can wash these clothes I got on, overnight, I'll pay extra." This was a huge treat, and one I thought I deserved.

I could afford it because I'd gotten everyone's pay. I pushed that thought away and went up the stairs. They seemed to have gotten steeper since the last time I was here. It took me three tries to unlock my room door. I pulled off my boots, and the smell disgusted me. That was the only thing stronger than my exhaustion. I decided to wash them out later, in the room sink. They'd have time to dry overnight.

This time of day, the bathroom in the hall was open and empty, and the hot water was working. I ran a tubful and lowered myself into the water.

I groaned at the sensation of the heat on my aching, abused body. I looked at it through the water. I was a black-and-blue person now, with a few white patches. I closed my eyes. I felt worse when I saw it.

For a few minutes I just let the heat seep into my sore muscles. A faint breeze came in the open window, and it smelled of good things. There were voices, but they weren't talking to me and they seemed far away. And it was so much quieter . . . finally. The relief of being alone was overwhelming.

I began to cry.

As I wept, I lathered up with the hotel soap. It did not have much of a sweet scent, but it got me clean, and clean smelled good. I'd hated my own smell for days. There was some shampoo, and though I didn't have much hair to wash, I used it. I massaged my scalp with the pads of my fingers, slowly, gingerly. I found the lump at the side of my head. It felt smaller. My ear was scabbed over. After a minute's cautious washing, it wasn't bloody anymore.

And still I cried. I could not stop. I put my arms around my knees.

Gradually I stopped. The water was dirty and cool. I didn't want to sit in it. I pulled the plug so it could drain. Then I ran a little more hot water to rinse myself off. I wasn't usually wasteful like this, but no one had knocked on the door to ask me to vacate the room.

I felt like a new woman as I patted myself dry with the scratchy hotel towel. I'd done the crying, and standing clean and whole and unburdened was simply great. Keeping back from the window, I turned in a circle, my arms held out, so the air could feel how clean I was. And then I staggered. I was weak with wanting sleep.

I wrapped the damp towel around me, grabbed up my filthy clothes, and peeked out into the hall. It was empty, and I scooted into my room, unlocking the door, stepping in, and shutting it behind me in a few seconds. On second thought I threw the clothes out of the room and called down the stairs to Edna that they were there. She'd already left a meal in my room. The meat was awful hard to chew, made my head hurt to try, so I ate the potatoes and the early squash and the buttermilk pie. My stomach hadn't been so happy in days. I put the tray outside the door, noting my clothes were already gone.

Edna had been real fond of Martin. She'd known his mom. I figured that was how come I was getting this kind treatment, and I was grateful.

I pulled back the chenille coverlet to climb between the clean sheets. Behind a locked door. Alone. Clean, full, and rid of responsibility.

I slept instantly.

But in the middle of the night, I woke up and cried for Tarken, and for Martin, and—maybe most of all—for Galilee. And then I slept again.

When I woke up, the sun was hitting my face. I hadn't drawn the curtains or pulled down the shade before I'd fallen onto the bed, and I could hear the sounds of the town below my window. Edna was scolding her maid for not scrubbing the dishes properly. The man across the street was talking about the new settlers who'd arrived yesterday, and wondering where they were going to live and if they had daughters of marrying age.

Not for a few years, brother. Not since the death of the oldest girl. I saw her again with the hole in her back, sprawled on the dirt, and I fought back a wave of badness; misery, anger, guilt. I did not know how I could have protected them better, and if I'd never talked to the girl's parents and her sister and her little brother, I would not have cared much about her fate. Because this was the kind of thing that just happened because times were hard and people were weak and bad.

When I'd gotten myself back into a regular frame of mind, I went downstairs in my clean clothes. They'd been folded and left right outside my door. Even my boots had been cleaned. I didn't think I'd left them out, but I was glad Edna had taken it on herself to come in and get them.

Edna had put aside some biscuits and sausage for me, with butter and blueberry jelly. I drank a cup of coffee, which I don't often get to do. It's hard to find in Segundo Mexia.

"This is real good," I told the landlady.

"Glad you like it. You need feeding up," Edna said, brisk and plain.

After I'd paid my bill, I accepted Edna's quick, hard hug. I carried all my firearms and canteens up the street to the dry-goods store and bought a leather bag, long enough for a rifle. I lined it with a new blanket and bought some washrags as well. I wrapped every gun in its rag before I placed it inside. Wouldn't do for one to snag on the other and fire. But unloaded, they were no good. I tossed in the spare canteens and filled two for the trip. I topped the bag with some dried fruit and meat and a loaf of bread before I closed it. I'd retrieved the sling from the bandit, and I'd wiped it off to remove his sweat, so I could wear Jackhammer across my back. And by a huge stroke of luck—I was due, I figured—there was a gun belt small enough for me, though it was very plain. Intended for a little boy, the shopkeeper said, but what did I care? I had the Colts where I could use 'em again.

Now I was ready to leave Corbin.

I circled behind the Main Street buildings so I wouldn't run into any of the Beekins party on my way out of town. I did see Jael, from a distance. She was playing jacks with her strong hand. Looked like she was moving without much pain. I nodded to myself and began the walk back home.

Now, alone, I had to be even more careful. No more eyes but mine. On the other hand, there wasn't all that chatter to take my attention away from what was important.

Only one man followed me out of Corbin, knowing I had money on me. I took care of him the afternoon of the first day.

After that, it was an easy trip.

I got to Segundo Mexia in three days, even though I was carrying a lot: six canteens, Jackhammer, my Colts, two rifles (one of them Galilee's Krag), and three pistols—Martin's, Tarken's, Galilee's. A fourth pistol would have to be cleaned before I even tried to sell it. It was a disgrace.

I'd used my new blanket the night before, but it was warming up to be a nice spring day when I walked into town. I went directly to Trader Army. Army was behind the counter, restocking his shelves. When the bell over the door rang, he turned.

"Aw, girl," Army said when he recognized me. "I'm real sorry." He looked as sad as his face would let him. Army had an old injury to his face, a white mass of scar tissue over his right eye. That side of his face didn't move too much. The skirmishes of seven years before had taken their toll on him. "Thomas told me he'd found your crew on the Corbin road," Army said. "Didn't find you, so I figured where you were."

"Thomas buried 'em?" Martin's brother, Thomas, was one of my least favorite men. I was glad they'd been buried, sorry that I would have to thank Thomas.

"Yep."

"What about Galilee?"

"Thomas told her son. He figured Freedom would want to take care of her."

I'd stopped by the site of the attack, early this morning. I'd been relieved the bodies had been removed—at least Tarken's, Martin's, and Galilee's. (The bandits were well on the way to being picked clean.)

"What did you bring me?" Army asked, wanting to get the look off my face.

"I got a pistol and a rifle and four canteens," I said, laying them out. I'd have to offer Galilee's son her Krag or her pistol. I might keep the filthy bandit pistol, I wouldn't know until I cleaned it up. I had to sell at least the extra rifle and two of the canteens. I was in for a dry spell.

We haggled for a while, in a halfhearted kind of way. Ended up the way most haggling does: neither side totally satisfied, but on the whole feeling all right about the deal.

"Anyone hiring?" I was ready to be on my way. But I needed to think about the future, and Army knew everything going on in the town.

"Lavender needs someone," Army said. His single eyebrow, about the size of three cater-pillars, was hiked up, showing what he thought of that. "Her gunnie quit four weeks ago."

"I'd sooner work for Big Balls," I said. Army laughed, his mouth going up at one corner. Big Balls was the pig owned by the butcher. Everyone was waiting for the day Frank Hacker put Big Balls down. That was one mean pig.

"Lavender's the only crew leader hiring."

Army, who'd been wiping off the canteens with a rag, paused. "But there's a kind of strange couple at the Antelope. They've been nosing around. They want someone."

"Not like people want the whores at Elsie's?"

Army laughed. " 'Capable' was the word the woman used. But when I asked her, 'Capable of what?' she didn't have no answer."

Army and I both knew that in Segundo Mexia you could find someone capable of anything you could imagine. And then some. Poor people can't be real choosy.

He looked to one side. The side where I wasn't. "They look like people in the grigori business."

He knew how I'd feel about that.

"I'll wait for a while, see if something else turns up," I said.

"Can't wait too long, Lizbeth." That was nothing but the truth. Army turned to put his new items up on his shelves. "If they come in again, I'll mention your name."

I started to tell him to keep his mouth shut, but suddenly I didn't have the energy. It didn't seem harmful to talk to them, and maybe I'd learn something interesting. "Well, all right," I said. I pocketed my money. "Tell Clarita I said hey."

"Will do. She's coming in this afternoon. Says she can't sit home no more."

Clarita, Army's wife, had been delighted when the store began making enough money for her

73

to stay home. But she hadn't taken to being a homebody at all.

"What are you going to do when she's working?"

"I don't know. Go fishing, I reckon."

I laughed, trying to imagine Army sitting in a boat holding a fishing pole. He would get antsy within ten minutes. "Bye," I said. All the miles I'd walked were suddenly pressing on my shoulders, and I wanted a bath. I had to make a quick stop at the grocery, and I had to let my mother see me.

As I walked to my mom's, now juggling the bag of guns with a sack of food, I was poking around my brain to think of a way to thank Martin's brother, Thomas, that didn't involve me lying on my back. That's what Thomas really wanted. That kind of thank-you wasn't going to happen. I'd feel too much like one of the girls and boys who lived at Elsie's. Their job was fine for them, but not for me.

I had to force myself to knock on my mom's door. I knew she'd want to lay eyes on me. I had always felt lucky she loved me. The way she got me, a grigori came through, putting on a magic show for the kids. He had his own little magic show going afterward, and Candle, my mother, was pretty and flattered by his notice, and only a kid. He took away my mom's will and had his way. Presto chango . . . nine months later, a

74

baby appeared. There were lots of comments, and since Mom was a cut above most people in the education and brains and looks departments, most of the comments were mean.

It's not like girls didn't get pregnant all the time. But my mom had so obviously been better than the normal run of girls . . . well, people are envious.

Mom didn't want anything to do with men for a long time, no big surprise. But she was still pretty, and she was honorable, and she was a hard worker. Men wanted plenty to do with her. Jackson Skidder won her over about the time I was twelve. It had seemed like a real unlikely match, but he had qualities that just suited my mom.

Jackson was smart. Not book smart, though he might have been that, too. He was business smart. He dressed for work, not for show. Jackson judged people pretty accurately. And he would kill to protect what he judged was his.

No one would think of crossing Candle Rose after she became Candle Skidder.

Not only does Jackson own the Antelope Hotel and a couple of other businesses, he looks like a bulldog and he's twice as scary. But he's gentle with Mom, and he's always stood by me, which has been a surprise bonus.

Jackson was at the house. He was the one who called to me to come in. I was glad to see him.

We weren't huggers, me and my stepfather. After he picked up his newspaper, he looked over his reading glasses at me and gave me a nod, which I returned.

"Candle, you better turn and see who's here," Jackson said.

My mom was busy making lunch. That meant it was the weekend; I'd lost track of where in the week we'd gotten to. On weekdays my mom still taught school, and left a lunch for her husband. When Mom saw me, her whole face lit up.

"Lizbeth," she said, and wrapped me in a hug, held me close and tight. "I am so glad to see you. I heard you had a bad time. I'm sorry about Tarken. And Galilee." Mom held me away from her, looked into my eyes. She rued what I'd become.

Mom had hoped I'd be a teacher, like her. I'd have as soon scrubbed toilets as been a teacher. I was glad to be a gunnie. I could shoot anyone who was mean to her now. For a second I rested my head on her shoulder.

I had to notice Mom had left Martin off her list of sorrows—but she'd never been too fond of him. He'd recruited me for the crew.

From behind the newspaper Jackson said, "The farmers all get to Corbin okay?" He was ready for the emotion to cool off.

" 'Cept one baby and one girl, who were already dead before I caught up," I said. I was more like Jackson than I was like my mother, at least in my nature. I had wished he were my real dad when I was a kid.

Jackson lowered his newspaper. Our eyes met. He gave me a sharp nod, his way of saying he approved of my conduct. "Good on you," he said. He added casually, "I gave Thomas a barrel of pickles." He raised the *Central Texoma News* to cover his face.

I felt a huge rush of relief. Now I didn't owe Thomas anything for burying my crew. That was a big burden I was rid of. "I thank you," I said, trying to keep my voice even.

He turned the page of his newspaper. That was Jackson.

"What will you do now?" Mom said as she returned to the stove and flipped the chicken over. She gave her head a little toss, to make sure her hair was all behind her shoulder. Hers is black and thick and straight, down to her waist.

I'm short, like her, and black headed, like her, but those are our only likenesses. All I had known about my father for a long time was that he'd escaped from godless Russia, like all the original grigoris. He had had an accent. I knew now that he had been a medium-tall man, and his hair had been golden and curly, and his eyes blue. I understood why Mom had been flattered by his interest. So my eyes are blue, and my skin is lots lighter than Mom's, and my hair is real curly. It makes ringlets as it dries. It's adorable. That's one reason I'd paid Chrissie to cut it off.

"Maude needs someone to work in the grocery," Mom said, not looking at me.

"Mom. Grocery?" Maude hadn't said anything to me while I was shopping. I was pretty sure that was proof enough that she didn't think I'd make a good grocer's clerk.

My mother laughed. "I know, it was a drug dream," she said. "But it surely would be nice to see you behind a counter instead of toting that Winchester."

I stayed a couple more minutes, then left, despite my mom's offer of lunch. Part of my good relationship with Jackson was knowing when to leave. As I walked home, I reminded myself to do something extra nice for my stepfather real soon for squaring me with Thomas.

Laden down with my groceries and my bag of firearms, I started up the path to my place. It's in the town limits but stuck off by itself. There's a hill rising to the east of Segundo Mexia, and in the middle of it a running stream has formed the ground into a crevice with steep sides. The stream's just a trickle in the summer, but now that it was spring, the water was running pretty good. We built a little bridge across the stream so we can live on both sides of it. There are other people living on my side of the hill, four families besides me. It's friendly.

I have a little house, all mine. I saved for the first year and a half I worked, living in a spare room in Galilee's place. It was spare because her son, Freedom, had moved out. The room was small, and it was very tight living. But it was worth it when I'd gotten enough put by to get everything I needed to build on an empty bit of land toward the top of the hill. Jackson and my mom had given me the lot. My friends came together to help me put up the building.

I paid for the plumbing and the electrical work. The rest was us, our hands. Luckily for me, Jackson's brother, Cedric, was a good planner and carpenter, and Cedric seemed to enjoy himself telling us all what to do. In the end, I had my own place.

There's one room that's my bedroom and my kitchen and my dining room and my everything-else room. And there's a small (tiny) enclosed bathroom, my big luxury. Segundo Mexia has a water system, mostly thanks to Jackson and some other well-to-do citizens maintaining the pre-Deconstruction system, and I'm hooked up to it, after many visits to our city hall. Sometimes I have electricity, depending on nothing in particular that I can tell. But we hill people also have an outhouse and candles, because sometimes things just don't work.

I was almost as smelly as I had been when I'd gotten to Corbin. I wanted to take off my filthy clothes and get in the tub, assuming the water was running. I wanted a door shut between me and the world. I wanted to be home. By myself.

The sight of two strangers sitting on the bench outside my front door seemed so wrong and bad I had to blink to make sure they were really there.

CHAPTER FIVE

My visitors, a man and a woman, were both tall and fair, though the woman was the taller of the two; she was maybe six feet. They stood when they realized I was coming to the cabin.

I didn't look at them too closely, because I wanted them to go away. Ignoring people never works like that, though.

"Lizbeth Rose?"

I nodded. No point in denying it.

The two seemed to expect me to say something, but I didn't. I waited. I didn't want to give them my words, much less my time.

I was sure these were the two grigoris Army had talked about. I had made a mistake, letting him mention my name to them. He'd seen them much sooner than I'd thought. I shouldn't have stopped at the grocery or my mom's.

The man was the younger of the two. He had a broad face with high cheekbones, a full mouth, long light-brown hair pulled back in a braid. The tattoos on his neck were just barely visible inside his shirt collar. Over his shirt he wore a vest with a score of pockets. Grigori vests contained herbs and spells inside the pockets, or so I'd heard.

The woman, somewhere in her late thirties,

was a blonde. I'd never seen a woman so tall. Her tattoos made his look modest. There were symbols on her face, crawling up her cheeks. It made me wince to look at them. She wore a vest, too.

Grigoris for sure. None of the magic users from the Holy Russian Empire liked to be called grigoris, though. They liked to be called wizards.

I disliked the two wizards even more because they were clean and they didn't smell. And the both of them looked rested. I was so tired my bones hurt.

Finally the tall woman said, "You're with the Tarken Crew?"

"I was until a few days ago," I said.

"You quit?" She tried to sound like she cared.

"The Tarken Crew quit living. All but me." I was surprised they didn't know. Could be they hadn't talked to Army long enough.

The grigoris glanced at each other, a little taken aback, but not for more than a second. "We need to talk to you," the woman said.

Maybe the man was looking a little harder, because he finally spoke. "We could come back in the morning," he said, his voice quiet and even.

She half turned to him to say something, and he made a little hand gesture. She shut up. But she wasn't used to taking hints. She was the boss.

"Any time is better than now. But most likely I won't do whatever it is you want," I said.

"Why?" She just couldn't stop herself.

I picked the simplest reason. "I don't want to have nothing to do with you," I said. My mother would have given me the evil eye for bad grammar, but she wasn't there and I was out of civil.

The woman opened her mouth again, but the younger man—he was maybe five years older than me—made a *stop* gesture with some force behind it. He must have had to quiet her a lot. "Tomorrow," he said. "In the morning. We'll be back then."

The two of 'em left, passing me on the narrow path, not getting too close. Smart.

At last I was able to go in my own place and shut my own door. And I locked it. I needed to clean myself, but I'd run out of energy and will. I turned the faucet to find the water was running, so I washed my face and arms and took off my shoes before I fell onto the bed. If anyone else came by or knocked on the door, I didn't know about it. I didn't dream, that I remember.

Next morning I woke up looking forward, not back at the catastrophe on the road to Corbin. I was still alive. I had to plan what I'd do next. I had to make my living. I showered, scrubbing top to bottom. I fired up the woodstove. It was one of the last times I'd use it till fall; when the weather got hot, I cooked outside as much as I could. I made myself a big meal—cantaloupe, oatmeal, bacon. I felt much better after that. Much.

I was feeling dandy as I started on the dishes, but then I had one of the black moments when grief stabbed me unexpectedly. I had to fight back. Tarken, Martin, and Galilee were gone, but with honor. I had to be strong, all by myself. I made myself look out the window at the peace of the hillside. A vireo was in a bush nearby, and it was full of bird conversation. I took a deep breath in and out, and returned to my job.

As I scrubbed the oatmeal pan, I began singing a cowboy song about beautiful women, loyal men, and plains covered with flowers. My scratchy voice wouldn't bother anyone, least of all the vireo. The little houses down the slope, they weren't real close and this time of day they'd be empty, except for Chrissie and maybe her little boys. I'd realized it had to be Monday. The other grown-ups were at work; kids were at school with my mother if they were old enough. In Segundo Mexia everyone has something to do.

I'd stopped school at sixteen, which was a little old to still be in a classroom. Being my teacher and my mother, Mom had wanted to pass along as much knowledge as she could. It had been hard come by, since in the middle of her teacher training, when she herself was sixteen, she'd come up with me. My grandparents had watched me while Mom rode the bus to Little

Bend to finish up. That bus hasn't run in the past five years, but then it ran to the larger town and back daily. Grandma and Grandpa died when I was six, and my memories of them are sketchy: worn, lined faces, kind voices, stern discipline. The influenza took them, but they left behind a daughter who could support herself and her child.

My mom was a good teacher and a good mother. She did not believe that ignorance was bliss. She believed just the opposite. A lot of people didn't want to talk about the past, because it was painful. But Mom thought I should know how things had gotten to be the way they were: the dead president, the dead vice president (influenza), the banks crashing, the drought, and the influenza . . . again.

The population had dropped, the government could not protect itself, and other countries had grabbed pieces of America.

"USA got big bites taken out of it: by Canada from the north, by Mexico from the south, and by the Holy Russian Empire from the west, where the Russian tsar settled when he fled his own country. To the east, the thirteen original colonies—all but Georgia—voted to form a bond with England, to keep from becoming part of Canada. They picked the name Britannia. The southern states banded together as Dixie. Georgia went with them." She was pointing out the new countries on the map.

"So what about us?" I asked, looking at the old map. She pointed to the place where we lived. "Texas and Oklahoma and New Mexico and a bit of Colorado became Texoma, where we live. We live in Segundo Mexia, in Texoma. And this big area north of us, the plains, that's New America."

My mother also told me no one had ever heard of real magic until the Russian Christians left their own country, driven out by the godless people, to wander until they found a home on the West Coast. The movie industry welcomed them with open arms and pocketbooks, and when the crash came, the army the tsar had brought with him convinced California and Oregon to unite under him.

The Russian royal family had brought the grigoris with them, and the grigoris rejoiced in the open under the California sun. Now the Holy Russian Empire rules with lots of show and lots of mystic bullshit. It's the only country in the world to openly admire magic.

And now there are all kinds of scum with a little bit of ability traveling around, putting on magic shows for the kiddies and selling "spells," and one of them spelled my mom to hold still long enough to beget me, was what I had been thinking as my mother told me about the map. I figure maybe Mom had been thinking about the same topic.

The mistake one particular grigori scum had

made was coming back to this area a second time. I smiled remembering that, but my happy minute was interrupted by a knock at my door. I dried my hands and reached for a gun. I opened the door real quick and stepped to the side.

I figured the odor of the soap I'd used—I'd found a scented bar in Corbin—had masked the grigori smell until they were real close. So much for my little talent.

The man and the woman looked the same as they had the afternoon before: tall, well nourished, well dressed, rested. Today they seemed a bit more worried.

Now that I was clean and had had a night's sleep, and some food in my stomach, I felt I could deal with them.

I'd cleaned one of my Colts already. All the other firearms were spread out on the table, on sheets of old newspaper, along with everything I'd need: clean cotton rags, Hoppe's, soft brushes. I was ready to work.

It was a good reminder to them.

"May we come in?" the woman asked. She didn't sound Russian, something I'd been too tired to notice the day before. I figured her for a British import.

I jerked my head, and they stepped in. I pointed to the bench on one side of my table, and they sat. I had a stool and my back to the wall, so I could see out the door, which I left open. It was a mild morning, and I enjoyed the little breeze coming in.

I didn't feel obliged to open the conversation. They were the ones who wanted something, not me.

I took apart Jackhammer first. My grandfather's Winchester was utterly familiar to my hands. The feel of the cleaning rag, the brushes, the smell of the solvent, the care I was taking of the tools of my livelihood, all felt good and comfortable to me. Plus, I'd had a good look at the neglected bandit pistol. It seemed basically sound. If I put in some work, I'd get a good price for it.

"I'm Paulina Coopersmith," the woman said. Yep, she had an accent. I'd only heard one like it at the movies. "Are all these guns yours?"

"Yes, they're all mine," I said. "I took most of 'em off the bandits who killed my crew."

"You killed them all," the man said.

I nodded. They didn't have anything to say about that for a goodly bit of silence.

"I'm Ilya Savarov," the man said finally. "Please call me Eli." No doubt about him being Russian. He had a slight accent. He might make his name more American, but I was willing to bet he'd been in the ships that had brought the tsar and his family to the West Coast after their escape in 1918 from the godless Russians. Though this Eli had probably been a small child then, since he looked in his midtwenties now.

"Lizbeth Rose," I said. But I realized they knew that. I almost told them not to call me anything.

Paulina and Eli and Lizbeth. We were pals now, for sure.

I finished the cleaning and reassembled and loaded Jackhammer. I set my cleaning stuff in a neat line back on a heavy pad.

"What do you want?" I said, satisfied with the job I'd done. I'd had my silence. Now it was time to get the conversation moving, so it could come to an end. So they would go.

I ran my hand down the walnut stock of Jackhammer one last time and laid it down. I made myself look directly at the grigoris. Paulina's eyes were frosty blue and fixed on me with no very pleasant expression. Her accent was English. A lot of English magicians had migrated to California after hearing how friendly the HRE was to wizardry. They were tired of being ignored in their own country. Looked like the court had given 'em a big welcome.

"We need a guard and a guide," Eli Savarov said. "We're hoping you can be both."

I looked at him directly. His eyes were green. I'd never seen that before, and it was striking. "For how long?" I said. I was going to turn them down, but not before I found out what they were doing in Segundo Mexia.

"For at least a week, maybe as long as three."

"While you're doing what?"

I began to clean the small parts of one of the bandit pistols, because I couldn't just sit and look from one to another. It was necessary to concentrate on my hands, but I wasn't so busy I didn't catch the look they gave each other.

"We're searching for a particular man," Paulina said. She was picking her words one by one. "And the last trace we have of him is in this area."

"Huh. No strangers here recently. You mean another one like you? A grigori?"

"We lost track of him some time ago," Paulina said. "And he is a wizard, yes." But her mouth twisted sour at giving him the title.

Eli said quietly, "He's an embarrassment to us."

"Yeah?" I didn't want to meet someone they'd be proud of. "So, who is this guy?"

"A Russian-born wizard named Oleg Karkarov."

Jackhammer was pointed at them before they could get to their feet.

"Get your hands up, now!" I said.

They made a great show of looking astonished and scared as they threw their hands up. You had to keep grigoris' hands in front of your eyes; you couldn't let them weave spells with their hands or reach for their vest pockets.

"What did we say?" Paulina said. She was pretty pissed off.

"You know he's dead."

But they didn't. Even I had to admit they'd been taken by surprise.

"But—but where? When?" The man, Eli, stammered as he spoke. He looked . . . dismayed. As if his world had taken a big turn for the worse.

"Five miles away in Cactus Flats," I said, not lowering Jackhammer. "Eight months ago. He your kin?"

"No," said Paulina Coopersmith, disgusted at the very idea.

"How did he die?" Eli asked, right on her heels.

"Gunned down," I said, glancing from one to another.

"On the head of the tsar," Paulina said, "we did not know." She was smart enough to see that their ignorance was real important to me.

I didn't doubt her after that. Holy Russians, that was a serious oath to them. Alexei I was the symbol of everything they'd left behind, and their hope for the future.

Eli and Paulina were smart enough to keep their mouths shut while I thought. After a minute I laid down the rifle, but I kept it close.

Meeting the eyes of each grigori in turn, I nodded, so they could lower their hands. I wasn't going to shoot them until I learned more. They wouldn't spell me until they did the same.

I sank back onto my stool, but I didn't relax. I continued to work on the filthy bandit pistol to keep my hands busy, because my fingers were all itchy to shoot. "You don't need me to go on that big search of yours, now you know he's dead," I said. Maybe this would be the end of it.

In the silence after that, I calmed myself by thinking of what my hands were doing, and I planned what I'd do next. When I finished this pistol, which would take a long time, I would set to work on Tarken's gun. Maybe I should give it to his boy. I was no favorite of the boy's mother, Leisel, and she wouldn't want to talk to me. But I was obliged to offer. And I had to talk to Freedom, Galilee's son, who worked at the tannery, the one whose room I'd rented after he'd moved out of his mom's.

The grigoris were murmuring back and forth in Russian, still being careful with their movements. It was a long conversation. I got a lot of work done.

All I learned was that they couldn't read each other's minds. That was good to know. Also interesting and of note was that Paulina had been in the HRE long enough to be fluent in Russian.

They stopped talking. They'd reached a conclusion.

"If Oleg is dead," Eli said, "we need to find his brother."

I was glad I was looking down, so they couldn't read my face. I was thunderstruck. It was news to me that Oleg Karkarov had family. Now that I knew he did, I didn't like it. My hands stilled for a moment. "Where is this brother likely to be?" I said cautiously.

"We know he was traveling with Oleg," Eli said. Paulina nodded.

That was another bit of news I didn't like.

"You need to talk to him? What about?"

"We need to find out if they were full brothers," Paulina said. "If they were, we need his blood."

I was able to look up at her with a genuine smile. "That's my kind of quest," I said.

Paulina and Eli both looked surprised that I knew an uncommon word. Fuck 'em. "My mom's a teacher," I said, before they could start trying to think of a nice way to ask.

"You've always lived in Segundo Mexia?" Eli said. I could feel he was trying to get me to relax, to like them, or at least to be at ease with them. Paulina didn't seem to care about that, and I kind of respected her point of view.

"Yes," I said, looking through the barrel of the pistol. My hands had been busy while the Russians talked. The barrel was clean as a whistle. I reassembled, loaded. Another job done. I still didn't want the gun, but at least it was sellable.

The familiar smell of Hoppe's oil was calming me. Instead of Tarken's pistol, I picked up Galilee's bolt-action Krag. It had bullets in it she'd never gotten to fire. That thought gave me a pang of grief. I put the Krag down and sat with my head bowed. I changed my mind about the Krag. I knew it was odd that I found it easier to face cleaning Tarken's pistol than Galilee's rifle. But I'd remembered Galilee's big smile.

And that was wrong. There were two wizards in my home, and I should not be paying attention to anything but them.

Eli cleared his throat. He'd asked me a question. "Do your parents live here, too?" he said again. Eli was asking if they lived in Segundo Mexia. It was easy to see no one lived in this house with me.

"Why?" I made sure to meet both pairs of eyes, blue (Paulina) and green (Eli), so they'd see how serious I was about not answering questions about my family. And since I was looking up, I saw a shadow. Someone had crept up to the door, and by the time he stepped fully into sight, his pistol up, I had jumped to my feet, Jackhammer ready. Since I'd had to waste a second by standing, so my bullet would clear the grigoris' heads, the other gunnie got off a shot. I felt my back hit the wall, and I slid down behind the stool.

"My God, it's the Tatar," Paulina was saying from far away.

"Was," Eli said briefly from much closer. "Come over here."

"She's alive?"

"Yes."

There was lots of shoving and clattering. They

were moving my table and stool out of the way. I was lying against the wall. I caught a flicker of Eli's face, broad and calm, but unhappy.

I could hear someone yelling in the distance. Chrissie. Sure, gunfire would get even Chrissie's attention. Glad she was here . . . I didn't want these two in charge of me. . . .

My mother was sitting by me when I woke up. I was on my bed. She was sitting on the stool, which had been pushed over beside it.

"Good," Mom said. "You're conscious." She sounded half-sad, half-angry.

"He was after them." I couldn't talk clear. But I wanted her to know it wasn't my fault.

"Yeah," Mom said. "He was a gunnie, like you. Josip something. Papers in his pocket."

I'd heard of him. "Josip the Tatar. He had a big name."

"Your name is bigger now. You killed him." She turned her face away, and I could tell she was biting back the words, *But that might have been you.*

"I'm okay?" I said, after flexing my muscles a little bit. I was pretty sure I was, but I had to ask what injury I had incurred. I hadn't exactly recovered from my bang on the head. Now my head felt bad again, sore and stiff.

"Bullet grazed your skull," she said. "And since you just cut off all your hair, it was easy to see the wound. It just made a messy . . . crease. Those two wizards had patched you up by the time I got here." Her face was all tight with trying to hold in stuff. "I have cleaned up all the blood," she added between gritted teeth.

Head wounds bled like a bitch. "Them two still here?"

"Those two," she said.

"Those two still here?"

"They're sitting outside. Jackson came to have a look at you. He talked to them for a moment. He'd seen them at the Antelope."

"You won't believe what they . . ." I'd been going to warn her. But then I was out again. My next little moment of consciousness, I realized I'd been ready to tell my mom something she shouldn't know about. I blessed the fact that I'd gone to sleep before I could. It went like that for what seemed like hours, a drifting time of sleep and dreams and hurting. I would be conscious just long enough to know where I was and that I'd been shot, and then I'd be out again.

When I woke up for real, my head was still hurting, though not as bad as I'd expected. Maybe I was just getting used to my head hurting. My mom was still there. Or there again.

"You better?" she said. "I made some soup while you slept. Chrissie went to the store for me. If you can get to the bathroom on your own, I need to be getting home."

"I can," I said. To prove it, I sat up. And though

it was in doubt for a moment, I didn't pass out. Another head injury, not good. But—I thought for the second time—I felt better than I had any right to feel.

I made myself look at Mom steadily. If I winced or closed my eyes, she would feel worse about leaving me, and she'd spent enough time here. If the sky outside the window wasn't lying, it was close to evening. I'd lost most of a day, drifting in and out of sleep.

And now that Mom had mentioned the bathroom, I needed to go bad. I got up, none too steady, and shuffled into the little room. I didn't shut the door. If I did, and I passed out, she wouldn't be able to get in because my body would hold the door shut.

While I was taking care of myself, Mom said, "The grigoris went back to the Antelope. They said they'd come back tomorrow. You get Chrissie to come for me if you can't manage." She looked like she'd say something more, but then she didn't.

"I will, Mom." Chrissie would get paid, as she'd already been paid for her trip to the store. She needed whatever cash she could bring in. I made my mouth turn up in a smile, so Mom could leave with a clear conscience. My mother looked at me doubtfully. I could tell she was torn. I gave her a nod, to let her know I was fine. After a moment's hesitation, she patted my hand and left.

Sure enough, there was a pot of something simmering on the stove, and she'd put a bowl ready on the table for me, spoon next to it, biscuits in the pan set beside the bowl. The smell got my feet moving. I was determined I wouldn't lie down again until I'd eaten. I swore only a time or two getting across the room to fill the bowl from the pot.

As soon as I sat down with the soup in front of me, and breathed the smell of it, I knew this was what I should be eating. My mom is a very good cook, and she knows how to season. This soup had chicken in it, and vegetables, and dumplings. The biscuits were bites of heaven. I tried to eat slowly, and with every bite I felt stronger.

When I'd broken up with a boyfriend, my first—he thought I'd neglected him, and I guess he was right—I'd asked Mom how she'd stayed with Jackson so long. She'd said, "From my side, this is how it looks. Jackson would stand by me if I poisoned his best friend. He never cheats. He works hard, he's a great provider. Just as important, he's been real good to you. That's my side. And from his side, best I can tell . . . he knows I'm loyal and I won't gossip about his doings, the sex is great, and the cooking is even better. Having both in your own home is damn near perfect." She'd grinned at me like a girl.

So this was why I was not put out that she

needed to go home to be with Jackson. I was glad she had someone who put her first.

It was pure pleasure to finish the soup slowly. I felt like a new person when I'd eaten the bowlful. I took the dishes to the sink, washed 'em up, put 'em in the drainer, smothered the little fire in the stove. I'd have to finish the soup tomorrow. I didn't have a refrigerator. Hardly anyone did, especially on the hill.

I gave myself permission to go back to bed.

The next morning I was brave enough to look at my reflection. I'd chanced on an intact mirror in an abandoned house where we camped on one of our jobs. I'd brought it home to hang in my bathroom. The electricity was on today, so I pulled the chain. The exposed bulb made everything in my bathroom glaringly clear. I took a deep breath before I turned to have a look.

It would have been better if the power had been off.

I'd been hurt worse since I started work. But I had to wince at the sight in the mirror. I looked exactly like someone who'd been shot in the head. I took off the little bandage real carefully in order to clean the wound. I said, *"Ew,"* from somewhere deep inside me. There was a raw furrow on the left side of my scalp. It had been stitched together real precise. I was kind of surprised at the skill of it. Had my mother done that? She'd said something about it, but I couldn't remember what.

Once I'd gotten used to the ugliness of the scalp wound, I moved on down to notice that the left side of my face was swollen and bruised. No surprise there.

After I had looked at myself enough, I told myself some hard truths. The Tatar's bullet could have taken off my ear—or the top of my head.

It hadn't. I should be grateful instead of dismayed.

Mom had cleaned my wound and put some thick, pink ointment on it, closed it with a sticky bandage that covered the stitches. I'd had to take the bandage off when I washed.

I leaned closer to the mirror and eyed the stitches. I was convinced Mom could never have done so neat a job. Sure of that now, I had to wonder about the bandage. It was purpose-made, not a rag with sap applied. There were clean ones waiting to be put on.

The grigoris had taken care of me.

I was sure the bandager had been the man, Eli. I didn't like the thought of him touching me, but somehow it was better than when I imagined the woman's fingers doing the job.

Shit. Now I owed them.

As if thinking about the grigoris had conjured their appearance, I could hear 'em coming up. They knocked soft and polite.

"Come in," I said, but I had my gun trained on the opening door, because all of a sudden I was angry. As soon as Eli saw me, he froze. Which was smart.

"I thought your mother might still be here," he said, trying to sound relaxed.

"No."

"Can we come in?"

"You alone?"

"Paulina and I," he said.

"Nobody followed you this time?"

"No." Eli sounded guilty and a little angry.

"Okay then."

Eli stood back to let Paulina precede him. They sat on the bench on the other side of the table, as before. Paulina looked . . . nothing. Her face was blank. I waited for one of them to open the conversation.

"We'd been here for a week without seeing him. We figured he'd given up," Eli said, by way of explaining.

"He likely to have anyone following *him?* Did Josip have a partner?"

"As far as we know, Josip the Tatar always worked by himself," said Paulina. She looked down at her hands. "That was a quick decision you made, to shoot. How'd you know he was an enemy?"

"*Your* enemy," I said, wanting us to be clear about that. "Around here, friends knock. Specially when they can hear you've already got company."

Her eyes kept returning again and again to the wound in my head. "Does it hurt?" she asked, and you could tell she'd been dying to ask.

"What the hell do you think?" *Of course it hurts, bitch. Get shot in the head and see how you feel.*

"We stopped in to see how you were," Eli said. "And to ask again if you'd work for us while we search for Oleg Karkarov's brother."

"And his name would be?"

"Sergei."

Of course. It would have to be either Sergei or Dmitri. Those seemed to be the most popular names in the Holy Russian Empire.

"And what do you need him for?"

They glanced at each other. Eli said, "As we said, we need his blood."

"On the ground? In a cup? Over an altar?" There were all kinds of religions popping up now. The old church had been half-broken in the Great Depression, when people had discovered faith would not save them from poverty and starvation. There were plenty of believers left, especially in Mexico. I'd heard there was a different kind of Christianity in the HRE.

Eli said, "No, we need him alive, so we can . . ."

Paulina scowled at Eli. He shut up. They sure did take turns hushing each other.

I thought of asking, *What's wrong with the*

tsar? But then they'd have to kill me . . . at least, they'd have to try. I felt pretty safe. The grigoris would never believe I could think it through. Here was my reasoning: It was expensive to send two grigoris traveling outside the HRE, to search for a man they didn't know was alive or dead. If the grigoris, finding Oleg dead, needed this Sergei alive for his blood . . . the only person I knew of who was both rich and afflicted with a blood disease was the Holy Russian tsar, Alexei I.

Even for a lowly gunnie like me, that was not so hard to figure out.

I didn't have any notion what Sergei's blood could do to help the tsar—but if the grigoris were involved, there was a magic ritual or some such shit.

My head began to throb with all this thinking. I wanted to sleep again.

"Does it make any difference what we need the man for, if we pay you to help us?" Eli asked.

That was a question I could answer, though I didn't have to tell the truth. "No," I said. "How long you need me for? How much you offering?"

"Considering we're not tearing you away from anything else," Paulina said with some quiet sarcasm, "here's what we'll pay per week." She named a price. In Holy Russian currency. That would convert to Texoman/New American bucks with an advantage for me.

The sum was enough to keep me for two months. If I lived to spend it. I had money at the moment, but I wasn't going to keep all of it. And I needed a stash. Hard times were always around the corner.

"As for how long," Eli said, "we'll keep searching until we decide we're not going to find him . . . or until we've got him."

"Minimum of three weeks, guaranteed." After all, if I was guarding and guiding them full-time, I couldn't be looking for another job, a permanent job, which was what I needed.

"Ridiculous," Paulina said.

I liked her not at all.

"I've already saved you from getting shot in the back. For nothing." I smiled at the grigoris, and not in a nice way. "Not even a thank-you."

Eli's mouth dropped open, and I could tell he was casting his mind back over the conversation and coming up with zero. Zilch. Nada. I raised my eyebrows, as if to say, *Right.*

He was mortified, but too proud to say so. She was too proud to even acknowledge their debt.

"You saved your own life," she pointed out, raising her nose in the air.

"Oh, you think he would have opened my door and shot at me if you hadn't been sitting there?" Josip had aimed at me only when I'd stood and offered to fight back.

Paulina shut up then. After a long moment Eli

said, "Thank you, Gunnie." It was stiff but pretty sincere.

"You're welcome, wizard. And thank you for taking care of my head. Good stitching. And I guess you had something to do with me feeling not as bad as I thought I'd feel." I didn't know how he'd done it, or how they'd done it, but I had to acknowledge their help.

After all, might as well be polite. They'd at least disposed of Josip's body, which was something. I started to ask what had happened to it, but then I realized I really didn't care.

"Where do you want to start looking for this mysterious brother?" I said. I could tell it hadn't escaped their notice that I hadn't said yes or no. I wanted to learn as much as I could. I figured that first on their agenda would be a trip to Cactus Flats, where Oleg Karkarov had been shot. (His death had been in the regional newspaper, which came out every week. It hadn't been any big secret. The grigoris couldn't be surprised I knew about it.)

"We should go to the place where Oleg died," Eli said. "Are the roads to Cactus Flats any good?"

"No," I said truthfully. "Best way to get there is by horseback. Do you both ride?"

"Yes, of course," said Paulina, looking down her nose. "How long will it take?"

"It will be a day trip," I said. "If we get started

early in the morning, we might be back here by midafternoon. Depending on what we find out, of course."

"We'll set out first thing in the morning," she told me. "Meet us at the stable." Without more conversation, Eli and Paulina left. Eli did tell me good-bye; Paulina kept her good-byes to herself.

Since I had the rest of the afternoon on my own, I paid the visits I had to pay. Though my head ached, I could walk and talk, and I should not put them off. If I was going somewhere with the grigoris, I might not come back.

I went to Freedom's little house when I figured he'd gotten off work. I gave him half Galilee's portion of the money, and I offered him her Krag. He gave me a hug, took the money, declined the rifle, but was glad to take the bandit pistol I'd cleaned.

"I know you loved her," Freedom said. I nodded. I wasn't going to cry anymore, but that was a hard resolve to keep. It helped that a stranger was there. She turned out to be Freedom's girlfriend, a shy and pretty youngster I'd never met. I could see she was pregnant. Freedom told me, "If it's a girl, we'll name her Galilee."

Next I walked back into the older part of town for the visit I was dreading even more, but for different reasons.

Leisel, mother of Tarken's son, disliked me

quite a bit. She and Tarken had been living apart for the past three years at least. I knew Tarken had had other women before he and I had begun being together, but I seemed to be the one Leisel objected to. No matter how Leisel felt about me, Tarken had been a good father, and I had to honor that by visiting his son.

"Well, it's you," Leisel said when she opened the door. "I didn't know if you'd come by." She was a tiny woman with red hair and a strong right hook, as I'd discovered when she'd come by Tarken's while I was there one night.

This evening there was no fire in Leisel. James Lee, who was twelve, and small like his mother and father, was deep in a shadow of grieving. He glowered at me.

"Why did my father count on you to protect him?" James Lee said, his voice all jagged with emotion. He was a quiet boy. He had always treated me with respect when he'd been with Tarken. Not anymore.

"Because I'm one of the best shots there is," I said. "But there were too many of them firing at us. I was the only one left. And I tracked them down and killed them all." That was all I had to offer the kid. James Lee ran outside and let the screen door slam behind him.

I thought about going after him, but Leisel said, "He needs some time. He's a brooder. He'll see it straight, sooner or later."

I gave Leisel Tarken's whole portion, for James Lee. That wasn't the normal thing to do, any more than giving Freedom some of Galilee's share. No one would have said anything if I'd kept it all. But I figured Tarken would have liked me doing that. I knew now that we hadn't been in love, but I'd cared about him something ferocious.

I had nothing more to talk to Leisel about. She did know where Tarken had been buried, but I didn't think I'd go to the cemetery, at least not yet. He wasn't there, to me.

Martin's wife and his daughter had been killed by a Mexican raiding party years ago. His brother, Thomas, wasn't entitled. I felt free to keep Martin's fourth, and I was glad to be spared another visit.

Early the next morning I took most of my money to my mother's. No one would dare to break into Jackson Skidder's home. Mom was at the school and Jackson was at one of his businesses, so I hid the money in a place I'd made in the wall behind the bed in the room I'd had growing up. Mom knew to check it if something happened to me.

I left her a bag of oranges smuggled in from southern Dixie. Army had acquired the bag (I didn't ask any questions how he'd done that), and I'd bought it before anyone else could. Mom would divide some of the oranges among the kids at school, but maybe she and Jackson would have one apiece. I left a note to tell her I was guarding the grigoris and where we were heading. If I didn't come back, Jackson might track them down. Maybe.

But if they got the better of me, they deserved to live.

I had assembled what I needed, a task that had taken me less than five minutes. If we were going to Cactus Flats, we wouldn't be there long. I liked riding a horse, and I liked going slow enough to see the land, but the trip would have been really interesting if the road there had been good enough for a car. Evidently, the grigoris had one. Though I'd been in a truck many a time, I'd ridden on a train once and in a car once. Those had been real events.

According to my grandmother, when this big space had been one country, a lot of families had had their own cars.

Tarken and Martin had saved for the truck, bought it piece by piece, searched junkyards, found old manuals, and put the truck together from old parts, new-fashioned ones, and imagination. Our crew's truck had been part Ford one-and-a-half-ton, part Kenworth, Martin had said.

I remembered the hours they'd spent building the truck, how proud they'd been. When I remembered what it looked like the morning after the ambush, I got angry all over again. There was a practical reason I regretted the loss of the truck, too. If it hadn't wrecked, I could have sold it for almost enough money to retire. Or I could have started my own crew, an idea both scary and exciting.

Right at this moment shade-tree mechanics all around Segundo Mexia were combining pieces of our crew's truck with their own vehicles. Eventually, most of our truck would hit the road again.

I was okay with that. Bodies could be claimed, but vehicles were fair game if no survivors were on the spot.

Long way around to say that when I met the grigoris in front of the stable, they were talking with John Seahorse, the owner. They were asking John to recommend the three horses least likely to give us trouble. I learned from their conversation that the grigoris had left their car in an unused room at the stable.

We set off at eight thirty or thereabouts, riding Briar, Star, and Birdie. We weren't carrying much besides ourselves—I'd brought a little emergency food, my guns (of course), and a canteen full of water, and Paulina and Eli had canteens only. The weather was clear and bright, the sky cloudless, and the talk . . . well, we didn't, besides a comment or two from Eli about some feature of the landscape from time to time. We reached the scraggly outskirts of Cactus Flats about two hours before noon.

Eli and Paulina told me to lead them to the sheriff's office first. This was going to be very interesting for the sheriff and me and all the inhabitants of the town. I was counting on the people of Cactus Flats to be cool with this situation.

The sheriff, Cal Trujillo, was sitting in the front room when we came in. He was gripping a pen. The day deputy, Maria Hannigan, was typing on a form very slowly. Her desk was smaller and side by side with Cal's.

Cal and Maria looked up with a certain amount of eagerness. The fact that there was paperwork on their desks may have had something to do with that.

Since both Cal and Maria knew me, it would have made sense for me to introduce my employers and explain their mission, and I'd opened my mouth to do so. That was wasted effort. It didn't seem to occur to either Paulina or Eli to step back and let me do this. They walked in ahead of me, taking it for granted that I was falling in somewhere behind them, just in case they needed me. They might as well have tied me up outside like one of the horses.

Cal shot me a quick look that translated as *What the hell is up with these people?*

From behind their backs, I shrugged, raised my hands, palms up. *I got no idea. I'm along for the pay.*

"Sheriff," Eli said, correctly identifying Cal, "I'm Eli Savarov, and this is Paulina Cooper-smith, my partner."

He did not introduce me. He did not refer to the fact that I was in the room.

"Yes," Cal said after a pause. He didn't think slowly, but he liked to let people believe he did. "Welcome to Cactus Flats. I'm Cal Trujillo, elected sheriff of this town. This here is Deputy Maria Hannigan."

Maria looked past Paulina at the fresh bandage on my head. She raised an eyebrow. I raised my hands again.

"How can we help you two this fine morning?" Maria said, deciding that since my employers were ignoring me, she would, too . . . for the moment. Maria, mother of three, wife of one, was a better shot than Cal, but he was a better tracker. They made a good law enforcement team.

Naturally, Paulina and Eli took the two good chairs in front of the sheriff's desk. They did not look to see if I'd been seated. I sighed, but real quiet. The gait of the horse over the rough terrain hadn't done me any favors. My head had been feeling better—a lot better—but now it wasn't so good. I found the only remaining chair, a wobbly one that had been pushed into a dark corner for good reason. I tugged it around so I could watch the door with my left eye and the people with my right.

"We'd like to ask some questions about a shooting that took place here," Eli said.

"Yeah?" Cal was trying hard not to look at me.

Paulina said, "Some months ago a man named Oleg Karkarov was killed here, we were told. He was a low-level magic practitioner. What you call a grigori."

"We don't get that many shooting deaths here," Maria said. "Lots of bar fights, with knives, things of that sort." She was trying just as hard not to glance my way.

"So you remember it well." Eli was doing a good job of looking relaxed and concerned. And he didn't seem to be picking up on anything.

"I do." With a creak of his old swivel chair, Cal rose and walked to the front of Maria's desk, where he parked his butt. He leaned against the desk like he had all the time in the world.

Maria opened her mouth to tell him to move, but then she thought again and bent back over the paperwork. I noticed her pen didn't move much.

"Can you tell us how Karkarov was killed?" Paulina said, as delicately as if talking about it would rake up terrible memories for Cal.

Cal covered his mouth with his hand for a moment. "I can do that," he said, real sober. "Oleg Karkarov had passed through this part of Texoma round eighteen, nineteen years ago. He made quite an impression then. People were real interested when he came back. He started asking some odd questions around town. But then, after he'd been here maybe three days, someone caught up with Oleg behind Skelly's place—that's a bar, Elbows Up—and shot him."

"He died right away?"

Cal laughed. "Yes, ma'am. He'd been shot four times before he hit the ground, so he definitely died right away."

Paulina turned to look at Eli, her eyes narrowed. She knew there was more to the story now. "Was Karkarov alone?" she asked in a much brisker voice.

"When?"

The grigoris looked at Cal blankly.

"He was alone when he died," Cal said. "Except for the shooter, of course."

"Did he arrive here with a companion?" Eli said.

"Yes," Cal said. "With two."

And here I sat up straight, because this part of the story was new to me.

"Oleg checked into the hotel with a whore. Becky Blue Eyes, her name is. Oh, and there was a man with Oleg, too. Oleg told the hotelkeeper he was his brother. But the brother—Sergei, I think, was his name—he didn't get a room at the hotel. He slept in the car. He said he was afraid thieves would pick on it during the night if he didn't stay in it."

"That true?" Eli asked.

114

"Possibly," Cal said. "Mostly good people here, but every now and then someone wants an item that ain't theirs."

"Did you have much conversation with this Sergei?"

"I only know what other people told me," Cal said. "I don't think I ever did more than nod to the man when I passed him on the street. Either man, really. I just heard who they were. And I kind of remembered Oleg. When I heard the shots and ran behind the bar to find out what was going on, I came upon Oleg, dead as a doornail. While I was examining Oleg's body, the brother, Sergei, took off in the car."

I hadn't known that, either.

"So Oleg was killed perhaps three days after he got to Cactus Flats?" Paulina was going to get it straight in her mind. That's the kind of person she was.

"Yeah."

"Someone followed him here."

"Or someone learned he was here as soon as he checked into the hotel," Maria said, as if she was determined to be fair.

"Was this Becky Blue Eyes a local?" Paulina said.

"She is now." Cal smiled.

"What? Why?"

"She didn't have any way to leave," he said. And that was that.

Becky Blue Eyes was "plying her trade," as Maria put it, from a back room at the bar across the street, Elbows Up. Many of the people in town (men) were pleased to have a "new" prostitute, since Miranda Redhead had passed away from a miscarriage, and Harvey Sweetcheeks was getting old.

Paulina and Eli both got this narrow-lipped look, like they were about to crawl down a sewer, even before we walked through the door of Elbows Up. I didn't know if it was the prospect of talking to a prostitute or going into a workers' bar that had stuck something up their asses.

Inside it was dark and there was music on the record player, some Mexican guitar group wailing about dead cowboys in Spanish. Since it was early in the day for drinking, there was only one person at the bar, a tall man with no flesh on his bones. He was a living cadaver, and locally he was known as Skelly. However, since we weren't dealing with locals, I introduced him to my employers as Jorge Maldonado, his christened name . . . if his parents had bothered to have the water put on his head.

"Can I get you something to drink?" Jorge asked, moving back behind the bar to the serving side. "If you don't want to start your day with something strong, I have tea or lemonade." Jorge had a refrigerator. I envied him. Someday I would save enough to get one, and by that time the electricity in Segundo Mexia would be more reliable.

While I stared at the refrigerator with longing, Eli and Paulina were polite enough to order some lemonade . . . or maybe they were just thirsty. This time Eli remembered I was a human being and offered me some, too. I accepted. Something cold might help my head.

Skelly leaned across the bar to hug me. He's tall, I'm short, so I had to boost myself up with one of the high stools. But the hug warmed me, after my stint of being invisible.

"You two know each other," Paulina said.

Couldn't get anything past her, no sirree.

"Are you kidding?" Skelly asked, and he was about to go on when he caught my warning eye. "Ah . . . Lizbeth here's one of the best-known gunnies in all Texoma. And I'm sorry for your loss," he added just to me. "I heard what you did. Tarken would have been proud. Heard you got 'em all."

I appreciated his kind words.

"We understand there's a prostitute named Becky working out of here?" Eli said.

"Becky might be up by now," Skelly said. "If you want her to take on the both of you, though, better give her another hour."

I would have kissed Skelly if I'd been tall enough. It was all I could do to keep the laughter inside my mouth.

"No," said Paulina, who sounded as though she were being strangled. "We just need to have a conversation with her."

At that moment the door to the right of the bar opened and Becky stepped out. I'd never met her, but the minute she appeared, I knew I'd seen her before. I tried to blend into the wood of the bar. When Becky saw me, she froze. I gave her a little finger wave, both hands open and empty. She relaxed enough to smile at the two grigoris, but from then on she kept half an eye on me.

"Becky, this here's Eli and Paulina from the Holy Russian Empire, and they want to ask you a thing or two about that man you came here with," Skelly said.

I was certain Cal had called the bar the minute we left the sheriff's office, and that Skelly had knocked on Becky's door two seconds after that. Becky's glossy brown hair was put up, with ringlets hanging down, all her makeup was on, and she wore a polka-dotted skirt that came just below her knees. Her red blouse had a big collar that was spread wider than it should have been to show her boobs. And she wore high heels, which not too many women in our part of the world did. Hard to find, really expensive, couldn't run in 'em. It was quite a production.

"Oh, what kind of thing or two would you like to know?" Becky said, sounding all flirtatious, though she flicked an anxious glance at me.

Since Paulina and Eli were looking away from me, I gave her a wink. The brilliance of Becky's smile increased. "Let me see. I was aiming to be a priestess in your Holy Russian Empire, but my bad, bad daddy spanked me for praying too long, and I developed a taste for it. I just love to be punished for my wicked ways."

Eli turned red, but he was also mashing down a smile. Paulina had turned to stone, far as I could tell.

"Not about your . . . livelihood," Eli said. "About Oleg Karkarov."

"May he burn in hell if there is one," Becky said, and spat on the floor.

The bar floor was used to way worse, but Skelly looked pained.

"Why?" Paulina had made up her mind this conversation would be on point.

"He brought me here from Juárez, where I was . . . vacationing. He said we'd be in this hick town a week while he tracked down a rumor he'd heard. Something he could turn to his advantage. Then he'd take me back home," Becky said. She turned to look at her host. "Scuse me, Skelly, them's his words. I didn't know no different. He told me he hadn't been hereabouts for nearly twenty years, time was ripe for him to visit again. He was sure no one would remember him from before."

Skelly and I both smiled.

"So here I am, stuck in beautiful Cactus Flats, and Oleg's in the graveyard, I guess. I didn't check to see where they put him." She raised an eyebrow at Skelly.

"Traveler's corner," he said.

"And I'm saving up enough money to get back to Juárez, or somewhere close," she finished. "I had me a good job there. I'm exotic, to the Mexicans."

"What about the man driving the car?" Eli sounded wary. Maybe he'd realized there was more to the story than he'd been getting from the people of Cactus Flats.

Becky yawned, a jaw-cracking gape that showed she was missing some back teeth. "Truth, I didn't talk to either of them that much. They wasn't interested in my conversation."

"Do you remember his name?" Paulina's voice was sharp.

"Oleg," Becky said, looking at the grigori with surprise.

"No, the driver," Paulina snapped.

"Don't take my nose off, bitch! You ain't paid me anything, you don't own my time." And Becky, who'd set herself down at a table, tapped the area in front of her. Skelly brought her a glass of tea. They had a routine.

I enjoyed the sight of Paulina's lip curling before she apologized. "I am sorry. We're anxious to know his name, the driver," she said more civilly.

"Hmmmm." Becky made a big show of remembering. "Russian name," she said thoughtfully. "I think it was Dmitri. No, wait, Sergei." She looked at them as though she was waiting for applause.

"Thank you, Becky," Eli said. "Do you have any ideas about where this Sergei might have gone? Or if it's true he was Oleg's full brother?" He didn't sound too optimistic.

To the astonishment of every person in the room, Becky said, "I reckon Sergei went back to Juárez, because there was a kid there he and Oleg took care of."

That bit of news set off the grigoris like a firecracker under their chairs. Paulina and Eli asked questions with a one-two punch. It was just like a fight on Saturday night at the gym. In short order they'd extracted every bit of actual information Becky had, and quite a few guesses.

But the upshot was the same, though with tiny details. Sergei—or Oleg, Becky Blue Eyes said she wasn't completely sure which one was the father and which the uncle—maintained a girl child in Juárez, of unknown age but not a baby. This girl had been left in the charge of her maternal grandmother during the men's absence. The mother of the girl was dead.

"Come to think on it," Becky said, looking at the two wizards with close attention, "Sergei sounded more like the girl's uncle. I think Oleg was the dad."

"Did Oleg and Sergei both have the same parents?" Paulina asked.

"I never heard them say anything different," Becky said. "Maybe, maybe not."

That riled up the two grigoris again. They pelted Becky with more questions. "Why would Sergei leave with such haste after his brother's death?" Paulina said. "Wouldn't he want to stay and get revenge? Do you think he knew the man who killed his brother?"

Becky looked very thoughtful. "I do think so," she said, not even glancing in my direction.

If the dad was Oleg, I had a sister.

And we were both in deep trouble.

"Do you want to see the grave?" Skelly asked. He was also the undertaker.

Paulina looked disgusted. "I don't see how that would do any good," she said. She turned to Eli and muttered, "We need a blood relative, not a corpse."

This time Skelly's eyes flicked toward me, but I looked down as if the scarred surface of the bar was the most interesting thing I'd seen in a long time.

Paulina and Eli slid off their barstools, talking to each other in Russian. I was getting used to them assuming I'd just follow them. I was *not* getting used to them not letting me be the first one out the door. It was my job to see who might be waiting there. We were going to have to have a talk, it was clear. But this one time it was good that they left first. When they were safely outside, I said, "Thanks, Skelly."

Skelly nodded. "Sure thing. Those grigoris may know a lot about magic, but they don't know shit about people."

"I'm seeing that."

"And about Oleg? If it hadn't been you, someone else would have killed that son of a bitch. We all recognized him, we all knew the things he done. Spelling Candle was just one of 'em."

Becky Blue Eyes cleared her throat in a pointed way. "I didn't tell them nothing. And I saw it all." I put a coin on the table in front of her by way of thanks, and she nodded like a queen accepting a bow. "Just between you and me, honey child, I'm not sure Sergei had the same mom as Oleg."

"But he had the same dad?"

Becky gave a big shrug. "He didn't look much like Oleg. That's no proof, of course. I don't look much like my sister."

"Thanks, Becky." I put more money on the table.

I gave Skelly a quick hug before I followed the grigoris out to the horses, after one more longing glance at the refrigerator. I was feeling grim, and I was thinking real hard. Looked like we were going to Juárez.

I'd better stock up on ammo.

The ride back to Segundo Mexia was mostly quiet, because the grigoris didn't want to share their real thoughts with me. Which was fine; I wasn't sharing mine with them. I'd find out sooner or later what they intended to do with the (possible) little daughter of Oleg (or Sergei) Karkarov. I wondered what the grigoris would do to me if they found out I was definitely the daughter of the low-level grigori they'd been tracking. I didn't know them well, but I was pretty sure whatever they would do, it wouldn't be pleasant. So I was keeping my little piece of news to myself.

After we returned the horses to their stable and settled with John Seahorse, Paulina made a detour to the Antelope, while Eli went to the room at the stable where the car was being housed. I trailed after him.

The local garage, right by the stable, kept in business selling gas and repairing and coaxing old vehicles to work. It also used an empty space at the stable where visitors could store their cars in safety, and that was where Eli went. When he unlocked the door and threw it open, I gasped. I'd never seen a car so fancy. This one was only a year or two old. It was black, with glossy dark-red bumpers. It had CELEBRITY TOURER on the hood in raised silver letters.

Tarken had dreamed about this car, had studied pictures in the few car magazines that had come our way. It gave me a pang to see it sitting in all its beauty. He would have enjoyed the sight so much. He would have pored over the engine like it was a Bible.

The manufacturer (in Michigan, now part of Canada) kept turning out incredibly sturdy autos for those who could afford them. This was well built and also deluxe.

In Texoma, backyard mechanics had endless discussions about rings and carburetors and rods. Keeping the truck running had been a full-time occupation. Eli, however, assumed the Celebrity Tourer would run just fine. He didn't even raise the hood. Paulina came along and joined him in the shed. As far as I could see, Paulina didn't think about the car at all. "What are you doing here, just standing and looking?" she said impatiently. "No one has touched the car."

"Nothing has been disturbed," he said, but as if his mind was on something else. "All my spells are untapped."

They'd booby-trapped the car. I was so shocked I barely stopped myself from lighting into 'em. "I hope you don't mean that anyone touching your car would be harmed," I said with as much control as I could summon up. "In these parts something as fancy as this car is a real attraction, and all kinds of people would love to have a gander at it. Not to harm it or take something from it. Just to look at it, and see the engine, and crawl underneath, and talk about how it works."

"We could not answer the questions," Paulina said without a trace of shame.

"Not even Eli?" I tried not to sound shocked. Sure, there were women mechanics, like Lavender. And I knew the parts of an engine well enough. But generally, the ones bitten by the lust for car parts were men.

"Not even Eli," he said soberly, but I could see he was almost smiling.

I gave the car as good a going-over as I could, in honor of the people of Segundo Mexia.

The Celebrity Tourer had a square cut in the roof, a big one, and there was some kind of a top to roll open and closed as the weather demanded, and a hard square to insert over that. The square locked into place on the inside, I noted with approval. It was April, only the beginning of the dust and sun season. I tried to reduce my anger at the booby traps. And the booby traps, they'd be handy in other towns.

I just didn't want anyone I knew getting hurt for being naturally curious.

It was a relief to watch Eli lock the shed door after he'd checked the gas and oil levels. At least he knew that much. I felt better someway.

When they were about to shoot off for the Antelope, I decided now would be a good time to tell them a few things. "You hired me to guide you and be your gunnie," I said. "I know you two are big bad wizards, but you have to let me do the job you hired me for."

They both stared at me without any expression. I waited for them to ask a question. Nope.

"So what I do is this. I leave a building first in case anyone's aiming at the doorway from across the street or on a rooftop. I go into a building first, same reason. I tell you to get down, you get down. I tell you to run, you run. Okay?"

More of the staring.

"In the morning," Paulina said, "we leave for Ciudad Juárez. Please be here no later than eight o'clock."

"I will," I said. And that was the end of our conversation.

The grigoris didn't seem to have any other use for me the rest of the day. I was glad to part ways with them.

I went home. My friend Dan Brick came by, and we went out in the desert to shoot, which always calmed me down. He'd brought a couple of pork chops—not from Big Balls, unfortunately—and I cooked them with some onions and peppers and made some biscuits and peeled an orange and topped some strawberries. That was a good supper. I felt so much better—since I'd gotten off the horse, my head felt like a normal head—I could actually enjoy the food and the company. It was a relief to be with someone I understood.

After we'd done the dishes, Dan left. I

packed again, this time with care. I didn't have many clothes, but I had to take what I could. I didn't know when I'd be home again, or what opportunities I'd have to wash.

More importantly, I packed up all my firearms and ammo. I had two extra magazines apiece for the Colts. I felt rich in guns right now.

When I'd gone over everything twice, and taken some strawberries down to Chrissie because they'd go bad in a day or two, I turned in, determined to enjoy my last night in my own bed. I hadn't expected to leave town so soon.

The next morning I walked away with a look back at my little house. I had a bad feeling that it would be a while before I saw it again. Of course, there was always the chance I wouldn't come back.

Paulina and Eli seemed surprised when I loaded my big leather bag of weapons and ammo into the back seat. Paulina looked outright scornful. "You brought more guns than clothes," she said.

"Am I not your gunnie?" I tossed the much smaller bag of clothes and other stuff into the trunk, where two suitcases were already tucked. I'd gone on trips before, sure, but had seldom spent more than two nights in a row away from Segundo Mexia. I told myself that this would be an adventure. I just hoped it wouldn't be too much of one. At least we'd packed big water bottles, and food, though it wasn't easy to have a good meal off things that wouldn't spoil in a hot car.

The way out of town led south past the schoolhouse. My mother was outside with the kids, and I waved. She lined up all the children and waved back, because seeing me in a car was an interesting moment.

"Was that your mother we passed?" Eli, who was driving, seemed to be curious about everything.

Mom did look different from the day I'd gotten shot. Her hair was loose, and she was with the children, which always made her happy. "Yes," I said.

"Her name is Candle, she said. She's young." Eli glanced back in the rearview mirror.

"Sixteen when she had me."

"Young to be wed," Paulina commented, but not as if she gave a shit.

"Old enough to be raped." That shut them up.

As I'd previously noticed, Eli and Paulina weren't anxious to share their plans. But as the day passed, they grew more comfortable with talking to each other in front of me. After all, I was just the hired help, along to keep them from getting killed in a mundane way. I began to piece their lives together from bits of their conversation.

Paulina had left England as a young woman, at least ten years before, to travel to the Holy

Russian Empire. By herself. That took some starch. She'd heard that wizards were welcome in the HRE; wizards were even admired.

Eli had been born in Mother Russia, but he'd come to our country—what used to be our country—on one of the boats in the armada that had carried the royal family, the remaining nobility, their surviving servants, and a lot of army, during the great rescue of 1918. Of course, Eli had been a child. He had living parents, and at least one brother.

I listened, and I watched and waited. That first day the country we drove through was calm but busy. We saw other cars and trucks, more people on horseback and afoot. It was about fifty-fifty Texomans and Mexicans, not that you could always tell the difference. I kept an eye out for trouble, but I spent a lot of time observing Eli and Paulina, watching the way they were with each other.

It was better than remembering Tarken and Galilee and Martin, or wondering what I would do when I returned home.

I'd never been around real wizards. I'd only talked to assholes with a smattering of talent, like the man who'd raped my mother. I could smell the power on Eli and Paulina. It didn't exactly scare me, but it made me cautious. Paulina was older and the leader of this little expedition, for sure, but Eli seemed to be almost equal. He had some edge over Paulina, at least from her attitude; she'd catch herself up short when she was about to stomp him in a disagreement. I couldn't figure it out.

We weren't anywhere close to a town around nightfall, so we camped. The weather was good, and we had a meal we'd brought with us, packed at the Antelope and kept cool by a chunk of ice, so the evening was easy. I didn't exactly sit with the grigoris, but I didn't sit too far away, either. No one had been following us, but there was never any telling who'd appear out of the desert. I kept alert.

Before we went to sleep, Eli cast a spell around our campsite strong enough to keep a bear out, he told me. His hands moved, and his lips, too. I watched. Paulina didn't. She trusted him to do it right.

I'd never seen anything like this. Eli seemed all wrapped up in strength.

"If this spell of yours will keep bears out, why do you need me?" I said.

"It won't keep out bullets," he said.

That was a good answer. "I'll keep watch tonight," I said.

"This night I don't think you need to," Paulina said. "I need to check your bandage while it's still light enough to see the wound." She stood and waited, none too patiently.

Feeling like a child, I went over to her. Gently

enough, she removed the old bandage and looked. "The healing went well," she told Eli. "It looks a week old now."

Eli looked, too. This was massively irritating. But now I knew what I'd suspected was true. I'd been feeling so much better than I'd had any reason to because they hadn't just bandaged me up. They'd hurried the repairing. I had accused them unjustly of being thankless, when they'd done something practical to pay their debt.

"You won't need the bandage any longer," Eli said.

"Good. Thanks for the help." I forced out the words.

I spared a cup of water to rinse off the healing furrow. Now that I could touch it directly, I could feel a slightly puckered new scar.

I used a little more water to brush my teeth, and that made me feel more myself. I'd been told (mainly by Tarken) that I was almost extreme about being clean, but the two grigoris spent more time on grooming than I'd ever known adults to do.

That night Paulina brushed her hair, and then washed her face with our precious water, before getting into her sleeping roll. First thing in the morning, Eli shaved, though his face hair was light enough that he could have waited another day. He, too, brushed his hair thoroughly. Before he tied it back, it hung over his shoulders in a light curtain. I'd never seen a man who wore his hair that long, except for the Indians.

I stopped myself before I could run my hand over my head again. I'd remembered my last look in the mirror. I could tell my hair had already grown some. Soon it would be long enough to curl. Then there'd be the damn ringlets. They made me look like a child. But now I thought it was lucky I had thick hair; when it grew back, maybe the scar wouldn't be visible. That was vanity, and it was ridiculous to think about my hair when I faced so many more challenges. I forced myself to get busy packing up the few things we'd used.

We got an early start, there being nothing else to do. I wasn't as familiar with this part of the country, but from my crew's previous visit I remembered that the terrain would get rougher. To reach a town sizeable enough to have a hotel by that night, we needed to make good time. We were able to gas up early at an isolated garage. I imagined the big trade there was fixing flat tires and taking care of overheated engines.

As the day went on, we sighted people less and less. When we did, they were almost always on foot and staying parallel to the road, but not on it. We were close to the Texoma-Mexico border. From time to time, to get a better view, I stood up on the floorboard of the back seat with my head out of the air-roof, or whatever it was called.

This annoyed Paulina, but I didn't care. Danger had sidled up to me and given me a nudge and a wink.

About an hour after noon—we'd had a quick lunch—we were driving on a dirt road that wound through low, rocky hills. There were stands of oak and some boulders on either side of the road. Great cover. I thought of the last ambush, on the Corbin road. My nerves were strung high and tight. I looked up to see a buzzard riding the air, wings broad and beautiful against the clear blue, as we were rounding a bend. So I got knocked around a little when Paulina put on the brakes.

There was a tree lying across the road, leaves still green. I could see the fresh cut on the trunk.

"Ambush," I yelled, and here they came. I was standing up on the rear seat, shooting through the air-roof, before I finished saying it. I shot two of them with Jackhammer, and they went down like bags of sand. That left two. I winged only one of those, due to a lurch of the car. I could see him squirming on the ground and got off a second shot, which killed him. I had swung around to drop the last bandit when Eli popped through the hole alongside me. He was reaching into one of his vest pockets, and pulled out a stone, which he clutched. He said a few words.

Before I could shove him to get him out of my way, Eli made the man's blood leave his body.

It was an eye-catching way to kill someone, that's for sure.

Eli dropped into the car like his feet had vanished from under him. Scared the shit out of me; I thought he'd gotten shot somehow. Turns out doing death magic takes a lot out of you, and some grigoris feel it sooner than others. Eli felt it sooner.

A fifth bandit leaped up from behind a boulder and began to run. I was so distracted by Eli that my quick shot just creased the bandit's shoulder. Paulina was out the passenger door and after her like a bullet looking for a body to hit. Paulina brought her down and left her moaning, by some means I couldn't see. Maybe she'd just tackled her hard. Then Paulina strolled back to turn off the car.

I climbed out. Though the surprise was still making my hands quiver, I had brought down our attackers. While Paulina's and Eli's help had been nice, I could have done everything myself. After the disaster on the Corbin road, my relief was enormous. I let out a deep, shuddery breath, and I smiled at Paulina. Out of sheer surprise, she smiled back.

Between us, we hauled Eli from the car and laid him under the shade of a tree. I was sitting by his side, my back against the tree trunk, when he came to, some ten, fifteen minutes later. Eli's broad face was a bad color, sort of gray, and his green eyes rolled toward me, checking who I was. I could tell he recognized me.

"Listen, wizard," I said. "Don't ever put your head between me and my shot again. I coulda blown your skull away."

"Sorry," he said, but he didn't sound sorry. He, too, almost smiled. "I wanted to try the spell."

"Yeah, okay." I handed him a canteen with the screw top removed, and he raised his head with some difficulty to take a swallow. I took the canteen and had a swig myself. "You needed a rock for that?"

"I invoked the spell with the rock. It was residing in the stone, I'd put it there, and I said a word of power to make it active."

"Quite a spell."

"Extreme," he agreed.

We had some shade from the bright sun. The landscape around us had woken up since the gunshots had faded. I could hear bugs moving and birds making their little noises. A few yards away I saw a quick movement. A very large spider was making its way to the west, getting away from us with good speed. It was kind of peaceful, now that our enemies were dead and we were not.

After a moment Eli said, "Where's Paulina?"

"*Interrogating* the one left alive." I had just learned "interrogating" was another word for torture.

136

"Oh. Just a bandit, surely? Not after us in particular?" He turned his head to one side as if he was looking for her.

"Yeah, well. She seems to want to make certain sure."

A voice rose and fell, babbling like a child's.

"Is that who's talking?" He looked at me.

"I think the gal's telling Paulina what she had for supper five years ago. Your friend can make people talk."

"Not you, though."

"I'll talk when I got something to say. Want some more water?" I said.

"Please." Eli lifted his head a little and I unscrewed the canteen again. This time he propped himself up on an elbow and took a bigger drink. He sighed and lay back down.

"How much longer you got to stay flat?" I said after a while, though I wasn't anxious to be in the car again.

"A little while." Eli's eyes closed, so I shut up.

After a minute he said, "You see how bright the sun is?"

"Yeah."

"But we are in the shade right now. Not just the tree shade, but we're in the shadow of the cloud overhead."

"Yeah. What of it?"

"Sometimes I feel like that," he said, sounding almost drowsy. "I serve the tsar, and he's the sun.

The people who turn and twist in their politics under him, they're the clouds. And we're the people who get caught in the shadows."

"That doesn't make a lick of sense," I said, but I knew what he was talking about. They had their mission, I thought with a lot of grimness. I had mine. I wondered what would happen to me if they discovered I'd deceived them about who my real father was.

Eli lay silent for a while after that. The breeze picked up a strand of his hair and blew it across his face. With a little hesitation, I brushed it to the side. He didn't move. Good.

The natural sounds of the land were interrupted only by the distant rise and fall of the bandit's voice. From her Spanish, she'd come across the border from Mexico. I'd checked the pockets of the others. One had Mexican papers, the others were Texomans.

The next time I looked down, Eli's eyes were open.

"You've had to do this often?" I said.

"Stop bandits? Only once or twice. You did very well."

"It's my living," I said.

"How long?"

"How long have I been a gunnie? Since I got out of school. At first with whoever needed an extra hand, and then with Tarken and Martin and Galilee."

"Your mother didn't have other plans for you?"

"Did your folks have other plans for you?" I said.

He laughed, just a little, and then winced. "Not this," he admitted. "But it was my talent, and the best service I could offer my tsar."

A shriek rose in the air and was abruptly cut off. After a moment Paulina came into view. She was wiping off a knife on the kerchief I'd last seen on the wounded woman's neck. Guess "wounded" wasn't the correct term anymore.

"Random bandit," she said. "If there was some kind of targeting, she didn't know anything about it."

The idea that they'd been waiting for us, just us, to come along . . . I'd wondered about that. This was a good place for an ambush, out in the middle of nothing, no witnesses. If I had been a thief, I'd have picked this spot. But you might wait for days for a good enough target to pass through. On the other hand, if you knew someone was very likely to use this road because it was the obvious route to Juárez . . .

We might not be the only people who'd talked to Becky Blue Eyes about the death of Oleg Karkarov. That was a question I'd never thought to put to her.

I'd used up some of Eli's unconscious time—while Paulina had been interrogating the former surviving bandit—by tying a rope to the tree and then to the hitch on the rear of the car. Very carefully I'd pulled the tree out of the way. Paulina seemed surprised to find the road cleared.

"You did that?" she said, looking down at me.

I nodded. Who the fuck else would have done it?

"You know how to drive?"

"Part of a smuggling crew," I reminded her.

"Then you can drive now."

"I can't drive and shoot at the same time, Paulina. You hired me to shoot."

She wanted to argue. She didn't like that I made sense. Her mouth got all puckered.

"Gunnie's right," Eli said. He struggled to sit up, and Paulina was on the ground instantly, putting an arm behind him. I didn't think they were lovers, but I knew it would be a mistake to touch Eli in front of Paulina.

I went over to the car, holding open the passenger door. He would not feel well enough to drive.

Paulina got him there and into the car, and then she took the driver's seat. I got into the back. We had spent well over an hour by this road. We wouldn't get to the larger town we'd hoped to reach by dusk.

If we didn't want to camp again, and I didn't, we'd have to spend the night at the next small settlement on the map. It was about two hours' drive away, and it was named Mil Flores—

Thousand Flowers. We got there about five. I spotted a hotel and a restaurant and a garage. That persuaded Paulina that Mil Flores was a good stopping place.

We might have driven longer, tried to make the larger town, if Eli hadn't been so ragged. He was still a little wobbly. The instant Paulina noticed this, she was determined to stop. Eli was clearly the center of her universe. If you'd asked me, I'd have guessed Paulina would be a ruthless boss to any apprentice or minion, along the lines of "Whatever doesn't kill you makes you stronger."

We went into the hotel, a weather-beaten two-story wooden building, to see about rooms. We were able to park right by the step up to the porch.

Comstock's Hotel was nothing much inside. I expected Paulina and Eli to stick up their noses, but they didn't. At least it seemed clean, if the wood was rough and splintery and the few carpets almost worn through. The man at the desk didn't have a gun out on the counter, always a good sign. Also, he didn't blink an eye at Paulina's tattoos or Eli's grigori vest, though you could tell he noticed those things.

Me, he ignored. I was getting used to it.

There were two rooms free. Paulina said she and I could share one, and Eli would have the other. That kind of surprised me. I would have thought she and Eli would bunk together. When she'd paid and gotten the keys, Paulina asked if the hotel dining room was open for supper and breakfast (it was).

She'd turned away when the host said to me, "Come down from the north?"

"More or less," I said.

"Uneventful trip?" he asked.

So he was more than just curious. "We saw a coyote and a buzzard and a few hundred snakes," I said. "Why?"

"Wondered if your friend here had been in a fight," the host said. Eli was leaning against the wall, looking like he needed a bed. "By the way, I'm Jim Comstock."

"Jim, my friend ate something bad," I said, smiling. "Nothing to do for that but get out of the car and let his stomach settle."

Paulina and Eli had their own bags. I picked up my gun bag and my personal bag and went up the stairs, which were wooden and noisy. You couldn't sneak out of here, for sure. On the other hand, we wouldn't be taken by surprise.

We came to Eli's room first. When he unlocked his door, I saw a double bed with a washstand. The next door was ours, and the door after that was labeled BATHROOM. I glanced inside to see it was clean and held a big white bathtub and toilet. Eli went directly to the bed, pulled off his boots, and was prone in less time than it takes to tell, leaving me to pull his door shut. Paulina and

I went into our room. It held two narrow beds but was otherwise the same as Eli's. I'd seen much worse.

Since Paulina avoided conversation by lying down with her eyes closed, just like Eli, I took clean clothes and my towel and soap to the bathroom. The window was open and a breeze was coming in, and that side of the hotel was in shade, so it wasn't horribly hot. Though I needed more alone time, I couldn't linger. Someone else might need the room. I quickly washed myself, and then I washed everything I'd had on. I pulled on some fresh Levi's and a sleeveless blouse with a bigger one over it to camouflage the gun belt.

Clean and wearing clean clothes, I felt like a better person. Back in the room, I opened the window to hang my clothes out. In the dry heat, with the breeze, they wouldn't be wet for long.

As soon as I lay down, Paulina got up. She'd decided I'd had such a good idea, she'd duplicate it. I took a nap while she was in the bathroom. I woke up ten or fifteen minutes later. My roommate was coming in wrapped in a towel, her clothes in hand. Not modest, then. She fished clean clothes out of her bag and began to dress.

When I spoke, she jumped a little.

"The hotel owner, Jim. Maybe those were his buddies, back on the road."

She sat down on her bed and stared at me while

143

she combed her long, pale hair. "Why do you think that may be so?"

"He didn't expect to see anyone driving in from that side of town. Might be another reason for that. Might not." I was pretty confident this little hole in the road didn't get more than a handful of visitors, just enough to keep the hotel, and the whorehouse next door, open.

So it could be that Jim Comstock knew there were bandits on the incoming road, and was pleased we'd dodged them so he could have our business. Or it could be he was surprised we'd made it into Mil Flores, because he'd expected we would be shot before we got there.

"We should have hidden the bodies better." Paulina's mouth turned down, sour.

I nodded. "We can hope three things. One, Jim Comstock doesn't know the dead guys from Adam. Two, if someone does find the bodies, maybe Jim won't believe it was us because we don't look that scary." Though if anyone talked to Paulina for more than five minutes, that wouldn't fly. Plus, the tats.

"The other thing?"

"Three, we can hope if Jim's in on it, no one else is. If they *all* know . . ."

The grigori stared at me without seeing me. "The whole town," she said slowly. Paulina was thinking hard, which was a good thing.

"Or even part of it," I said.

If the town knew about the bandits—if they were Uncle Willy and Cousin Bart and Aunt Freda to half the people of Mil Flores—we were as good as dead if the bodies were found before we left.

"If we tried to leave now—after paying for the rooms—we might as well hang out a sign saying, 'We Did It.' " I wasn't really joking.

"I'll tell Eli," Paulina said. There was an interior door between our rooms. She knocked on it softly. After a moment Eli answered. He'd cleaned up a little. He looked as though he felt much better. Paulina beckoned him to come into our room. They sat on her bed, so she could keep her voice soft while she explained the situation to him. "This is what the gunnie thinks," she said to begin with. Somewhat to my surprise, it didn't sound like she was advising him to take it with a grain of salt. More like she was giving me credit.

"We should stay, and get as early a start as we can," he said, though he didn't sound sure.

"Tonight," I said, "after we eat, we come up here, we take turns sleeping. Or I can sleep in the car, make sure no one lets the air out of the tires tonight. In case they come for us."

Eli met my eyes. I had no idea what he was thinking. Paulina, however, was real straightforward. She said, "What if they kill you before you can yell, and *then* let the air out of the tires?"

"I guess I won't care too much what happens after that," I said, and she flushed, red flaring up her cheeks behind the blue tattoos.

Eli smiled before he could stop himself.

"We can make sure everyone in the town knows we're here," he said. "It's not a great idea, but it's better than doing nothing. If there are townsfolk who know nothing about the bandits, they might help us if we need it. At least they'll be able to point our people in the right direction, should we go missing."

"I can try to kill them all, take them unawares," I said. "Myself, I think that's a mistake, but you're the bosses."

Paulina looked at me in a weird way, as though I'd crawled out from under a rock.

"I said I thought that was a mistake," I told her after an uneasy moment. This was the woman who had tortured a bandit to death that afternoon.

"Maybe it would only take killing the man downstairs," Eli said. "That Jim Comstock."

I spread my hands as though to ask, *Do you want me to do that?*

"Let's go down to supper," he said. "See how Jim smells."

After a second I got that he wasn't referring to food. I wondered what he could pick up from a person's smell. Since I'd always thought my ability to catch the smell of magic was unique, I didn't like the idea that all people with grigori blood could smell things about other people. Put me firmly in the grigori camp.

It would have looked very strange to carry Jackhammer when I went down to supper. I did wear my Colts as a polite camouflage.

Downstairs the ceiling fans moved the limp air around in a halfhearted way, and the smell of fried chicken came from the kitchen at the back. I had been hungry, but now I was all geared up inside, kind of twitchy, ready for action. Jim appeared, with an apron wrapped around him, and waved his hand to indicate we should sit anywhere we liked. There were only two other people in the room, a plain woman in her forties in a conservative dress, and a man who looked like he chewed nails for a living.

All the tables were picnic style, with long benches on either side. Hard to get out of quick; that wasn't good. I sat facing the kitchen door, and the grigoris sat across from me. There were tablecloths covering the planks of the table; once, the blue-and-green stripes might have looked nice. Now the cloth, though clean, was marked with countless stains and holes. My mom would not have used them for rags.

At least the droopy cloth provided cover. I drew my right-hand pistol to have it at the ready. I laid it carefully on the bench right beside me. That way my hands were visible and empty.

When Jim pushed through the swinging kitchen

door, I tensed, but he was carrying only a platter with fried chicken piled on it, and a bowl of mashed potatoes. In another trip he brought the gravy and the green beans. Third trip, biscuits. He served the three tables the same way, except the single people got smaller bowls.

I made myself eat. This was good food, and anytime good food was in front of you . . . you ate. The wizards cut up their chicken with knives and ate it with a fork. Picking it up was fine for me.

Jim came by to chatter every few minutes, inquiring about the food, how our rooms were. He stuck in questions about where we'd come from and where we were going. He directed all his palaver at Paulina and Eli. He'd definitely put me in the hired-help category.

Jim might have been naturally curious. Or he might have been calculating how many people would know or care if we disappeared.

When we finished eating, Paulina asked him if there was a store that had women's blouses.

"Well, there'll be shirts and such at Godley's Store, across the street and one north," he said. "Should be open for a little while."

"We'll go there," she said. We all got up at once, as if we'd practiced. My gun was back in its holster by the time I stood.

As soon as we came out onto the wooden sidewalk, right by the Celebrity Tourer, we saw the sign reading GODLEY'S. We sauntered across the packed dirt of the road, looking around as if the quiet street deserved some studying. I checked the rooftops. I checked the windows.

We came to the barbershop, which had a big glass window. We beheld the biggest gathering we'd seen in Mil Flores: four men, all eyeing us hopefully.

"I think I'll get a shave," Eli said, as if an evening shave was simply a great idea. I didn't like us splitting up, but before I could speak, Eli had pushed open the door. I could see him nodding to the men, who nodded back, smiling. They were pretty excited at the prospect of talking to a stranger, and a real exotic one at that.

Paulina and I went into Godley's Store. Though it had a narrow front, it ran deep, a real cave of anything you could want. Everywhere I looked, there were goods for sale. Every inch of space, except what had to be left open for walking, was lined with shelves and racks and bins and barrels. I found that Godley's sold dry goods ranging from clothes to pots and dish soap and clothespins.

Paulina was enthralled. I had to figure she'd never been in a country store before. While she slowly browsed through stacked shirts and ladies' underwear and frying pans, I made common ground with the girl behind the counter, a Godley daughter named Manda. She was quite the flirt, and interested in flirting with me, which was a mild surprise. So I was pleasant in return. Why not? Paulina came to the counter with a couple of things and got out the money to pay.

While Paulina was counting her change, Manda stared at Paulina's tattoos. If Paulina was having a new experience, so was Manda. She'd clearly never seen a grigori. I sure wished Paulina hadn't been so proud of being a wizard that she'd gotten inked on her face, and it wasn't the first or last time I'd think that.

"Ain't you scared of being with her?" Manda whispered after Paulina had walked out the door. First. Before I could check.

"I'm getting used to it," I said. "They pay me good money." I bid farewell to Manda as though I'd enjoyed talking to her, and that was the truth, as far as it went.

"Friendly girl," Paulina said as we walked back to the hotel in a very leisurely way.

I nodded. "Seemed okay," I said. "Paulina, do you have to get the tattoos? Is it part of the job?"

Paulina debated for a minute over whether to answer. "My guild rules tell me what tattoos I should get, and in which order," she said, deciding to tell me the truth. "At least in part. They all have some magical significance. To put some on my face, that was my decision. I am committed to my craft."

That was a pretty bold commitment. "Guilds.

That would be like a union? How many are there, for wizards?" I might as well ask, since she was in what passed for a chatty mood with Paulina.

"Earth, Air, Water, Fire, Healing, Death," she said. "But a death wizard can deliver a baby and heal small wounds, an earth wizard can provide wind to get you across an ocean. Or take that wind away. It's not that you lack power in other areas, but you specialize in what is your strongest talent."

That was the longest speech Paulina had ever made in my presence.

"So your guild is . . . ?"

"If you see this symbol"—and here Paulina tapped her face, against what looked like some jagged mountain peaks—"you know the person is a fire wizard."

"I would have thought you were a death wizard." She knew her way around a torture.

"No. It's simply one of my talents." Paulina smiled. It was as unpleasant a smile as I've ever seen. "If I were a death wizard, we wouldn't need a gunnie."

And that would have suited Paulina just fine.

I could smell Eli coming out of the barbershop from ten feet away. "Yow," I said, unable to stop myself. The plain woman who was also a guest at the hotel, out for an evening stroll, turned her head and tried not to smile too broadly.

Paulina's face tightened like someone had

pulled a string on her head. "Smells like a whore-house," she said.

Eli looked embarrassed as we got closer, prob-ably because we were making gagging noises. "Some friends you are!" he called in a hearty voice. I caught a glimpse of the barbershop men, laughing fit to burst as the plain woman stepped inside the shop, still smiling. There was *really* not much to do here.

Eli fell into step with us. Paulina showed him the shirt she'd bought at Godley's. We all smiled at one another, because everyone (meaning maybe six people) was looking at us, the strangers. I was glad to see other townspeople around. Meant nothing was about to happen, I thought. "Did you learn anything?" she asked.

"I learned a lot," Eli said. "If you want to know how Hank Murphy's cow got out and ate everything in Sister Butter's garden."

"We had less luck than that," Paulina said. "Unless you want to count the fact that Gunnie could have a bedmate tonight if she so chose."

I shrugged. "Just working my personal charm with no wizardry at all," I said modestly. They were a little startled, and then they laughed. For a flash of a moment, I felt comfortable, back with my crew. Just a flash.

Then Paulina drew us under the awning of a dilapidated restaurant across the street from the hotel. Come to find out, Paulina had been brooding as she looked through shirts in Godley's. "Those men today on the road, they could have done us in if you hadn't been quick and we two hadn't been lethal. We *cannot* be killed by some drabs here so far from home. Our holy father has sent us on a mission."

Paulina didn't mean that the two of them couldn't be killed, period. She meant that two powerful grigoris like her and Eli simply couldn't afford to be killed before they'd done their duty.

"Listen to me, Paulina," I said. "All it takes is one of these 'drabs' on a roof with a rifle, like that one over there, and your damn mission is up in smoke."

"Truly?" Eli said, smiling at me as if I'd said something amusing. He wanted us to act like we'd noticed nothing. That was a good idea.

"Truly," I said, smiling back and ignoring his little moment of surprise. "He can't see us right now because of the awning, so he's not going to shoot. I don't know if Mil Flores keeps a guard up there all the time, or if this is more of the same incident. Josip the Tatar. The ambush on the road. Adds up."

"Can you kill him, and we'll jump in the car and go?" Paulina couldn't bring herself to smile, but at least she didn't look completely grim. "Are you good enough with the pistol?"

"Of course I am. But I'll have to leave my rifles

if we do that," I said. They were up in the room. "Don't want to."

"Got the car key?" Paulina asked Eli.

"Sure." The friendly smile was still on his face.

But their bodies were getting all tense. I could tell which way the grigoris were going to jump. "Listen to me," I said, gripping Eli by the elbow. "What if they've disabled the car? If we jump in it and don't go anywhere, that's as good as a signed confession that we're guilty of something. And we'd get shot real easy cooped up in the car."

"Tires look okay," Eli said after a sideways glance.

"Isn't there something dripping underneath?"

The car was parked in front of the hotel's porch like an obedient horse. A horse that had peed. There was a dark puddle of something under it.

"Damn!" Eli exclaimed in a normal voice.

"My goodness!" The plain woman passed us again on her way into the hotel. She was everywhere. She stood in the street, looking at us huddled under the awning. "What happened to your car?"

"Don't know yet," I said tersely, and she nodded. When we didn't move, the plain woman said, "Aren't you going to go see?"

Yeah, that would be the next step. We couldn't stand under this awning forever.

"We're trying to decide if we want a piece of pie," Paulina said, nodding at the restaurant door.

"Oh! Well, it's not as good as Jim's." The plain woman gave us a doubtful look and went across the street and into the hotel.

My right hand was on my gun, in what I hoped was a casual gesture. My skin itched, reacting to magic somewhere, maybe just the two grigoris shedding power because they were anxious.

"We need to get across the street," I said, not able to stand this dawdling any longer. I drew both guns. Something was about to happen, my kind of something.

Eli and Paulina looked at me. They were actually waiting for me to tell them what to do. I didn't want this to come to a shoot-out. I wanted us to get out of here in the morning without being killed. Without killing anybody.

My guns held down by my side, I stepped out from under the awning, keeping my head turned toward the car. But my eyes were looking up.

The man was still on the roof of the house directly across the street. Now he stood up.

But he would wait for the grigoris to venture into the open street. I turned my head slightly so he could see I was talking to my companions. "Come on!" I said cheerfully and loudly. "Let's see about dessert." They hesitated, then stepped into the open.

He snapped his rifle to his shoulder. I could just make out his brown face under the brim of his hat, focused, intense. But I'd dropped to a crouch, my pistols came up faster, and I shot him square in the chest. He fell (with a lot of drama) over the low parapet surrounding the roof, after which he slithered down the tin awning in an awful, limp way. Finally, his body landed in the street with a thud, and his rifle bounced beside it.

Once heard, never forgotten, that sound.

For just a moment, after he'd sprawled in the dust, everything was silent. Paulina and Eli stared at the body while I turned in a quick circle, scanning the rooftops, guns up. There was no one else.

After those seconds people came boiling out of the buildings like fire ants from a mound. Where had they all been earlier?

His trigger finger had pressed down when I'd hit him. I looked at my two charges; they looked fine, just startled. At least the shot hadn't hit either of them. I wondered where it had gone. A quick look didn't find anyone else who was bleeding.

There was a lot of shouting, but I was too busy watching all the hands to pay any attention. Seemed sure we'd have to move fast.

I had my doubts that the car would start, not with that puddle of fluid underneath. As I'd told the grigoris, abandoning our bags would be a heavy blow. I was going to need all the firepower I could muster. And who knew what the grigoris had in their bags, besides clean underwear?

The hotel proprietor had rushed out onto the

porch. Jim Comstock bellowed, "Shut the hell up!" And pretty quick everyone did. If they had a mayor here, Jim was it.

"Are you all okay?" Jim asked.

I had to assume he was asking us. I didn't look at Paulina and Eli. I'd seen they weren't bleeding. I was too busy being sure no one else was aiming at them.

"I'm real nervous," I said, to point out how quick I'd be to use the guns again, "but I'm not shot."

"You two?" he asked Paulina and Eli.

"I'm missing some hair," Eli said, his voice calm. "That bullet passed close. But I have plenty to go on with." He even sounded a little amused.

I could feel the heat coming off Paulina after she heard how close the stray bullet had passed. Yep, her hands were twitching. She was ready to exercise her own talent.

I didn't stop scanning the crowd. The tension was getting to me, though, and I knew I couldn't keep my alert much longer. If they swarmed us . . .

"Who is it?" Jim called to the people who'd formed a cluster around the body. If he already knew, he was a good actor.

"It's a stranger, Jim," said Manda, all bright eyed and bushy tailed. She was loving the drama. She was bent over the body. Strong stomach. "I never seen him before."

There was a murmur then, passing through the crowd: surprise.

"He's got some tattoos, not as many as the lady," Manda called.

You could hear the breaths drawn in. This was better than a movie.

Paulina said, "Let me see." She didn't have to say it twice. Every person between Paulina and the dead man stepped aside to form an aisle.

The dust underneath the body was soaking up the blood. He'd landed on his back, so the wound was bleeding out through the exit hole. Paulina squatted and looked at him hard.

"Gunnie," Paulina said, like I was her hunting dog and she was calling me to heel. I felt like biting or growling, sure enough. I went to stand by the body. Paulina's white, bony fingers were unbuttoning the top two buttons of the dead grigori's shirt. She glanced up at me, like she was saying, *What are you waiting for?*

I was supposed to help her undress the body.

I was less than dust in Paulina's view, I understood that. Also, she was paying me more than I'd ever been paid for a job. But her attitude that I had to jump to any task (besides shooting) when she said *jump* was beginning to poke me like a sharp stick. Two things held me back from telling her that. It wouldn't be good policy to start a snarling contest in public. And I had a respect for her abilities. Also, it was smart to keep on the good side of Paulina. If she had one.

So I knelt on the other side of the dead man, and I eased the shirt apart so she could see his tats. The symbols covered as much of his chest as I could see, which was not a lot. But I knew a few things about him after I'd looked at them.

The crowd did a lot of oohing and aahing. Good background talk.

Paulina looked up at Eli, who had come to stand by us. You could tell that for her he was the only other person there. Then they both looked down at the man's skin. "He's not a wizard," she told Eli, as if there weren't thirty or forty people listening who should not know our business. "Almost all of these are unskilled tattoos. But one of them is a protection symbol, that's from a guild."

"Then it's lucky I shot him," I said.

She looked at me thoughtfully. Once again I misliked the feeling that I'd gotten her notice. "Yes," she said. "Lucky."

I leaned over close to her ear. "Maybe we should save this conversation for later, after we look at the body in private."

Paulina gave me a good hard stare. She nodded.

"Do you know him?" Jim Comstock asked from behind me.

"No," said Eli. "I've never seen him before." Paulina and I shook our heads.

There was more rumble among the townsfolk.

"Well, he didn't take a shot at you for nothing," Manda said. Lots of sense, that girl.

Paulina brushed her hands against her pants as if she could remove the dead-man cooties. She stood in one swift move, like an animal. Eli reached down a hand to help me. I had more sense than to take it, with Paulina standing right there. I stood, too, but I couldn't match her ease. It was like she'd oiled her joints.

"Is there a sheriff?" she asked our host.

There was a kind of ripple of chuckling, and it made its way through the little crowd. "No," Jim said. "We got enough troubles without a sheriff."

"Then it doesn't make any difference what we do with the body," I said to Jim. "You got no beef with me killing him, I take it."

"He wasn't shooting at none of us," Jim said, and there was a lot of wise head nodding. This had been our problem to solve, the people of Mil Flores agreed. How I'd solved it was my business.

"Where can we take the body?" Paulina was looking around like a funeral parlor would pop up in front of her. "I need to look at him more closely."

This plan did not make a good impression on the people of Mil Flores. Of course, Paulina didn't care, if she noticed at all.

The plain woman had drawn near. She'd

picked up the shooter's rifle and was holding it at a distance from her body, as if it were a dead animal. Her flower-patterned dress came to the middle of her calves, and she'd thrown on a broad-brimmed straw hat with a white ribbon for decoration. Other than the ribbon, and the rose and pink of the dress, she was as blank a woman as I'd ever seen. Medium everything: looks, build, coloring, age. "I've got a wagon out back," she said. "You just want a gander at this fella, you can use it to get him off the ground and out of the view of these good people."

"Thank you," Eli said. "I'm Eli Savarov, my companion is Paulina Coopersmith, and the gunnie is Lizbeth Rose."

"Belinda Trotter," the woman said, but her voice got drowned by a few exclamations of surprise.

"You're *Gunnie Rose?*" Manda said, her voice rising with every word. My traveling companions stared at her. Then at me.

I nodded, hoping it would stop there. But of course it didn't.

"I've heard of you," Jim Comstock said slowly.

"Is it true that—" Manda was dragging me to disaster.

"I don't care to talk about my living," I said, turning to look directly into her eyes, to share my dislike on the way this talk was going.

To give her credit, she stopped dead. "Of course not," she said. "Your business."

"Where's that wagon, Miss Trotter?" I wanted to get the conversation going in another direction.

"Through the alley and turn right," Miss Trotter said. "Horses are in the stable, but the wagon is standing empty."

Eli stepped into position to pick up the dead man's feet, so Paulina made a move toward the head, but a man (surely the blacksmith, from his arms and shoulders) leaped to the task to spare her. Paulina tried to seem pleased and grateful, but she looked more like she'd sucked on a salted lemon.

Paulina liked to carry her own bodies, I figured.

I trailed behind the little parade, keeping an eye out, which is what I do best. I'd checked my ammo, of course. The rooftops were clear. The sidewalks were clear. Even Manda had left, after a last longing look at me.

The alley lay between the hotel and the whorehouse. The prostitutes were at their windows, woken by the sound of the gunplay. It was still a bit early for their working day to be beginning. This late in the spring, the sun would go down around seven thirty. They had the time and inclination to have a good look-see. There were three women and one young man, two more than I would've guessed for a place the size of Mil Flores. I could feel their eyes on us as Eli and the blacksmith made their way to the back of the hotel, where an open yard contained a couple of wooden chairs and a table and Miss Trotter's empty wagon.

The two men swung the body up onto the flat bed of the wagon. The dead man's head was at the rear. His shirt was spread wider now. It's always something to recognize, how still the dead are. Ten minutes ago he'd moved and breathed and thought and wanted, and he'd done his best to kill us. Now all that didn't matter to him. I spared another look around, checking the crowd for intent and weapons, in case anyone else wanted to get that way. But the people of Mil Flores had had enough of the drama, and they were melting away.

Unless the whores were hostile, and they sure didn't seem to be, or the blacksmith went crazy, we were secure this moment. I scanned the back windows of the hotel and saw only the man who'd been sharing the dining room earlier. He scowled when he saw me mark him, and he turned away right quick. I made a note in my head to find out who he was.

Paulina appeared to expect Miss Trotter would leave once she'd escorted us to the wagon, but that didn't happen. Donating her wagon had been the price of admission, apparently. The woman stood waiting for whatever would happen next, and her silly, flowery dress made her look even more out of place, especially since she was still carrying Marcial's rifle. Which was mine now.

"Need me anymore?" the blacksmith asked Eli. Eli thanked him and slipped the man some coins. The smith made his way back to whatever he'd been doing before, glad to leave us with the dead man.

Paulina looked at Miss Trotter, and I could see Paulina hoped Miss Trotter would profit from the smith's example. Not going to happen. Miss Trotter met Paulina's gaze with a bland look.

The wagon bed was high for me, so I used a mounting block to finish unbuttoning the body's shirt before Paulina could tell me to. I unbuckled his belt, too, and slid it out of the loops. It was a good piece of leather, and undamaged. I rolled it up and put it aside, catching Eli's look of surprise from the corner of my eye.

Paulina pulled the corpse's boots off, which didn't surprise me. I climbed down from the block to take them from her, and I set them aside to examine later, along with the belt. When Paulina grabbed a leg of his pants, I waited to see if Miss Curious Trotter would take the other—she was standing right there—but she just waited with the same bright-eyed curiosity.

So I obliged with that, too.

I'd never taken the pants off a dead man. Wasn't pleasant.

Then Paulina did something I actually enjoyed.

She reached into one of her vest pockets and withdrew some dried herbs. She tossed them over the corpse and said something in a tongue I couldn't make out, and the smell vanished. That was a very useful spell. I wondered if I could learn that one. But most likely, I wasn't qualified.

While I was appreciating the nicer air, I went through the dead man's pant pockets. "His name was Marcial Montes," I told whoever wanted to listen.

The grigoris shook their heads at the same time. Not a name they knew. Miss Trotter didn't blink.

Paulina leaned over the wagon on one side to study Montes's tattoos in more detail. Eli stationed himself at the other side. They muttered to each other (in Russian, I guess) and pointed to this or that. The whores, crammed in two windows, were fascinated. The young man came out onto the porch and beckoned to me when no one else was looking. After a glance around I went over to him. He was maybe seventeen, slim and blond, and cute enough I was surprised he wasn't somewhere busier.

"Andy," he said after he'd had a good look at the healing furrow on my scalp.

"Lizbeth Rose."

"*The* Lizbeth Rose? The one who shot her—"

"Big ears here," I cautioned him.

"Ohhhhhhkay. So, what are the grigoris doing?"

I shrugged. "The dead man tried to kill us.

They're looking at his ink. Means nothing to them. As you can tell if you look at Paulina's face."

"She's a tall drink of vinegar," Andy said after he'd had a look at Paulina. I guessed he had to be a good judge of character in his profession.

"You ever seen the dead man before?" I asked. "Montes, his name is."

Andy shook his head. "The woman who owns the wagon, she's been in Mil Flores two days," he said. "She didn't bring anything in on it. No one knows what she's planning on taking out. Had to bring it along with her for some reason. Why?"

This was good information. "I appreciate your taking the time to tell me," I said politely. "Please let me give you something for your trouble." I handed Andy a couple of the Holy Russian coins Eli had given me for expenses, and the boy slipped them into his pocket with a happy smile.

Paulina glanced over our way once and looked back at the body with no change of expression.

"She'll be over tonight," Andy said.

"No!" I said, truly surprised. "For you or for the ladies?"

"Me," he said with the same certainty. "She'll act like she's in charge, but she'll be glad when I let her know I am."

Well, he'd be the expert. But before I went back to join my little corpse-stripping party, I

166

said, "Andy, you watch out for her. She's a killer, and she can do some gruesome shit."

Andy looked at me and smiled. "Well," he said, "you oughtta know. I'd be happy to see you later, if you want to come over."

I was real popular in Mil Flores. Maybe I should move here, after this was over. I laughed and bid him good-bye.

Now that the two grigoris had backed off, I had a look at the dead man myself. I wanted to be sure what I'd noticed earlier was true. Montes did have tattoos, and one of them looked similar to the wizards', but the ones on his chest had not been made by the same hand. They were colorful, and they consisted of animal figures. The blue one, the one that looked grigori-like, was a symbol, and Paulina had already identified that one.

"Eli, Paulina. Look here. Lobo Gris," I said, tapping the snarling canine head in the middle of his chest. They turned from their quiet conversation to join me at the wagon. The Trotter woman was still observing with bright-eyed interest. I had to show them this. It was hard to ignore her.

Paulina gave me the look I was coming to know, the dog-is-talking look—wonder crossed with irritation. "What do you mean?" she asked.

These HRE grigoris didn't know shit. "Lobo Gris, Gray Wolf. It's a criminal crew in Mexico, where gray wolves live. Marcial Montes was a member."

"Gray wolves are different from the wolves in Canada?" Eli looked down at me with nothing but interest, at least that I could tell.

"They're smaller. But their size doesn't make them less dangerous, 'cause they hunt in big packs. Which is the point of naming a crew after them."

Eli should have been concentrating on what I was saying, because it was important, but I felt his eyes wandering to my scalp. Was he sidetracked by the puckered scar? It was healing well, but it wasn't pretty.

Miss Trotter said, "I've heard of them." A second later she was exchanging remarks with Paulina, who was trying to be subtle about persuading the woman to leave the yard. They looked good to talk at cross-purposes for a few minutes.

"Ask Trotter what she has the wagon for," I said on the quiet.

"She must have brought cargo in on it," Eli said, as if I was missing something real obvious.

"No, she didn't," I said. "One of the whores said it came in empty." I didn't look up to get his reaction. He'd believe me, or he wouldn't.

I stepped away from him to spend a little more time looking at the body of Marcial Montes. I identified not only the crew tattoo, but a few more. "This is his nagual," I told Eli, who was sticking with me instead of doing what I'd asked. I touched one outline.

"That is?"

I would have thought a grigori would know this. "His spirit animal, in the old language. In Spanish, *zopilote*. That means vulture."

"The spirit animal gave him special talent? Protection?"

"He might have believed so." He'd been mistaken. "I don't know what . . . attributes . . . go with each animal. *El chamán* tells you. He figures out your spirit animal by using your birth date. It's not cheap." When you're in my business, people talk about protection a lot.

"So what does this tell you about this Marcial Montes?" Eli asked, as if he really wanted to know the answer.

"He was hired help. Someone approached his crew and asked to hire someone for a murder, and the crew boss picked Montes for the job. See? He's got the death symbol." I touched the skull on his left shoulder. "So he was okay with killing. He'd done it before. And he'd made a decent amount of money doing it. The tats and his clothes and his rifle were expensive. He was good." I glanced over at the rifle, another Winchester, newer than my grandfather's. I was pleased to have it in my little arsenal.

"You're better."

"So far," I said. "Maybe Montes hired the bandits from this afternoon, too. He himself would be the fallback, in case the bandits didn't stop us."

"Who do you think he was trying to kill?" Eli asked.

"You and Paulina," I said, trying hard not to sound like I thought that was a stupid question. "The bullet came mighty close to you."

"Because I would have sworn he was trying to kill you," Eli said in a calm and conversational way, and I felt a shiver down my back. "I think you hit him enough to make his aim go wide."

I had. I just hadn't looked at it that way.

"Don't know why he would be aiming for me, unless he thought that'd leave you unprotected," I said, trying to cast off that creepy feeling. "What are you going to do about fixing the car? It's getting on to dark."

I needed to give him something else to chew on before I walked away. We'd ventured into dangerous territory. If Eli was right, someone knew everything about the grigoris' mission, and everything about me. If that was so, I'd have to tell the grigoris everything, too. I sure didn't want to have that conversation.

Eli took the hint and headed off to the only local mechanic's shop, hoping to talk to the man before it turned dark. I left Paulina and Miss Trotter still talking, though Paulina was looking very impatient. I got the rifle and took it in with me.

Jim Comstock was sweeping the lobby. He stopped when he saw me.

"Good with a gun," he said, by way of greeting.

"My job. You know why that Belinda Trotter is here?"

He wasn't surprised I was asking. "She says she's on her way to Juárez to pick up a load of medical supplies for her clinic." That was a believable reason for her trip. Medicine was cheaper in Mexico. The only other major manufacturers of medicines were in Canada and Britannia, so it had to travel a far way, which jacked up the price. Of course, those medicines were purer.

"Where is it? The clinic?"

"In Texoma, north of here," Jim said. He was smiling. Everything in Texoma was north of here.

"But she's lingered," I said.

"Says her mules were tired out, needed a rest." Which Jim didn't believe any more than I did. "You all going to stay the night, or are your friends spooked?"

"Depends on them," I said. "I'm just the help. I guess they'll tell me before I start to climb in bed."

Jim nodded and went back to his sweeping. The lobby was clean. I figured he'd been waiting for me to come in to see if I had any questions.

I glanced out the door again, to see Eli and a dark man I figured for the mechanic standing beside the Celebrity Tourer. The dark man had looked under the car, I could tell by the dust on his jeans. Eli looked pleased at whatever the mechanic was telling him, so I figured the mechanic had the right part to fix the car, or it hadn't been bad broken.

Dark fell soon after that. The grigoris and Miss Trotter came in and joined the single man, who was sitting in the parlor. There were some lamps on. The electricity was steadier in Mil Flores than I'd expected. Several things about Mil Flores were not square with the appearance of it. The well-stocked stores. The number of barbers and whores. The presence of a full-size hotel. I was thinking about that while I sat in a corner chair in the parlor.

I didn't want to talk myself, but to listen. In my opinion, these four new friends were doing enough chitchatting for seven or eight people.

Miss Trotter talked about the hospital in Juárez where she bought her medical supplies, and about her clinic. Though she never pinpointed the location of this clinic.

Mr. Parsons, the single man, talked about the notions he had in his sample bag: needles, thread, thimbles, patterns, scissors, shears, powder compacts, perfume, fancy writing paper. He was trying hard to interest Paulina, but soon she looked even more bored than I was. Mr. Parsons didn't seem to be a very good salesman, if he was targeting Paulina as a woman who needed a thimble.

Belinda Trotter told us she'd already seen Mr. Parsons's wares. For a minute I thought the woman was making a bawdy joke, though not a very funny one. But Belinda went on to tell us she'd bought a pattern and a pair of scissors. She turned to smile brightly at me, as if she expected me to get excited about her purchases. I gave her a flat stare. She looked away right smart.

But before long Miss Trotter was back in the conversation again, asking about our plans. She tried to find out when we were leaving Mil Flores. Neither Paulina nor Eli gave her a definite answer, and I had to admire the way they dodged the woman. The two grigoris were so smart in some ways, so scary.

But they were so dumb in others.

So far I'd done well by them, though I was on my own personal mission. It would take only one big mistake, like Manda blurting out my most notorious act, for the grigoris to find out more about me than I wanted them to know. I was walking a tightrope with my employers. I would never forget Eli making the blood leave the man's body this morning. I'd never forget Paulina's interrogation.

After one of the longest hours I'd ever spent

in my life, Eli and Paulina decided we'd turn in. As I'd expected, they didn't give me a hint of what they'd decided to do the next day, or what they wanted done with Marcial Montes's body. Paulina didn't tell me anything even when we were alone in our room, and I was irritated enough to not ask a single question.

Usually, when my head hits the pillow, I'm out, but this night I stayed awake a little while, thinking about Lobo Gris and the vulture nagual. I made myself relax and breathe evenly. That usually worked, the few nights I didn't drift off quick.

My roommate must have believed I was deep asleep. She got up and left our room, quiet as a shadow. I heard the back door of the whorehouse open and a voice bid her welcome three minutes later. Sounded like Andy's.

He was right, I thought. And somehow the fact that Andy had found it easy to read Paulina made it easy for me to sleep.

I didn't hear Paulina slip back into our room, but she was there in the morning when I got up and washed. She didn't move as I dressed and left the room. I hoped she needed her rest, that her night of pleasure had softened her a little. Or something. Made her happy for a few seconds.

I was surprised to find I was very hungry, and to my pleasure I could smell that breakfast was ready. Jim had just served Mr. Parsons and Miss

174

Trotter, who were sitting together. They invited me to join them, but I said, "You'd be sorry. I'm not a morning person," and set myself at a table on my own.

That was a flat-out lie; I was a morning person, for sure. But I'd listened to them talk enough the evening before to last me for a good long while. I ate some eggs and some bacon and some pancakes. I didn't know Jim Comstock's true purpose, or what he was doing in Mil Flores, but he was a truly great cook. Right up there with my mom.

Paulina and Eli came down together a few minutes later. Sure enough, Paulina looked very relaxed. They sat with me, and Jim hustled in with some plates for them, and some coffee. They were quiet. I got to enjoy that for too short a while.

"What will happen to the body?" Paulina asked out of the blue.

"Good morning to you, too," I said.

She ignored that. "I begged an old sheet off our host and covered Montes last night."

So Montes's body was still lying in the backyard on Miss Trotter's wagon. Interesting that Miss Trotter hadn't insisted on his removal. "I doubt Mil Flores pays a gravedigger," I said. "And no one does that for free. I reckon they'll throw him out in the desert."

The two grigoris stared at me. I wouldn't say

they were horrified. It would take a lot to horrify these two. But they were for sure taken aback.

"What?" I said. "The dead from the ambush are out there. You never asked about burying them." I'd made a point, I thought, even though I'd had to do it in a whisper. "In fact, since the body on the wagon is there because of us, we should do the disposing of it, I figure."

I could see both of them, especially Eli, struggle to come up with some kind of sensible reply that would end up in Montes's being magically buried by someone else. But in the end neither could find anything to say.

"Hold on a minute," I said, and swung my legs free from the bench. I went to the door at the back of the passage and opened it to look out. Andy was getting water from a pump behind the whorehouse, and we waved at each other. I returned to the dining room.

"He's gone," I said.

"What?" Paulina didn't keep her voice down.

"He's gone. They came and got him in the night."

"Lobo Gris?"

So she had been listening. "Yeah, I reckon it was them. I don't guess he got up and walked away on his own."

"That means . . ." Eli stopped while he thought. "That means someone here told them one of their members was here, dead."

176

I nodded, ate some more pancake. "Yep."

"Could have been anyone in the crowd," Paulina murmured. "Someone else who belongs."

"Could have been whoever hired him," Eli said.

"That, too. You talked to the mechanic last night?" We were all keeping our voices very low, but it was time to change the subject. We couldn't know who had tipped off the crew that Montes was dead, and might not even want to know, I suspected, at least right now. "How is the car?"

Eli said, "Mechanic says that only a cap was loosened, and he replaced the oil and tightened it. He was going to come over this morning and take a slower look to be sure. I'm going to talk to him as soon as I finish eating."

I nodded. A good precaution.

Eli added, "With the car parked in front, it seems unbelievable that no one noticed the man fiddling under the car."

"It all ties in," Paulina whispered. "The car out front, any number of people could have seen whoever was trying to sabotage it."

I didn't really believe everyone in Mil Flores was willing to ignore such a strange thing because they were all in a criminal crew. That was possible, but not probable. "Most likely some people did notice, but it wasn't any of their business. Why would they be on your side?" I said with some reason, considering Paulina and Eli were openly grigoris. Even I didn't necessarily think grigoris were good guys, but they were not criminals. Maybe. And they were the ones who were paying me.

As scary as Paulina and Eli were, and lethal as they were, I had to stick with them until we found the remaining Karkarov brother in Juárez.

That ended our conversation. After I'd gone up to brush my teeth, I went out to the car, since Paulina and Eli were lingering over their coffee. The hood of the Celebrity Tourer was up. The dark man from the evening before was scrambling out from under the car. When he'd gotten to his feet, he lowered the Tourer's hood.

"Good morning. I hope you got some good news?" I said.

"Morning, Gunnie. Yeah, I'm Desmond. And I do have good news."

"I'm ready for it." And that was God's truth.

"I just had to put in some more oil and screw the cap back on the pan. Might have been a little problem if the asshole had made off with the cap, but it was lying on the ground under the car. Couldn't be bothered, I guess. And the engine looks fine to me. No interference there."

"That simple. Great. How much do we owe you?"

"Couple of dollars will do me."

I handed it over, plus a little more. "We'll probably come by to fill up as we're leaving."

"If I'm not there, my wife can pump the gas. Or either of the kids."

Desmond was a man who stuck to business. I wished more people were like him.

While I was outside, I strolled between the whorehouse and the hotel. I noticed the fresh footprints in the dirt. Four men had walked here the night before. They'd gone in light and come out heavy. Carrying the body.

Eli came out onto the porch a minute later. "What did he say?"

"Car's ready to go. He's got gas if we need it. I think we should fill up."

"Then we might as well start."

"Okay." I went upstairs to fetch my bags.

I would not be sorry to leave Mil Flores. I did not feel I could let my guard down here, not for a second. I had a gloomy feeling that the tension might not get any better when we left. It wasn't only the town that made me jumpy, it was my employers.

If I could have been back in Segundo Mexia just by wishing, I would have been home. At the same time, I thought more and more about the chance that I had a half sister. I didn't know if I wanted one or not. I wondered how it would feel if I did.

CHAPTER SIX

The good thing about that morning was that no one tried to kill us. The bad thing was the road. It was paved. Well, it had been paved, once upon a time. But it hadn't been repaired any time in the recent past, and we lurched around like we were in a wheelbarrow.

Paulina was driving, and when Eli got impatient, she snapped back, "If we go any faster, we'll break the underparts of the car, and then we'll be out in the middle of Bumfucking Nowhere and we'll have to walk."

That was an entertaining way to put it. I had never heard a woman say that word out loud. I have to admit I'd *thought* it, after I'd learned it from Tarken.

Eli took a deep breath before he said, "Given our current rate of speed, when do you think we might reach Juárez?"

"I am not even going to try to guess," Paulina said, sounding a little less angry but just as disgusted.

She wasn't the only one.

All I had to do was look, and there was nothing to look at. The land was flat and full of nothing. So much nothing. Scrubby trees, sparse plants, lots of rocks, little deer, and probably thousands of snakes. The only good thing about this terrain was that there was nowhere for ambushers to hide. No daytime attack could be a surprise, unless the attackers dropped from the sky. And if anything was rarer than good cars in this area of our planet, it was airplanes.

When we stopped to eat—Jim had packed some food into a little box with an ice compartment, for a pretty penny—Paulina and Eli hunched over the map, trying to find a place we could reach before nightfall. They came up with nothing.

We drove and drove the rest of the day, taking turns at the wheel. I didn't mind driving when there was so clearly no one else around. While I was at the wheel, Paulina and Eli both fell asleep after they were sure I was competent. I didn't have anything to think about that I hadn't already gone over in my mind a million times on this trip, and it was hard to push off the sadness. I was still grieving for my friends, but I didn't want to talk about it to anyone else . . . if there'd been anyone around who cared. It was my own grief. I could feel it fading away into something I simply accepted, because that's the way I am. I knew I'd feel better. It was living until then that was hard.

By dusk I was so ready to get out of the car and stop being bounced around that I could hardly bear it. I did not mind spending the night out in the open, because at least we would get to be still.

After the long silences of the day, I was ready to talk to someone, even them.

We made a fire and heated up some stuff from Jim's provisions. "What is your home like?" I said, aiming the question somewhere between Eli and Paulina. They were both surprised I was starting a conversation. For a moment neither spoke.

"I live in San Diego, close to the palace of our tsar. I have a room at my guild house," Paulina said. She spoke real carefully, like she was testing the information lest she reveal any big secret.

"How big?" She looked blank. "How big is your room?"

"About as big as both the bedrooms we had last night put together. It has a sink. There are big bathrooms with toilet stalls and shower stalls, shared by all. We eat in the guild dining room."

That sounded real . . . institutional. "Did you get to pick your own furniture?"

"I picked the furniture, yes." She was warming up to the topic.

"Can you do your own cooking?"

"I eat in the dining room, almost always. But I can make tea in my room, and sometimes when I am out, I go to the bakery and pick up something for a meal."

"What about your washing?"

"All my clothes and sheets, I take them to the laundry in the basement of the guild house."

"Do you clean your own room?"

"No, there are cleaners who do that. They are all men and women who are relatives of wizards, so we have a hold on them if they steal or if they are bribed to take hair or any body waste from one of us."

That was charming.

Bottom line was that Paulina had almost no responsibility for her own upkeep. I hoped she was doing a great job at whatever she did day to day, to make her worth being waited on like that.

My mouth was full, so I pointed at Eli to indicate it was his turn. "I live at the palace," he said.

I'd expected his story to echo Paulina's. I glanced at her, but she'd ducked her head to look at her food. Okay, I was learning something now.

"I have a little room, very humble, in a wing far, far away from our tsar's. My mentor, Dmitri Petrov, lives closer to His Imperial Highness." Eli smiled and tried to catch Paulina's eye.

"That's funny?" I said.

"He is so close to the tsar that he has the honor of being wakened very often in the night when the tsar is in pain." He was still trying to get Paulina to look at him, to share his little bit of humor that living in the palace was a real big pain in the ass. But Paulina wasn't having any of that. She would have given a finger or two, it was easy to see, if she could have been inconvenienced by Tsar Alexei waking her in the night.

"Alexei's sickly with the bleeding disease?" I said cautiously. It was no big secret anymore. Couldn't keep things under wraps in the Holy Russian Empire the way you could in imperial Russia.

They both nodded. "His wife is pregnant with their first child to be carried this long," Eli said.

"That's big news, I guess." What I didn't know about the Russians . . . well, it was a lot.

"Yes, very big, to us," Paulina said, her tone telling that "us" was all that mattered.

"It's the second time he's been married, right?"

"Yes," Eli said. "His first wife died of influenza."

"She was the rich one," I said, knowing as soon as the words had left my mouth that I shouldn't have said it.

"Yes," Eli said without any expression. "She was from the Ballard family."

The Ballard family pretty much ruled a lot of Dixie. Family members had made huge fortunes on cotton, sugarcane, and timber, planted and harvested by the labor of people who were real poor and really unable to leave their situation. My friend Galilee had been the daughter of such a man. He owed the company store so much he could never discharge his debt, though he worked day in and day out. There was nowhere for him to go that the debt would not follow him, unless he somehow got a huge amount of money and could get out of Dixie with speed. That wasn't going to happen.

But when Galilee had come up pregnant, her mom and dad had scraped together the money to get her out of there. They'd hired an Indian, a Choctaw, who seemed to be invisible to white people. He hadn't been a bad man, Galilee had told me, but he'd been a man, and sometimes it had been a harder journey than she'd ever counted on, until they reached a place she felt safe and she could tell him to leave her.

And I was not going to think about Galilee now. I put my mind back on the tsar's situation.

I could see how the grigoris would try to maintain a sort of militant silence about the tsar's first wife. Thanks to that marriage, the Russian royal family could act royal again, since they had the padding of the Ballard money.

"None of the tsar's daughters have this bleeding disease?"

"No. But Olga and Tatiana each have a son who does."

The most memorable thing about the previous tsar, Nicholas, was that when he'd fled the godless country, he'd formed engagements for all his five children within two years, starting with his oldest daughter and working down to Alexei, his youngest child. At least as far as we

Texomans were concerned, that was the most memorable thing.

Thanks to his daughters of marriageable age, the tsar who'd escaped the rebels in his country had flourished, especially after he'd landed in America. And he'd had some real shrewd advice in farming them out. There had been people who'd wanted to connect with royalty—even royalty in exile—so bad they'd practically drooled at getting one of the grand duchesses yoked into their families. Even at the risk of having grandchildren who stood little chance of living to grow up.

"So it's only boys who get this bleeding thing?"

Paulina and Eli looked at each other. "It's not certain," she said. "But it looks that way."

"But *some* boys don't get it."

They nodded simultaneously.

"There's no way to know, if the woman's going to pass it to her baby?"

Again the nod. Tsar Alexei and his second wife, a Danish princess, were probably praying every day for a healthy boy who didn't have the bleeding disease. What if the tsar's wife had a girl, and then the tsar died?

My stepfather, who read every newspaper he could get and also listened to the radio, had told me it was a miracle the tsar had lived so long. Alexei'd almost passed so many times there was probably a coffin and a plan of the funeral somewhere in a drawer in the palace in San Diego.

I thought about it for a few minutes that night, lying on my blanket in nowhere, listening to the little sounds of the two grigoris sleeping, the movements of small animals in the sparse brush. No matter what glorious marriages Alexei's sisters had made, they could not rule if Alexei died. His baby boy—if he had a boy—would inherit the throne.

Babies were fragile. I could see why it was so important to keep Alexei alive and breeding. But why was the blood of one half-assed wizard essential, the point of this search by Eli and Paulina? Why had the guilds sent these two on this quest? They needed the blood of Oleg Karkarov specifically, and that was just weird. And since my father was dead, his kids' blood would be the best substitute, apparently, given the grigoris' reaction to the idea that the girl in Juárez might be a daughter of Oleg's.

If this child in Juárez was not Oleg Karkarov's, I was his only living child, as far as I knew. Or at least the only living person who *knew* she was his. If Eli and Paulina figured that out, and sooner or later they would, I was going to be made to go someplace I didn't want to go, to serve someone I didn't want to serve. And maybe my life would be taken.

There was no point wishing the grigoris had

never heard my name or come to my door. Wishing never gets you anywhere.

I had a practical idea. If I were smart, I'd just kill my companions right now, while I could catch them by surprise. It would have to be one killing shot apiece, *bam bam*. If either one had a chance to work magic, I was done for.

But by the time I went to sleep, I hadn't killed them.

CHAPTER SEVEN

The next day was grim. The sun beat down, the car needed gas, we didn't have coffee or tea or much water, breakfast was sketchy, and the two grigoris were stiff from sleeping on the ground. Paulina out-and-out ordered me to drive. I slid behind the wheel. Though the land was changing, becoming hillier, with more places of concealment, I didn't protest. If they wanted to get shot more than they wanted to drive, I was in the mood to oblige them. We jolted and bounced across the land, following what was more a track than a road.

I knew we were going in the right direction, but Eli felt he had to pull out a compass to show me that we were. Paulina's quick eyes picked out my exasperation, and it pleased her. She didn't want me to like Eli. She would love it if we quarreled.

I could not figure out Paulina. I thought, *When she was underneath Andy, maybe she called him Eli.* Or maybe Paulina and Eli were related somehow? If I asked them, she'd know I'd been thinking about their relationship, and that would make her hackles rise. Better not to risk it.

Around noon we stopped to get out of the car for a while. By sheer luck, I spotted a huge jackrabbit. I brought him down with Marcial

Montes's rifle. It would be dumb not to eat while the meat was fresh.

I built a fire and put up two little towers of rocks, skewering the carcass on a stick and laying the stick ends on the little towers. While I went a short distance away to pee, Eli turned the skewer.

Paulina had taken off in the opposite direction. She returned with some green stuff she said was edible and good for you. It was a plant I'd seen before but never tried to eat. I watched her take a bite first; that was how much I trusted Paulina.

The leaves didn't taste bad, a little peppery. Since they were fuzzy, the feeling of them in my mouth was not pleasant. But fresh green stuff is hard to find the farther south you go, and my mom had always told me it was important to include vegetables in your eating habits. I hoped I was healthier after I'd made myself swallow a mouthful. It was like chewing a caterpillar.

The jackrabbit tasted even better after the leaves, though. It was done just right. I cut it into pieces with my knife and shared it around. Only the bones were left when we got back into the Tourer.

This time Eli drove, so I was in the back seat. I tried to stay alert, but the long day and the heat and the jolting made me feel stupid. I hated the car by the time we stopped. We'd have to spend another night on the road.

We'd been going south-southwest steadily, and

the plants and scrubby trees were getting farther and farther apart, though the hills were higher and closer together. Eli located some water by his witchy ability, but it was not clear water. We filled up our canteens but had to let the particles in it settle before it was fit to drink, and it was warm and bitter going down our throats.

But any water was better than no water, and any food better than no food. That night I killed two snakes it was safe for us to eat, and they weren't too bad after roasting. Not a lot of actual meat, though. I was about to wrap up in my blanket, since the night was getting chilly.

I heard something that made me sit up so sharply that Paulina jumped. I held up my hand, telling the grigoris to be silent, and they did, for a wonder. I listened hard. I heard the sound of metal clicking against metal. That wasn't going to happen unless people were around. I stood and drew my pistol.

A strange woman stepped into the firelight. Her hands were empty and held wide apart, so I didn't shoot her. She smiled at me, then at Paulina, and then at Eli. That was just creepy. Most people didn't smile at a gun unless they were simple, or unless they knew something you didn't know. I didn't like either of those ideas.

We all waited for the stranger to speak, but she didn't. She had rippling black hair and big, dark eyes. Her white blouse was spanky clean. Her silver earrings made tinkly sounds. She looked like a woman men dreamed about.

The newcomer crossed her arms over her chest in a deliberate way. It was a signal. Not one I recognized. But Paulina did.

After a long hesitation Paulina said, "Welcome to our campfire. I'm Paulina of the Fire Guild, and this is Eli of the Water Guild." Paulina was well aware this creature was not regular, not at all. There was badness all around us.

I wanted to shoot this woman. But I held off, thinking Paulina would give me a signal if that was what she wanted. Paulina and Eli were too completely focused on her to spare me a thought. At least, Paulina couldn't seem to look in my direction. But then, neither did the newcomer.

I glanced at Eli and grew more worried. Maybe they couldn't spare me a thought for real. Eli seemed to be under a spell. His face was blank and his eyes half-closed, and from the state of his pants I could tell he was physically ready to jump on this stranger right in front of us.

"I can tell none of you will harm me." She smiled with a real awareness, kind of *I'm so beautiful*. "Wizarrrrd," she said coaxingly, "come herrrre." She swung her head, and her earrings clicked.

An alarm sounded inside me as I felt a horrible, creeping fuzziness in my head. It was like the leaves we'd eaten had gotten into my brain.

Moving with terrible slowness—at least in my mind—I drew one of the Colts and I pulled the trigger.

She gave me one totally amazed look as a big red stain spoiled that white blouse.

Eli screamed. With a huge effort Paulina broke free from whatever had grabbed her to launch herself forward. She grabbed the witch's skirt as if she feared the woman would run away; instead the witch fell backward. Paulina sprawled on her stomach—way too close to the fire, still clutching the skirt—and panted for the space of three breaths. But after that, flinging off whatever had held her still, Paulina leaped on the witch, her face right above the witch's, like she was going to kiss her. Instead she began sucking out the few moments the witch had left.

I could see the remnants of life flowing out of the dying woman's mouth. I could see her ghost, a white, shadowy thing rising up out of her, being sucked into Paulina's open lips.

I was sickened. Paulina had stepped across some line in my head. She should die, too.

My finger was actually tightening on the trigger when Eli threw himself on me, much the way Paulina had thrown herself on the witch. At least he didn't seem to want to take my soul. His interest lay elsewhere. I could feel . . . oh, God, he was hard as a rock. I did not move even a tiny bit. His arm was pinning down my gun hand, but

I could still manage to shoot him if I had to. "Eli Savarov," I said. He blinked. "Eli Savarov," I said again. "Get the hell off of me."

I watched his personality flowing back into him.

"I . . ." Eli's expression was dazed. He could not come up with words.

"Off."

Eli stared into my eyes a moment longer. It was a very long moment. Then he rolled off and lay panting like a dog, looking up at the stars. I looked at them with him. He took my hand and squeezed it. He released it quickly. It was an apology. "Not like this," he whispered.

While Paulina finished her spiritual cannibal act, I calmed down. If Eli's breathing was anything to go by, so did he.

"You okay?" Paulina was standing over me.

"I am."

"Why are you lying on your back?"

It was real clear Paulina had been totally wrapped up in her soul-sucking, since Eli landing on top of me with a big hard-on was not something she'd miss or let pass, ordinarily.

"It seemed like a good idea," I said, and struggled to sit up. Paulina reached down to help me, and it *didn't* feel like a good idea to refuse to take her hand. I looked to my right. Somehow Eli had already resumed his seat by the fire. I'd lost a minute or two.

"When I signed on to do this, I didn't realize I'd be so damn busy," I said, trying to reenter the world as I knew it. "Out in the middle of this nothing, that *thing* pops up acting all *I'm so sexy.* How?"

"Look," Paulina said, pointing at the body. Though I didn't want to, I followed her finger. A woman in her eighties stared at me sightlessly. It was the same woman. She was still dressed in a white (but red-stained) blouse and a blue skirt. My stomach gave a lurch.

"Is that the way she really looked, or did she wither when you sucked her soul out?"

My question startled Paulina, and Eli, too. They both stared at me. Shit. I'd said something interesting again. "You could see that," Paulina said thoughtfully.

If there was anything I didn't want, it was for Paulina to think about me.

"I saw a cloudy something," I said. "I'm not going any farther than saying that." I'd already said too much.

"When one of us is dying," Eli said, "we can take the power."

"Like I take the gun," I said.

"Just so," Paulina said approvingly. "The gun is your weapon and your livelihood. Magic is ours."

Well, I just loved being like Paulina. I was so glad she'd noticed.

"How'd she find us?" That was the most

important thing we had to settle. I walked a few steps to the rock I'd been sitting on before the witch had shown up. I sat down a little harder than I'd planned on.

"In the morning Eli and I will find out."

After I'd become sure I was in the here and now, the witch was dead, and Paulina and Eli were unharmed and in their right minds, I lay down on my blanket and wrapped it around me. I'd folded up my jacket to be a pillow. Shortly, the other two did the same. The fire was dying out, but when I turned on my side, I could see Eli was looking at me.

I looked back.

He'd landed on me when the witch had made him horny. Not Paulina. He'd gone where he had *thought about* going. I couldn't unthink that. I didn't want to.

Then I willed myself to close my eyes. After a few minutes I slept.

"How come Lizbeth didn't fall under the spell?" Paulina was saying, very low, when I woke up. "She has no power. She should have been out of the action completely. The witch took you under in a few moments."

"Maybe she's a null." He didn't appreciate being ranked just above me, his voice said.

"Maybe. But the witch slowed me for a few seconds, and I'm very strong." Paulina wasn't bragging. She was stating a fact.

"Don't tell me Gunnie has any magical blood," Eli said. He meant it—he doubted it—but he wasn't entirely certain.

Shit.

I should never have agreed to come with these two grigoris. It had seemed like a good idea, tracking down my maybe-sister, finding out why my father's half of my blood was so interesting to these people. Now I wondered if I'd set my own death in motion. I imagined Paulina hovering over me, her mouth open. It made me want to throw up. Or kill her.

"No," Paulina said, but after a pause. "Of course she doesn't. How could she? We saw her mother. That man who looks like a bulldog is her father. No magic there."

They did not know Jackson was my stepfather. A huge wave of relief rolled over me. I felt better all of a sudden. My smoke screen was still up. I would find out what I needed to know. Then I would go home to Segundo Mexia, and the wizards would return to the Holy Russian Empire, and all this craziness would vanish from my life.

The relief was so great that I did go back to sleep for a very short while, enough to make it credible when I yawned and stretched and told them how sorry I was for oversleeping.

I was lying through my teeth, especially when I saw that Eli had started breakfast preparations, and the witch's body had been dragged several yards away, two things I wouldn't have to deal with.

Eli had some oats and some dried apples. We had enough water—assuming we could find another source later today, and there were towns on the map—to boil the oats and apples together in a metal pot, one I hadn't even known Paulina had. We each had a bowl of sweetish cereal that would fill your belly and make you feel strong. I felt able to face today, and face Paulina, after I'd eaten.

There were some questions we had to answer.

"Where did she come from?" I kind of talked to the air between the two wizards, because I didn't want to favor either one. "And how did she find us?"

"We don't know," Eli said. "But we're going to find out. We're going to search the car."

"Tell me what you want me to do." Assuming guns would not be involved, I stacked Montes's rifle and my gun belt with the Colts neatly by the rock I'd been sitting on last night.

"We'll start going over the car inch by inch," Paulina said. "It would have been easier to put something on the car than on our bodies. I'll take the front seat, Eli will take the back seat, you take the trunk. Then we'll all examine the outside."

The day was getting hot by the time we'd peered at every inch of that car. We went over the seats, the cavities behind the seats, the trunk, the floorboards, under the seats, in the glove compartment, under the engine, in the wheel wells. I'm no mechanic, but I'd spent enough time watching Tarken and Martin to at least recognize I was looking at the normal innards of a car.

We found nothing. The grigoris tried with their own eyes, and they tried magic. Paulina took a pinch of this and that from pockets in her vest, and said a few power words and tossed the stuff from her pockets over the car. I was really hoping to see something happen, but nothing did. So the car search was a bust.

Next we all emptied our bags. Then we searched the icebox Jim Comstock had sent with us.

After another hour we'd come up with nothing. If we wanted to reach anywhere by noon to refill our canteens and check the car, we had to be on our way. I gathered Jackhammer, my pistols, and the rifle I'd gleaned from the hired killer.

"Wait," said Eli. I stopped. I'd been about to toss the rifle into the leather bag I'd brought with me. "That's a new thing. The dead man's rifle."

I handed it to him as quick as I could. I hadn't had a chance to clean it, as I would have if we'd been in a hotel last night. "It's a good rifle," I said. "A bolt-action Winchester, like Jack-hammer, but newer."

Eli looked blank, but he nodded to show he accepted my opinion. "Is it loaded?" he asked.

Good to be cautious. "Yes," I said.

"Then while I'm holding it out, you look at it, and tell me if you see anything odd about it."

I'd never thought of checking the rifle, a tool of my trade and one I was glad to have, for . . . well, I didn't know what they were looking for. Some extra item added to something familiar, something magic could stick on to. A map we couldn't see, one that led right to us.

Now that Eli had suggested the rifle might be the bearer of the homing device, I found it right away. "On the stock," I said. After I glanced up at the grigoris, I pointed. "This here is the stock. The shiny wood. Mine is walnut. This Winchester is stained darker. You see this little pimplelike thing? This bump?"

They bent over to look at it. There was a bump in the wood, close to the bolt action—not something so big you'd notice it, if you weren't a gun person, if you weren't looking, if you weren't in the bright sunlight.

"Better unload it," Eli said.

I did. "Look down the bore," I said, just so he'd be reassured, and he peered down the barrel.

Eli nodded. The rifle was unloaded. I laid the weapon on the hood of the Tourer.

With the point of his knife, Eli gently nudged the rough spot while Paulina squatted down to get very close to the rifle. Eli dislodged some crumbly brown stuff, almost the same color as the wood but not the same texture. This dab amount of brown, whatever it was, had covered a tiny piece of metal, thin as a shaving, sticking it to the rifle.

"That's a piece of tinfoil like you wrap food in," I said. You couldn't get anything by me. Except a sabotaged rifle.

The tinfoil came out, too, very delicately. We all peered at the shallowest scrape in the wood. My eyes were sharper than theirs.

"There's hair in there," I said. "From when you had that shave in Mil Flores, I bet you."

"But you killed the man who had this rifle very soon after Eli left the barbershop," Paulina said.

"If he had this little hole prepared, he could have nipped in, gotten the whiskers, stuck them in place, and pressed this brown stuff over it to hold it all still."

"How could he know that we would end up with the rifle?"

"I got a reputation," I said, trying to hit the middle between boasting and being overmodest.

"But still."

I had another idea. I was sharing them right and left. I might have kept my mouth shut, but I wanted to live through this plagued expedition. "So . . . you two would know if you were with another wizard, right? You'd put out your magic feelers and know what they were?"

I looked off in another direction while I waited for an answer. I didn't want to know if their eyes were on me.

"You think the person who put the hairs in the rifle was Belinda Trotter," Eli said. "Not the gunman."

I shrugged. "Her or the traveling salesman. My money's on Trotter. She had a wagon handy. She had no reason to be there. She was way too helpful."

"You think she hired Josip. He failed. Then she hired the ones who ambushed us," Paulina said, thinking as she spoke. "And when that missed, her gunman was waiting in Mil Flores for her directions. But by then she knew your reputation, so she stepped into the barbershop to get some of Eli's whiskers. I'm not sure how she knew Eli'd go in. Maybe she was simply waiting for any opportunity to get something off one of us, and that was a golden one. Then—she'd have to be prepared for this part—she stuck the whiskers, as she might have fixed any other tiny thing, on the rifle. And she got that opportunity when she picked up the rifle after Montes fell to the ground from the roof. So that if he missed, and you killed him, we'd take the rifle with the find-them spell." Paulina did not sound angry at herself— or at me, which surprised me. She sounded very,

202

very thoughtful. "So was that creature last night the real Belinda? Or was it another hired hand?"

"I guess we'll find out," I said.

"What do you mean?" Eli asked.

"If someone else tries to kill us, we'll know Belinda Trotter is alive."

"Maybe there's more than her in this conspiracy," Paulina said.

I took the rifle over to the body of the witch, which was drying out into a mummy real quick. Of course that wasn't normal, but was anything with these two, in their world? I used Eli's knife to scrape out every tiny whisker. Then I spat on the knife blade to make sure anything on it would be wiped off, and I rubbed the blade of the knife against the witch's blouse. I was leaving a message . . . if anyone came to read it.

My whole life I had hated the magic world. I knew grigoris were unreliable and dangerous, if not outright evil. Now I was surrounded by the very thing I hated. But I'd gotten myself into this fix. I had to get myself out.

And I also had to do everything I could to protect the lives of Paulina and Eli, because that's what I'd contracted to do. You don't have to sign a paper to have a contract. I might be a crew of one right now, but I was still bound.

CHAPTER EIGHT

We loaded up the bags and started driving after that. It was going to be another long, jolting day. It was hot, it was windy, and we needed water and gasoline. According to the map, we would pass close to Dalton in the afternoon. If we turned west, the town would be only a mile out of the way. Also according to the map, Dalton was larger than Mil Flores. It was our best chance. Clear choice.

Except outside of Dalton there was a roadblock. There were two men and one woman standing guard. They were professionals, or at least they looked like they were. I said, "You two stay in here, and don't do anything hinky." Paulina and Eli looked a little offended, but screw 'em.

I slid out of the car and advanced to the wooden barricade. I held my hands out, empty.

"Can we come into town and get water?" I said.

"Who you guarding, Gunnie?" The woman was older than me, her blond hair in a long braid running down her back. The two men were grizzled and bearded, hard to tell one from another except one was shorter and his hair was darker.

"Two strangers from Holy Russia," I said.

"They grigoris?"

Thanks to Paulina's face tattoos, there was no way to lie about it. "The woman is," I said.

"Nope. We don't let none of them in," the shorter man said.

The barricade was weathered. This had not been set up to stop us specially. This crew was paid to stop grigoris and other suspicious strangers from entering Dalton. No point arguing.

"I understand," I said. "You got any water we could have? We'll just go back to the main road, with or without. Peaceful. But I'm asking."

They looked at one another, had a silent palaver. The woman said, "We can spare some. Bring us your canteens."

Keeping my hands up, I went back to the car to fetch 'em. Eli and Paulina looked at me, questions all over their faces, but I shook my head. "We ain't welcome," I said. My invisible mother gave me a poke in the head. "We *aren't* welcome. They're giving us some water, though. Smile and nod." I gathered up our canteens, including our spare.

Though Paulina's face made it clear she would rather have done something painful to the guards, she inclined her head like a queen, and Eli produced a passable smile. It was clear these two had never been told they weren't welcome somewhere, so I guessed they hadn't been out of the HRE real often.

I walked back, my arms still extended, two

canteens hanging from each hand. If I'd stuck a pistol in my back waistband, I could have dropped the canteens, pulled the gun, and shot the three of them. They hadn't been challenged by a professional in a while.

It was like the shorter man read my mind. "Stop!" he called, and I obeyed instantly. "Turn in a circle!" he told me. I did, keeping my hands out far. "Okay," he said when he'd had a good look. "You can come on."

They had a big barrel of water. I saw it when I got close enough to hand over the canteens. The taller man turned on the spigot and filled 'em, all four. The tall man handed the canteens back to me over the barricade. He wasn't going to come out. Maybe something about me spooked 'em. Maybe they were always this cautious.

I offered them six bullets, as goodwill for the water. The blond woman accepted, with thanks. So we were square with them.

We didn't linger. No point, and discourteous. Paulina made an efficient U-turn and we returned to the main road . . . though calling it a road was a big compliment.

At least we could take a drink, and if the car overheated, we had some water to put in it.

We jolted along. I am used to tough living, but I was getting worn down. The movement, the heat, and the long day—after a night that hadn't been exactly restful—made me dull. But maybe the biggest lack, as keen as that of water, was that I had no one to talk to . . . at least, no one I could trust.

No friend.

It wasn't that the two grigoris were killers that bothered me—Tarken, Martin, and Galilee had all been killers in the line of work. I hated the idea that people could be not what they looked like. The witch the night before, she had been both a beautiful woman and an ancient crone, and I didn't know which was her real face. The not knowing, it made me queasy.

Not only that, but the grigoris could take life in weird and horrible ways. Removing the blood. Sucking away the soul. In comparison, gunshots seemed honest and straightforward. I knew that wasn't fair. Dead was dead.

Anyone who'd been gutshot would be glad of having his blood extracted instead of writhing in agony for terrible minutes. Someone whose wound had become infected, whose blood was being poisoned, might be glad to have her soul removed rather than suffer a slow death. It would be an easy death. Well, an easier death. I'd seen this, and my head knew it to be true. But I couldn't change how I felt, even though I knew it didn't make sense. At least, not now.

While we headed southwest, I studied the map some more. We might be able to reach Paloma. We were going up and down hills again, and the road was winding and sometimes steep; but the paving was a bit better, and if our gas lasted, we'd be fine.

For once, we were fine.

The road was suddenly a real road instead of a suggestion of one; it had been built well and patched, and we were able to go faster. The ride was smoother. Before it fell dark, we saw Paloma. After Mil Flores, it looked like a city, though it was only a couple of streets of stores around a courthouse, surrounded by a few more streets of smallish homes. But there was a choice of hotels, there were restaurants, and there was running water and electricity.

Best of all, there wasn't anyone standing guard to tell us we couldn't come in.

We stopped at the first hotel, one of the new kind, one story with parking spots in front of each door. It looked pretty busy. Since I looked more like a regular person, I went into the lobby to ask about rooms. There was only one available, with one bed.

I went back out to the Tourer to consult with my bosses.

"We can make do in one room," I said without any enthusiasm. "If you want."

But we'd all had a bad night the night before, and some good rest was high on my list of wants. Paulina and Eli agreed to look further, so we drove on a little ways. At the second place, a large, two-story wooden structure a block off the main square, there were three rooms available on the second floor.

"And we got four bathrooms up there," the owner, a middle-aged woman named Margaret, said. It was hard to stop myself cheering.

We took all three rooms, and my relief was so great that, again, I wanted to cheer. I needed some time to myself.

The second floor was one long corridor. I took a quick look at the other two rooms before I stepped into mine. They were all more or less the same: a double bed without any trough in the middle, a lamp on the bedside table. As a backup, there was a candle in a heavy candlestick (harder to sneak out) on a little wicker table beside a matching chair.

Nothing looked suspicious in any room.

I'd done my duty. I was able to shut the door of mine, the grigoris on the other side, without any guilt. I could not grab a towel and clean clothes fast enough. The hall bath closest to my room was in use, but the second one was not. I pulled off my dirty clothes and ran a big tub of hot water. As soon as I was clean, I washed my nasty clothes, quickly as I could, and wrung 'em out.

I put on a shirt and pants that didn't smell, returned to my room to hang out my wash, and looked forward to eating some decent food.

I would have enjoyed exploring by myself, but

the grigoris had told me they'd meet me in the lobby.

They were my bosses. I met them.

Margaret was still at the reception desk. "What's the best place to eat?" Eli asked her.

"You want to eat? Or you want to eat and drink?" Margaret was a plain and plainspoken woman.

"Eat," said Paulina.

I could have used a drink or two, but it would not have been smart to drink around the grigoris, or while I was working.

"The Angora, two doors down, is the cleanest place in Paloma," Margaret said. "Dusty's, off the square, is good, too, but sometimes you pay for eating there by staying up all night."

Without discussion, we went to the Angora. The sun was just on the edge of going down, and some streetlights came on while we were walking. I'd seldom seen such a thing. It was real convenient to have a little light to see by, but at the same time it felt funny, as in unnatural. The restaurant had its own light pole outside, and a million bugs were whirring and bashing into the yellow glow. People spilled out onto the sidewalk, some of them with glasses of whiskey, or cigarettes, or both, in their hands. The Angora was doing a good business.

Paulina made an impatient noise. "I will see how long we must wait for a table," she said, and vanished into the brightly lit dining room.

"I'm sorry," Eli said the minute she was out of earshot.

"What for?" So much had happened, it was hard to pick out exactly what he should apologize for.

"For landing on you like that last night."

So we were going to talk about it. "I didn't know if you were going to kill me or have sex with me."

"I didn't know, either." There was a moment of silence while we both tried to figure out where to go next in this conversation.

Eli said, "If you hadn't shot the witch, we'd have all been under her control in another minute. How did you do it?"

I didn't know. "She wasn't really focused on me," I said. I was just thinking out loud. "She was after you and Paulina."

"She didn't focus on you because she knew you were not a grigori," Eli said. "You should have fallen under her spell right away, faster than Paulina and I did. Instead you pulled away enough to kill her."

This was becoming real awkward. I shrugged uneasily. "That's what you hired me for."

"You saw Paulina harvest her."

So that was what they called it. "Yeah. I saw that."

"Not all of us . . ." He trailed off. I didn't know if he meant he would not have done that, or if he could not have done that. Either way. Bad.

"Does she do that often?" I really wanted to know if that sucking thing was a common practice.

"It's supposed to give you a lot of power." He looked away.

Not really an answer.

"Why is everyone trying to kill us?" I thought I might as well ask while I could. I could see Paulina turning from the host to come outside.

"Isn't that why you're along?" He smiled, just quick and gone. "To make sure no one does?"

Eli was big into not answering.

"That's why you're paying me," I said, and if I sounded grim and grumpy, I figured I had good reason.

Paulina beckoned from the door. "There's a table," she called.

The food was good, just as Margaret had said. Grilled steaks, fresh bread, onions cooked in butter in the skillet, snap beans. My stomach hadn't been so happy in days. As soon as I was full, I wanted to sleep. I thought of the bed, of being alone in a room.

That sounded so wonderful it was hard to keep myself seated with Paulina and Eli. They were talking about nothing more important than whether or not they should order pecan pie.

The answer was obvious (yes), so I let my eyes wander through the crowded restaurant. The bar was visible against the north wall, and I looked at the mirror facing me. I could hardly believe it when I spied a face I recognized. His eyes met mine in the mirror, and his weather-beaten face spread in a smile.

We were moving toward each other the next breath. "Chauncey Donegan!" I called, and we wrapped our arms around each other.

"Lizbeth," he said to my scalp. "Jesus, girl, what did you do to your head?"

"If you're talking about the scar, I got clipped. If you're talking about the hair, it's growing back," I said, pulling away from him. I ran my hand over my scalp; yep, it was coming in thick. "What you doing here?"

He nodded to two men sitting together at a small table near the front window. They were staring. When they saw me looking, they turned away quick. "Guarding them two. They're from Britannia. They got some business here."

"What kind?"

"Who the hell cares?"

Chauncey had never been too interested in the underpinnings of his job. He was a surface kind of guy, and he'd done well that way. He was at least fifteen years older than me, and still alive. Gunnies don't live too long, mostly.

"How's Martin?" he asked. "That truck still running? And the rest of the crew?"

"They're all gone, Cee. Killed on the Corbin road."

"You all on your own? Come here for work?" he said, after giving the dead a minute of respect.

"I got me a job for the moment. I'm taking the grigoris somewhere." I tilted my head, indicating Paulina and Eli.

Chauncey gave them a hard look. I didn't check to see if they were looking back. "Jeez, gal, they're some kind of scary," he said. "How'd you find them?"

"They found me. My lucky day." My voice told him it was just the opposite. "But it's paying well."

"Smooth trip?"

"Not so far. Yours?"

"Quiet as the grave. Nobody seems to want to kill Mr. Harcourt or Mr. Penn." He sounded kind of regretful.

"Even you?"

"Only every other minute." He laughed, but it was forced.

Well, that makes two of us, I thought. "Don't get too bored," I said. Being bored means being sloppy.

"I guess you all are staying the night?" Chauncey asked hopefully.

"Yeah, we're at the Palacio."

"Maybe we can have a drink after we put the clients to bed?"

I was powerfully tempted. "That would be so

great. But we've had shooting and whatnot and I can't leave 'em alone. How's Nancy?"

Chauncey looked away. "She passed of the pneumonia last winter."

I shook my head. "Hard times, Chauncey. I'm real sorry."

He shrugged. "Least I still have my boy, Milton. He's fourteen now. He stays with my mom while I'm working, helps her out."

I gave him another hug, a quick one. "It's great to see you, Cee. I got to get back to the grigoris. You keep your two Britannians safe. You got to get back to that boy of yours."

He gave me a whiskery kiss on the cheek and returned to his spot at the bar, where he could keep an eye on Mr. Harcourt and Mr. Penn. After their first quick look, they hadn't glanced our way. Chauncey could have been dancing with a voodoo queen, for all they knew, or he could have had a snake wrapped around his neck by an enemy. They cared as much about Cee as my grigoris did about me. Well, maybe the jury was still out on Eli.

Paulina and Eli were making for the door, so I made haste to catch up with them. Looked like we weren't going to have pie. They didn't speak, but I could tell they knew I was right behind them. When we were out on the sidewalk, which had grown a lot quieter, Paulina said, "Are you going to spend the night with your friend?"

"I am not, because I am working," I said, biting out each word. "I don't recall asking you who you were spending the night with, Paulina."

"He just seemed fond of you," she said with a real cold innuendo.

"Yeah, fat damn lot you know," I said. "He just lost his wife. Not that you ever asked, but my man got shot and killed on the Corbin road less than a month ago. So you just go take your ideas about me and stuff them somewhere you have a hole to fill."

I hadn't realized how angry I was until I let this fly.

There was an awful silence. I should have stopped with "He just lost his wife." They didn't need to know about Tarken, or any part of my personal life.

"I spoke from anger," I said, and though I was trying, my voice was stiff and unrepentant. "But you should know I don't leave people I'm guarding, especially when the trip's been as busy as this one has." And I walked away, hoping like hell they'd follow me.

CHAPTER NINE

For once, they did what I wanted them to. And they didn't say a word. That was damn near perfect. If I could have locked them in their rooms, I would have, and been happy to do it. But I had noticed a whorehouse two blocks down from the Palacio. Maybe Paulina would be going over to see what there was to play with.

I didn't have the slightest idea what kind of whore would appeal to Eli. I didn't know if he'd want a man or a woman, a real young one or a granny. I had a strong feeling, after the incident in the desert, that grown women were his preference.

If my clients ever started talking to me again, I had a few questions I wanted to ask. I'd heard of prostitutes who had some magic in them, for whom sex worked as a kind of feeding. If that was true, maybe grigoris sought them out. It was hard to believe this little town would have any such. Thinking about prostitutes got me all the way to the Palacio, and past Margaret standing vigilant at the desk, and up the dimly lit stairs.

Paulina went to her door, Eli to his, and I pulled my key out, but then I noticed something. I clamped my hand down on Eli's arm and poked Paulina with my free hand. She whirled around

217

to snarl at me, but I pointed to the line of light showing under Eli's door. It had not been dark when we left for the Angora.

I'd stopped him from unlocking the door and pushing it open, but now I wasn't sure how to proceed.

I could shoot through the door, but I might kill a maid or a thief or a friend who wanted to surprise Eli (that would be one stupid friend). None of those people should be in the room, but shooting them dead was the kind of overreaction gunnies got hung for, time to time.

Paulina had a plan, which didn't surprise me one bit. She pointed to a spot to the left of the door. It was clear she meant me to stand there and stay still. Then she beckoned to Eli. They consulted in near silence.

Paulina took something out of her vest and knelt in her smooth way, putting the pinch of whatever it was just under the door. When she stood up, she and Eli began moving their hands and whispering. I could not understand the words, was not sure they were even English, and I was grateful for that. I was real busy praying no one needed to walk by us. By chance or by magic, the hall remained empty.

Paulina waved a finger at my gun belt.

So my part in this was to be ready to shoot. I drew a Colt and began breathing deep, emptying out my head.

When someone appears out of nowhere and starts shooting at you, it's easy to shoot back. It's not so easy to stand there waiting.

There was a thud inside the room; something had hit the floor. Could be there was someone in there smart enough to feel the magic, smart enough to play possum. But the chances were better that the grigori magic had worked.

Paulina stepped back and swept her hand from me to the door. Of course she wanted me to be first through, when it was her magic that might not have worked. As I stepped past her, I thought how great it would be to stomp on her toes, accidentally on purpose. Someday Paulina and I were going to have a showdown.

But not today.

I took the key from Eli's fingers and turned it in the lock with my left hand, pushed the door open, and stood back, my Colt at the ready in my right.

Nothing moved in the room. The glow of the lamp showed a man sprawled on the floor. He was very young.

"Peter!" Eli jumped past me on his way to the body. Paulina wrapped her arms around Eli from behind and lifted him up off his feet. I admired her quickness and strength.

I could hear boots coming up the stairs, so I stepped fully into the room and shut the door behind me.

"Gunnie," Paulina snapped. I was supposed to

understand my orders from that. I circled round the grigoris to look down at the man—no, the boy—on the floor. I sniffed the air. I moved the lamp so I could see him better. Nothing suspicious . . . aside from the fact he had no reason being where he was, and Eli thought it was someone named Peter.

I took a deep breath, let it out. I knelt down. Lightly. I laid my hand on the boy's back. Eli's breath left his lungs in a groan.

"He's alive," I said, real calm and quiet.

Paulina let go of Eli, who didn't dive for the fallen boy like I'd thought he might. Eli'd gotten control of himself.

"I'm gonna turn him over," I said, and laid my gun on the bedside table, by the lamp. "You be on watch," I told Paulina, looking up to meet her eyes.

She nodded.

That was as much reassurance as I was going to get. I leaned over the body, gripped the clothes on the boy's left side, and heaved backward. Though the situation hung in the balance for a second or two, I got him flipped. His eyes were shut. His mouth was twitching. This Peter looked a lot like Eli, but with all the character sanded off.

Eli couldn't keep away after he saw the boy's face. He was crouching on the other side of the body before you could say lickety-split. "Peter," Eli said, low but urgent. "Talk to me!"

The boy's eyes opened. They were blank and white and horrible. As his hands shot up to grab Eli, I shoved Eli with all the strength I could muster. He fell back on his ass. "Pau—" I said, and then the boy was on me.

This was it for me. Upstairs room in a hotel in Paloma, somewhere on the border between Texoma and Mexico.

I tried to reach the night table to scrabble for my gun, but I couldn't get to it. For the second time in two days, I had a determined male on top of me. But this Peter was not interested at all in being inside me. He wanted to kill me.

His fingers clamped on my throat. I brought my hands up between his wrists, hitting out as hard as I could, and I loosened one hand. I rolled in that direction and pinned his wrist with my elbow, but his other hand was still digging into the flesh and bone of my neck, and I was seeing spots. I saw a flash of something coming down and heard a nasty crunch, and the boy fell away from me, limp and lifeless.

I could not move. I lay bonelessly on the floor, feeling pretty limp and lifeless myself.

Gradually my breath got regular again. The pain in my throat and chest eased up just a little. I wasn't going to die.

"Gunnie?" Paulina said. "How are you?" She was holding the candlestick she'd hit the boy with. It wasn't clean. Eli had left the room hastily, and now he came back in and leaned against the wall. His broad face was pale and clammy. He'd been sick. At least he'd made it to the hall bathroom.

I could think only of a play we'd all had to read in my mom's school. " 'A plague o' both your houses,' " I whispered, and I rolled to my feet, retrieving my gun. It was the only smart thing I could think of to say.

They could handle this from here on out. With great care I walked out of the room, went next door to mine.

I had to lean against the wall while I turned my key in the lock. After I pushed the door open, I made damn sure the floor was clear. I looked up at the ceiling. I checked every corner and opened the wardrobe, too.

I even crouched to look under the bed. That might have been a mistake. It took me a very long time to get up.

Finally I was sitting on the bed instead of staring underneath it. I pulled off my boots, and my shirt, and my pants, and I lay down in my underwear. My neck hurt like hell. I didn't even want to think about swallowing, or talking, or coughing. A little air stirred in the open window, and it felt good, helped me breathe.

Some time later, maybe ten minutes or a couple of hours, I don't know, there was a knock at the door. I hadn't locked it behind me, which lets you know what kind of shape I was in. I was scared to speak. I used my knuckles to knock on the wood of the table. Even that sounded feeble.

Eli came in. He pulled over the rickety wicker chair. He leaned over me to have a look, but my room was as dark as the night outside. He made an impatient sound and turned on the lamp. His face got all tight. Yep, my neck was bad.

Eli looked away, and we stayed like that. He didn't want to talk, and I couldn't.

After a while I got bored with all the silence. I tapped his hand with my finger. When he looked at me, I pointed left to his room. I turned my hand palm up to ask, *What happened?*

"It wasn't my brother Peter," Eli said. "Though it was a good likeness. No telling who it used to be. It's dead now."

I raised my hand again. *What are you going to do with it?*

He shrugged. "We dropped it out the window. I pulled the car around and loaded it in. Paulina's going to drive out of town a little way and dump it."

I sighed, tried to sit up.

Eli put his hand on my chest to stop me. "You don't need to go," he said. "She can do this."

I decided not to argue. I lay back on the pillow. His hand didn't move, though. It was spread on my chest bone. Gradually I got a warm feeling there, and the pain burst into blossom. I was scared to move. My eyes flicked to his.

"This is going to hurt some, but it'll help you heal faster." He could have told me that at the start.

I could not stop the tears rolling from my eyes to the pillow.

"I'm sorry," he said. "Sorry." At last the warmth began to feel good. With a great effort I put my hand on top of his. And the healing went quicker. I went to sleep with that glow in my chest.

When I opened my eyes, the room was empty and the sun was bright. The limp curtains were shifting in the wind. I needed to pee in the worst way. Getting up was painful, putting it mildly. I pulled on my pants and shirt as quickly as I could manage, and I inched my way out of the room and down the hall to the bathroom, encountering two men in business suits. They saw my throat and looked away hastily. And this was the time I had to wait for another customer to leave the bathroom, of course.

After I'd gotten in, locked the door, and eased myself, I had to struggle to stand. I leaned against the edge of the tub. "Good morning," I said very, very quietly. The discomfort was definitely hanging around, but I didn't think any bones were broken in my throat. Looking in the mirror was downright horrible. My neck was wearing a circle of bruises. *A choker of bruises,* I told myself, and felt my mouth twitch.

It was a real adventure to pull my clothes off and take a bath. I wished I'd just walked to the bathroom naked. I brushed my teeth real gently. Feeling human again, I resumed my clothes, and I slowly made my way from the bathroom. I should check on my employers.

The doors to Paulina's and Eli's rooms were open, and a maid was stripping the sheets from Paulina's bed.

CHAPTER TEN

I had a second of real shock, followed by a mixed kind of hope. Could I be rid of 'em? I'd still go to Juárez. But maybe nobody would try to kill me for a day or two.

I packed my weapons and dry clothes in two minutes. The bag of guns weighed down my arm, the Winchester across my back felt heavy and hard, and my neck ached like hell. But I could get around. More or less.

I went down the stairs slowly, casting looks around like someone was going to jump out and yell, *Boo!*

No one did, but I spied Paulina and Eli sitting on a bench across from the desk. Shit. Margaret was yakking away at them. She was in the middle of a long story, judging by the glazed look on Paulina's face.

"And don't no one know who he is," she said. "Looks like he's been dead two, three days or longer. Dumped by the road."

"What killed him?" Eli asked, showing a polite interest.

"Skull bashed in, I heard," Margaret said with relish.

Paulina glanced at me, and her eyes widened. That was enough to tell me I should have covered my neck somehow. Sporting an unusual injury after a dead man shows up . . . not a good idea. I slipped my hand into my pocket and pulled out a bandanna I used when the dust was blowing. I tied it around my neck and picked up my bags again.

"We wondered where you were," Eli said cheerfully. Our hostess looked at me with a little surprise. She'd been so excited by her story she hadn't heard me, and so she hadn't seen my neck . . . which was good.

"You done missed breakfast, young lady," she said.

I was going to have to talk. It would seem too weird if I didn't. I said, as quietly as I could without sounding peculiar, "Overslept."

"I can get you some leftover oatmeal."

I nodded, smiling. Doling words out as sparingly as I could.

"You have something you can put it in?" Eli said.

"I got a box," she said, nodding. She vanished for a couple of minutes, returning with a cardboard cigar box lined with wax paper, and cup of hot coffee.

I accepted the box. "Thanks," I said.

Margaret said, "You don't sound like yourself. You better take it easy."

Gunnies didn't take it easy, ever. Not when they were on the job.

"Drink your coffee while I go fill the car," Eli suggested, and Paulina and I settled into a calm silence. She could have talked at me, but she didn't, and I was grateful. The hot coffee felt both good and bad going down, but I did perk up as I drank it. By the time Eli returned with the car, the cup was empty.

"Bye, Miss Margaret," I said, and Paulina gave the older woman a bob of the head as we emerged into the sunshine. I stood on the porch in the strong morning light, and I shut my eyes. I had not thought I'd see this morning, or any other morning, ever again. I opened my eyes to find that the grigoris were waiting for me and looking grim.

We got into the car, me in the back seat. I put Jackhammer across my knees. I would really enjoy shooting someone today, if the occasion arose. At the very least, I wouldn't mind.

Paulina drove out of town. I spared a thought for Chauncey and his two indifferent charges. I hoped he was more comfortable and relaxed than I was.

I took one look at the congealed oatmeal and pitched it out the window. I kept the box. Boxes were always handy. The bright landscape looked empty and serene today. We climbed up hills and wound around them to come down the other side. We saw deer out in the broad, flat area, but they were lost to sight in a moment.

I hadn't been sure if Paloma lay in Mexico or Texoma, but early that morning we saw a border marker. It was leaning to one side and the paint was peeling. Casual.

I liked it.

I also liked the silence. None of us was in a chatty mood. At least I had a good reason, given the state of my throat. I didn't even want to imagine what it would feel like today if Eli hadn't done his healing. I did wonder who the Peter look-alike had been, and why his body had been transformed to look like Eli's brother. But I was giving my throat the morning off, and my wondering was silent.

Not a word was spoken until we stopped for lunch in a thriving Mexican hill town called Ciudad Azul. I don't know if the city had been named for the paint job, or if the name had inspired the decoration. At least half of the buildings were painted some shade of blue. It was strange and cheerful.

There was a festival going on in Ciudad Azul, going by the blue and green banners and streamers hung everywhere at the top of the hill. Much of the town lay around the bottom, but the big public buildings were on a mesa on top. Even on the elevation the banners and streamers weren't doing much fluttering today, but there was plenty of other movement. A large crowd was strolling around, taking in the decorations and air of celebration. All these folks were dressed in their brightest and best. I felt dusty and sweaty as I climbed out of the car.

At least it would be easy to get a meal. There were food stalls and makeshift bars set up around the square.

In Texoma and Mexico, if a town is any size at all, it has a square. The church, or the courthouse, is in the middle of the square. Whichever institution doesn't get the middle spot, that one's always nearby. In Ciudad Azul the courthouse had claimed the middle, so the church had grabbed the whole west side of the square. It was huge.

I looked around at all the bright colors and the hum of activity, all the bustle of buying and selling. Normally, this degree of celebration meant that it was some saint's day. My mother had cooked at saint's-day festivals while she was single, to bring in some more cash. I could almost taste her churros, and recalled the pleasure of watching a parade.

I felt a little hum inside, like my motor was starting up again.

Then I saw the gallows on the courthouse lawn.

Public hangings were bad news. Two separate people, Jackson and my friend Dan Brick, had told me about being in towns on their judgment day. It was a miserable spectacle in and of itself. Even worse, the excitement of it often churned the crowd into a frenzy.

No stranger could gain any benefit from being present on judgment day. I could pass for a native, but Eli and Paulina could not. The Mexican attitude toward wizardry was *very* unpredictable. On a feast day I wouldn't have worried. On a hanging day . . .

"You need to get out of here," I whispered to Paulina. I jerked her arm to pull her back to the car. I didn't know where Eli had gotten off to; from the way he'd hustled off, I guessed he was visiting the town latrine.

"We have to eat," Paulina said in a loud voice. "I smell good food!" This drew the attention of the closest food vendors, as she'd intended. They all began talking to her in Spanish, which she did not understand. I spoke some Spanish, like nearly everyone in Texoma, but I couldn't keep up with the Ciudad Azul rapid delivery. Paulina, having committed to a role, let herself be drawn over to the food stalls. She studied the offerings with deep interest, as if she were some kind of expert. (It looked like goat and grilled snake to me, and the usual beans and rice. Tortillas, salsa, sopapillas, churros.) She hadn't noticed the gallows, or else she just thought I was being silly.

Eli appeared at my side. He said, "What is she doing?"

"She decided to be the big spender and make the crowd like her," I said. "Don't know why. But today's a hanging day, and we need to get the hell out of here." I nodded toward the gallows, and his eyes widened.

A tiny woman wrapped in a bright shawl began to talk to us, and I tried to follow along. Finally she said, "*¿Es este tu amante?*" looking from me to Eli in a meaningful way.

"*¡Sí!*" I said brightly, wrapping an arm around Eli's waist.

"*¡Dale un beso!*" the ancient woman said to Eli with the air of a captain giving an order. She waved a wrinkled claw. She was clearly drunk.

"What did she say?"

"She thinks you're my fiancé," I said. "She expects you to kiss me."

He gathered me up and laid one on me. I was real surprised, but I couldn't very well push away. After all, there are worse things than being kissed. I did my best to look enthusiastic. If stretching up hadn't made my neck ache so much, it would have been real nice. Way too nice.

"Hey, you two, not in front of everyone!" Paulina called gaily. She would have enjoyed cutting my heart out at that moment, her eyes told me. Eli and I went over to her, me clinging to his arm (but very lightly), and he said, "You found something good for our lunch?"

"This beef looks good," she said.

"Goat," I murmured.

"Goat," she said, giving me a look that would have shrunk my balls if I'd had any.

For the first time I wished I could speak Russian. I needed to explain a few things to my companions, and the chances were good that most of the people around us had some English. I had a little French. "*Madame,*" I said, smiling, "*voyez-vous l'echafaud?*" *Do you see the scaffold?*

Her jaw dropped down for a gratifying moment, and she glanced toward the courthouse lawn. This time she registered what she was seeing. "*C'est une structure pour pendre les gens?*" *The structure is for hanging people?*

"*Oui.*" I nodded. I was sorry the second after, when my throat throbbed. I gasped and put my hand to the bandanna. "We need to skedaddle," I croaked.

"What does this have to do with us?" Eli said.

"They all get drunk and excited and things get crazy," I said.

The grigoris looked at me without understanding.

"Surely we can get some food and be on our way." Paulina eyed me narrowly.

"This is the most fun these people have all year," I said. "They're going to get pretty riled up. You're infidels here. We got to get out."

"So far everyone has been friendly." Paulina literally looked down her nose when she said this.

"*Take my word for it.*"

"And if I don't?"

233

"Then I'm just gonna drift away from you two in the crowd, and leave you to get out of this yourself. Or not. I can't kill this many people."

The massive front doors of the church opened, each needing a man to push it. The inside of the church was a dark cavern, but the procession moved into the light, beginning its progress to the gallows. It was led by a man carrying a cross on a rod, and after the crucifer came an armed guard. Behind the guard shuffled the condemned prisoner, his face covered with a white hood. His hands were bound in front of him. He was escorted on either side by two priests, both wearing long black cassocks. An armed guard walked behind them, too.

A woman screamed and lunged forward. Maybe she wanted to see the prisoner one last time because she loved him, or maybe she wanted to gouge his eyes out because he'd killed her husband. Either way, she went for his face. The prisoner, who could not see the woman hurtling toward him, turned his head in the direction of the scream. The priest on the prisoner's right backhanded the lunging woman. She went staggering, and the people in the crowd grabbed her arms, to keep her from trying again. But she kept shrieking, and the crowd began moving restlessly.

"Okay," Paulina said abruptly. We began to drift between the little clumps of people. It was good they were milling around, so our retreat was not obvious. As we went, I dropped some money on the table of a baker and smiled at him as I picked up some rolls (at least that was what I guessed they were). And I grabbed up some meat, skewered and roasted. The meat seller was so involved in the spectacle that he only glanced down at the money and nodded.

I had my canteen over my shoulder, as well as Jackhammer, and I made sure we passed by a pump. Eli filled up my canteen, and his, while I kept watch. Paulina, of course, hadn't brought hers. Because she was always safe, since she was the mighty wizard Paulina.

We progressed cautiously, steadily, keeping smiles on our faces, while the condemned man continued his slow progress to the gallows. The crowd's excitement keyed higher with every step he took. More people began calling things to the condemned man, though I couldn't understand the words. It sounded like wolves howling. Even Paulina looked alarmed at the way the crowd ebbed and flowed . . . almost in unison.

Finally we were back at the car. I gave a happy wave to the drunken scum of the earth leaning against it. They smiled back, showing their broken teeth. At least one of them had a pistol, held loosely in his hand.

If I killed them, the crowd would come down on us.

"Give them money, Eli," I said. "Now."

He pulled out a wad of money and handed it all around. The men were delighted and tipped their sombreros or cowboy hats. Three of them made their way to a nearby liquor seller.

The armed one stood his ground. We couldn't waste the time. I worked my way around the car. It was easy because he only had eyes for Eli. When I was behind him, I held a knife to his back, the tender part below the ribs.

"*Alejate! O sufriras.*" I hoped my Spanish was clear enough. I was telling him to get away or he would suffer. My throat hurt every time I opened my mouth, and I wanted my words to count.

He nodded, just a jerk of the head. To sweeten him, I handed around the cash I had in my pocket, and he took it so fast I wondered if it had ever been in my hand.

"*Alejate,*" I said in a deadlier voice, and I'm sure my expression matched, because it really hurt to produce that angry tone. Off he went. God bless him. He saved his own life and maybe ours.

I got in the driver's seat. "You two crouch down," I said. No sense reminding the locals that there were tattooed wizards present at this glorious and holy moment in the history of Ciudad Azul.

I drove very slowly out of the square, trying to be invisible. The throng parted before me—once they noticed the car—and leaving wasn't as hard as I'd feared, since we were heading away from the central attraction. The screaming increased in frequency and intensity. Then there fell a few seconds of breathless silence. I did not have to look back to know that the man danced on the end of the rope. The crowd roared. The gallows of the Blue City drank another life.

Very soon I was driving through an empty town. And then I was out of Ciudad Azul, into the countryside. I drove as fast as I could. I wanted to put miles between us and the town. When I figured we were a safe distance south, I spotted a clump of trees that would provide a bit of shade. I pulled underneath. There was a long silence.

"You speak French," Paulina said, sounding just as surprised as I'd expected. Again, the dog that could stand up and talk had confounded her. To her, this was the most notable thing about our visit to Ciudad Azul.

I started laughing, and it hurt like hell. "*Un peu.* Right?"

"I think so," Eli said. "I'm not fluent."

"Me either," I said. I took a big drink of water, and that helped a lot. "We had a French priest at the Catholic church in Segundo Mexia. He taught any kid who wanted to learn, for free." I didn't add that my mother had made me go. Free learning was precious to her, not always to me.

"Is there any other hidden talent you have?" Paulina said, sounding the opposite of admiring.

I shook my head, sparing my throat.

"Anything else we should know about you?"

That was harder to answer. "I've saved your ass so far," I said. She had no reply for that. But my conscience was nipping at me. "Thanks for hitting that thing on the head last night," I said. "I thought I was going to die."

"I think that was the idea," she said.

I had nothing to say to that. Whether it had been me or Eli or Paulina who was the primary target, that false Peter had been designed to lure us in and do some damage.

I got out of the car and stretched, trying to relieve the tension. I was weak in the legs. "We need to eat and get on our way," I said.

We sat in a little circle, me with my back against a tree. I divided the food. Eating wasn't going to be comfortable, but I needed food. I chewed real thoroughly, and I swallowed with care. I ate until the pain got too nagging. Finally I stopped, worn out from the effort. I took a long drink of water.

"Let me look," Eli said.

I pulled off the bandanna and stuck it back in my pocket. Paulina looked uncomfortable when she looked at my neck, and Eli tried hard not to wince. And this was after he'd worked some healing. Eli got some goop out of Paulina's bag and smeared it on my bruises. It stunk, of course. But after a few minutes, I was able to think about talking, which we needed to do. Dammit.

"Who is Peter?" I whispered. It came out hoarse.

"My younger brother."

"Whoever left that false thing in your room, it was someone who knows what he looks like." I was glad we were out in the middle of nowhere, so they could hear me without me raising my voice.

"I was going to find a telephone in Ciudad Azul so I could try to call Peter," Eli said. "I'm really worried. He should be back at school in San Diego, after his stay with my parents."

"You didn't know the dead man? When he went back to his real . . ." I hadn't seen the man's true face myself.

"I'd never seen him. Paulina?"

"Nor I."

"Now you're just lying," I said, meeting her cold eyes.

Paulina waited too long to deny it.

Eli said, "Who was it?" There was an edge to his voice I hadn't heard before, at least when he spoke to his buddy Paulina.

"It might have been Timofei Bazarov," Paulina said. "The body went bad so fast I can't be sure."

That explained the odor hovering around the car. The stink must have been terrible if Paulina's odor-away spell hadn't conquered it.

"Could Timofei have been following us all this time?" Eli seemed both puzzled and outraged.

239

"Who could have put such a powerful spell on him, and to what purpose?"

Sometimes I just couldn't understand these people. "Who would run to a body that looked like his brother?" That was a lot of words, and it hurt.

Eli muttered, "Me."

"Who would have been choked?"

"Me." He shot to his feet to pace restlessly up and down in the scant shade, not looking at either of us. "And I would not have fought back as hard, because I believed it was my brother. So I must thank you, Gunnie."

I didn't want to look at anyone, either. I closed my eyes. My neck hurt. I felt tired. I felt used up. I thought of my cabin with a longing I could almost taste. If I'd been a wizard like these two, I'd have sent myself home.

All this was my own damn fault, because I'd been curious. And angry.

"Are all hangings like that?" Paulina said. I opened my eyes a slit. Yep, she was talking to me.

"You don't have hangings in the Holy Russian Empire?" I let my eyes close again.

"Only people guilty of treason are killed in public. The rest are put to death in privacy."

"In a lot of Mexican villages, the remote ones, the church is in charge of justice. It got that way when the depression hit, and it stayed that way. People get excited about executions. It's a holiday, civil and religious. They don't have a lot of 'em. It puts a scare in 'em. And they can be relieved it's not their own neck in the noose." There's a lot of joy to be found in *I'm not dead.*

"Why did you think they'd turn on us?" Eli sounded just a little hurt.

"You're grigoris. The Catholic Church in Mexico, specially the church in remote areas, again . . . it doesn't approve of witchcraft or whatever you want to call it. Magic. Your Rasputin isn't their kind of holy man. Not a Catholic monk." I rested for a minute. "It would be real easy to get caught up and decide that if one hanging was a cleansing, two would be even more fun, especially if there were barbarian grigoris to be strung up."

"They wouldn't have hung you?" Eli was thinking this over.

"I'm short, I have black hair, I don't look rich. No tattoos. Maybe I could have gotten away." And taken the car with me. I wondered what I could have sold it for.

"Why didn't you do that?"

"Oh, Eli. Jesus. Because I have standards."

I didn't bother opening my eyes to see their faces. After a minute or two I said, "If you all don't want to tell me who has it in for you, particularly for Eli, okay. But the more I know, the better the job I can do."

"We didn't hire you to think, but to shoot," Paulina informed me.

I shrugged. "Suit yourself. We need to go now. We got to get gas and find a place to sleep."

"Then whenever you are ready, Your Highness, we can go," she said.

I was on my feet in a flash and had a hold of her upper arm, disregarding the pain. I was so angry I couldn't speak. Tall as she was, and healthy as she was, she could not break free of my grip. She didn't want to lose her dignity by trying very hard, though.

Eli said, "I beg your pardon, Lizbeth. For her insult."

I took a sharp breath, pulled myself together with every bit of self-control I could muster up, and let go of Paulina. I could not get rid of these two. I had told them that gunnies had standards, and it was time I showed I would stick to them.

I got into the driver's seat. I wanted them to sit in the back, where I couldn't see them, for a while. I opened the map to make sure I knew what we were doing. For the first time in hours, soon it would be possible to make a wrong turn. Another road crossed the one we'd taken out of Ciudad Azul.

"Poorly done, Paulina," Eli whispered to his companion as they got into the car. She didn't answer, of course.

I figured he was throwing a bone to the dog

242

(that would be me), but I decided I would take it. "We'll get to El Soldado in maybe three, four hours," I told them. "There's nothing after that. Ciudad Juárez, the next morning before noon, if nothing else happens." There was no response, yea or nay. I started the car. We had just enough gas to get to El Soldado if nothing happened—a big if, given the way this trip had gone so far.

CHAPTER ELEVEN

No one tried to kill us all afternoon, I didn't say another word, and the gas held out until we stopped at a garage on the outskirts of El Soldado. We had to add some oil and water, but everything else was okay. The mechanic seemed to know what he was doing.

El Soldado was situated in the middle of a long, shallow basin surrounded by high, rolling hills. The basin stretched into the distance, broken only by one broad, low hill, after which the road ran straight as an arrow out into the barren land.

With a little more water, El Soldado would have been a pretty sort of place. It wasn't bad the way it was, if you liked one-story whitewashed houses, dirt streets, and cactus in your yard instead of grass. There were chickens and goats and a pig or two in pens behind most houses, and there were children everywhere. I stopped beside a crowd of the kids and asked them where a hotel would be, in my slow Spanish. They laughed and told me to drive on through the town, that on the other side of the square would be the Hotel para Desconocidos. Señora Rivera ran it, they told me. The walls were yellow and white; we couldn't miss it. Then they offered to go with us.

I declined with a smile, handed out some coins, and began searching.

The kids had been right. We couldn't miss it. The hotel was distinguished by its paint job, which was not only white and yellow, but *striped* white and yellow. I liked it. I told the grigoris I'd see about rooms. I didn't wait for an answer. I pulled the bandanna back over my bruised neck, and I left my guns in the car. I didn't want anything to shake our chances of getting a place to spend the night. I needed to get away from the grigoris, especially Paulina. In fact, I handed her the car keys, hoping she'd decide to drive away while I was in the hotel.

Señora Rivera was delighted to rent us three rooms, and was even more delighted to be paid in advance. She did not have a dining room, she said with a good imitation of deep regret, but there was a café one block away—or if we wanted to drive, there was a place to eat a few miles south. They were both excellent. She handed me the room keys with a great smile and flourish, and I went outside to collect Eli and Paulina. Who were still there. Dammit.

Señora Rivera was not as delighted when she saw my companions were wizards, but she was polite enough (or cautious enough) to keep comments to herself.

I hadn't even asked if our rooms were together, which showed how rattled and ill I felt. My room was on the main hallway past the señora's desk. Two rooms after mine, the hallway turned right to another block of twelve rooms, six on each side of the corridor. The second and third rooms on the northern side of the corridor were Paulina's and Eli's; at least they would be side by side. I walked back to the desk to ask the señora if there were rooms closer together that we could choose, but she told me that we had rented the last three vacancies.

I returned to Paulina and Eli, who were standing in the hall outside their rooms, looking impatient. I told them what the señora had told me. I said, "You sure you want to stay? I didn't count on us being apart from each other."

"You're that fond of us," Paulina said, sneering.

"You're the reason I'm here."

"Yes, and you have *standards,*" she said.

Even devout farm families, who'd tried to get me to see the error of my ways while they were paying me to shoot people for them, hadn't been this irritating. I took a deep breath. "Paulina, if you don't think I'm doing a good job, fire me," I said. "Pay me what you owe me. I'll be gone tomorrow." I didn't add how happy that would make me. I didn't need to.

She was genuinely taken aback.

Eli opened his mouth, but I glared at him until he mashed his lips together. Good choice.

"We are better with you than we are without

you," Paulina said after a goodly pause. "I hope you will stay."

I didn't hear an apology in those words, and I started to make that clear. But I remembered Paulina had killed the not-Eli's-brother creature who'd been trying to choke me to death. She'd saved my life.

"No mocking me," I warned her.

"You have no sense of humor?"

"Not where you're concerned." I gave myself a mental shake, got back down to the present moment. "If you want to stay here, I think you and Eli should share a room." I looked from Eli to Paulina, making sure they knew I was serious.

"All right," Eli said. "We've done that often enough."

Paulina's face turned a dull red. She nodded, just a jerk of her head.

"Don't give up the extra room," I said. "Give me the key to it. I like being close to the front door, but we might need the room . . . for something."

Eli shrugged and handed me his key. After a brief talk about dinner, we went our separate ways for an hour.

We went to the cantina down the street. It had been an easy decision. No one wanted to get back in the car. We ate in silence. By the time we finished our supper—beans and rice, of course, and some chicken—the streets were mostly empty. This little town rolled up the sidewalks—well, there weren't any—early.

I wore my guns openly, and I wasn't the only one. People were cautious in El Soldado, seemed like. Even if I'd been the only armed woman in the town, I would have carried my Colts. Someone had been dogging our trail and sniping at us. It was only a matter of time before that someone got lucky.

After Paulina and Eli retired to the room that had been assigned to Paulina, I cleaned up and I settled in my own room to listen. Two hours after darkfall the hotel was quiet. Then someone wearing spurs went past my room whistling a cowboy song. I was not waiting for anyone who would announce he was coming.

The whistler had a room close to the grigoris'. His steps stopped after the opening and closing of a door.

I kept seeing that boy's body on the floor, the body that looked so much like a younger Eli. It had been a booby trap, a good one. I'd never thought I'd die any way but by the gun; choking had never been my picture of how I'd leave this world.

When no one had stirred in half an hour, I took off my boots and stepped out of my room in my socks, Jackhammer in my hand and my gun belt on. I left my door unlocked.

Señora Rivera did not believe in wasting money

on electricity. There was only one dim bulb at the conjunction of the halls, just enough to let a guest see the numbers on the room doors . . . if he was sharp eyed.

I stood still and listened, got used to the little sounds. In the lobby someone had turned on a radio, keeping the volume low out of consideration for the patrons. From a room across the hall, I heard the slapping sounds of sex.

When I was sure I knew what was happening around me, I began to scoot along the inner wall. I looked around the corner. Nothing. I kept moving—real quiet, real slow. No sound from Paulina's room. I unlocked Eli's room, didn't like the little click the key made. I slid inside real quick, pushed the door almost closed behind me. When I'd given the room a good once-over, I turned the knob very slowly and pushed the door shut, releasing the knob just as carefully.

The curtains hadn't been drawn in this room, and the moonlight flooded in. Jesus, did I have to tell these people every little thing? Eli should have pulled the curtains to. I half expected to hear a challenge from Paulina's room next door, but there was no sound. They were sleeping. For a minute I hated them. More.

Keeping out of the line of sight, I slunk over to the window and looked out from the right side. Nothing but moonlight, and a dog trotting down the dirt-packed alley with something in its jaws. I dropped to my knees, crawled under the window, repeated, looking left. I could see the end of the alley where it met the street in front of the hotel. In fact, I could see the dog pause at our car and sniff the tires before leaving his own message.

Nothing was out of place. But the silence was getting to me. My skin was crawling. Magic prickled at me. Was it just the nearness of Eli and Paulina? I was sure something was wrong. What if the grigoris weren't asleep? What if they were dead? When the idea crawled into my brain, I couldn't make it go away.

Maybe someone had killed Paulina and Eli while I waited in my room. After keeping them alive this long, maybe I had been outwitted.

I could go back out into the corridor and knock at Paulina's door. Or I could try the connecting door between the rooms, which I hadn't expected, since my room had none. It should be locked, of course, since Eli had never been in this room. But I stole over to try it . . . and it opened. My skin crawled so hard I thought it would leave my body. I whispered, "Eli? Paulina?"

The curtains were closed in here, but the moon streamed in from the other room. There were two beds, one against each side, and they were both empty.

No suitcases. No clothes.

The grigoris weren't here. Their things were

gone. But they hadn't left town. The car was outside.

"Huh," I said, and sat on one of the beds to think.

After a moment I checked the window. It was shut but not locked. They could have gone out the window and closed it behind them. The window in the other room had definitely been locked.

I felt pretty dumb.

If Eli and Paulina had been stolen, they'd have put up a fight, and it would have gotten noisy. Right? But why sneak away when I'd practically begged Paulina to fire me?

I could not figure this out. I wasn't sure what to do.

Those are not my favorite feelings.

I grabbed my Winchester and left the room. There was a lamp on in the lobby. From his resemblance to his mother, the night clerk was a son of Señora Rivera, and no more than fifteen. He was sound asleep, his head on the check-in desk. I opened the front door and stepped out onto the rock-paved entrance.

Yes, the car was still there, and yes, it was definitely the right car.

I was back in my room in a minute, and thinking as hard as I could.

After a short while of coming up with nothing, I went back to the empty rooms. This time I searched. I had to be quiet, and I had to be careful, but I was no longer concerned with there being light in the window.

The señora kept a very clean hotel. I know because I crawled on the floor while I looked behind and under the beds. Same with the little chests of drawers, the seat cushions, the throw rugs and bathroom fixtures . . . everywhere.

And finally I found something in Paulina's room: the keys to the car. They'd been jammed between the mattress and the box spring. Nothing would land there by accident. If Paulina had wanted to hide the keys from me, she'd have taken them and pitched them out the window. It would have taken me hours to find them in the debris of the alley.

So she'd been hiding them from someone else. And that someone else had stolen Eli and Paulina, two powerful magicians who could kill with a few gestures.

So that someone was pretty damn dangerous.

I could figure only that one thing for sure. So why would have to wait.

I went back to the lobby. I hated to wake the boy, but I did it anyway. In my faulty Spanish I asked him if he'd seen the two tall people leave, the ones with the tattoos. Yes, he had.

"I was not sure when they were leaving," I said. "Was someone with them?"

At least he didn't seem suspicious. "Yes, señorita," he said. "There was another woman with them, very short, she had long blond hair." He sighed. The hair had been beautiful, and the woman underneath it, too, seemed like.

"Of course," I said, as if that was what I'd expected. "Our car is still here. They must have gone in her car."

"*Sí*," he said. "They all got into a big car. Someone else was driving."

"I'm surprised I didn't hear them. I must have fallen asleep."

The boy looked uneasy. "I could not hear them, either, señorita. I don't know how they were so quiet. If I hadn't woken up a little bit, I would never have known they'd walked through the lobby."

"You were very tired," I said with a smile. A silence spell of some kind, I guessed. And it was lucky that the boy had kept his wakefulness a secret. I gave him a few coins and I went back to my room. He was asleep again when I came through with all my bags five minutes later.

Before I started the car, I looked around. There were a few streetlights, not many, but I could see the packed dirt of the road, and there was one track that seemed to override all the others in the dust. There was only one way in and one way out of El Soledad, so I had a fifty-fifty chance of going in the right direction.

When I was at the intersection where I could turn left or right on that main road, I closed my eyes and took a guess, based on the very faint prickling of the magic. For once, my little talent might come in handy.

I went south because it felt right . . . and prickly.

The Tourer's headlights cut a sharp path through the scrubby desert. There was one low hill in the long valley where the town lay, and it was between me and a long straight. For now, if there was a car ahead of me, the driver couldn't see my headlights. I needed them to get up all the speed I could muster.

The last time I'd been in a vehicle at night, my whole crew had been killed or mortally wounded, leaving only me behind. And here I was, tracking through the night again, after my cargo had been taken hostage . . . again. I'd never imagined being in the rescue business. People hired me so they wouldn't have to be rescued.

From now on that would be the case.

I was clear in my mind about that.

And since I was being clear, I wasn't going to trouble myself with second-guessing. I was on the right road. Going the right way. I knew it.

I could drive without lights if I went slow and steady, and I decided to do that soon. If I figured correctly, the people who'd stolen Paulina and Eli had at the most an hour's head start, maybe much less.

They might get out of town and stop to get some sleep, not counting on me. Maybe they believed I was asleep in my room. Maybe they were laughing about the stupid gunnie who'd left her clients to be snatched. Jackhammer was on the seat beside me, and I reached over to touch it. It was fully loaded. So was the other Winchester, and the Krag. And my Colts, slung around my waist. I was ready.

My chances were not outstanding. They might drive like bats out of hell until I was hopelessly behind. But their car weighed more, loaded down with people, and it might not be as good a car. Couldn't know.

After I rounded the one low hill, I'd be visible.

Halfway to the other side, I switched off my lights. Time to run dark. The road would be straight from now on. I couldn't help but wince a bit about the damage the Tourer would take.

When I'd been part of Tarken's crew, I'd never made the big plan. I'd never weighted profit against loss. Not my job. But it stood to reason Paulina would rather be rescued and have occasion to buy a new car than remain captive.

Far ahead I saw the taillights of another car.

I was pretty damn happy.

If they stopped, I'd have a chance to surprise them. Right now they were moving, but not real fast. I tried to creep up on them gradual.

It was like the answer to a prayer when the taillights stopped moving.

I wondered why they'd pulled over, but I drove

faster than before. As long as they held still, I could catch up with them.

Then I thought of the sound this car must be making in the silence of the night, now that the other one had shut off.

I gently braked to a halt and turned off the engine. I leaped out, Jackhammer slung to my back, Marcial's Winchester in my right hand. I ran. It's hard to run quiet, not falling, even with the help of the moonlight. When I got closer, I stopped, listening. I heard voices, raised in dispute. Holding the leather bag tight under my arm to prevent clanking, I moved forward, real quick and light.

The headlights of the other car were illuminating a big drama. A woman was yelling at the top of her lungs. "Our father will crucify you for this! You will die a traitor's death!" Yep, Paulina, all right. She was at the center of the light, her hands held in front of her, ready to cast spells. She was not wearing her vest. She was alone. Maybe they'd already killed Eli. My heart pounded so much I thought it would punch out of my chest. I was seeing, hearing, thinking, more clearly than I ever had in my life. Rifles were no good tonight. I laid them down and pulled both Colts.

I got as close as I could, dodging the light, concealing myself. When I was close enough, I could see Paulina was doing a good job of keeping the three—shit, *three*—kidnappers busy.

Eli was down on the ground, bleeding at the shoulder. A grigori, a little blond woman—the beauty seen by the desk clerk—was standing over him with her hands at the ready, looking down every few seconds, but dividing her attention by taking quick glances at Paulina, who didn't have her grigori vest. Neither did Eli. What had they done with the vests?

Paulina had a lot of fight left in her. She'd gotten a tactical position, her back against a tree. Trust Paulina to find the only tree of any girth in the miles around. The other grigoris held back as though they feared her, and rightly so. One of the men, the white-haired one, was already injured, bleeding from one leg. The younger man was listing to one side, since one of his legs was clearly the worse for Paulina's attack. But the two men were standing far apart. They weren't dumb.

Paulina was pitching a fit. Her voice was loud and her words were furious. But her body told me she'd had a beating, magical or with fists. She needed the tree for support, not just to keep her back guarded. I didn't know how long she could keep it up.

A lot of things happened very close together. I saw Eli's hand move, and I knew he was waking up from whatever had happened to him. While Paulina was keeping their attention, I moved behind the men. I was finally in her line of sight, and I stood up. Our eyes met. She saw me. She nodded.

Then Paulina carried out her own plan. Didn't matter what mine might have been.

"Thanks be to God!" she yelled, pointing where I wasn't. When one of the men wheeled to look, she killed him. He died, screaming. The other guy was smarter; he didn't waste any time watching the spectacular death of his buddy, or turning to see what was behind him. He unleashed some big magic, and Paulina hit the ground like her strings had been cut. But then I shot him with a Colt, and the grigori hit the ground himself.

The blonde wheeled to fight me, and Eli's hand seized her ankle, making her stagger. I shot her. She'd already launched a spell at me, but thanks to Eli, I dodged most of it. It spun me around by the left shoulder as though I'd been shot, too. So I was on the ground with everyone else.

After a minute or two, I got no idea how many, I was able to move. I got to my knees, then to my feet. My shoulder was numb, but I was otherwise okay. I staggered over to the blonde. She wasn't quite dead. I shot her in the head. I would have left her whatever minutes she had remaining, but with grigoris you could never be sure what they could pull off in their last moments.

Eli looked at me, and he made a move of his hand that I thought meant he was going to be fine. I was glad to accept that just now.

Very slowly I worked my way around the scene to check on everybody else. The two male grigoris were dead, for sure.

Paulina . . . if she was alive, it wasn't very. There might have been a very weak heartbeat, already stuttering. I went back to Eli, my best bet, and sat beside him. Then it seemed like lying down would be better.

I didn't ever pass out. But I wasn't all there. The headlights of the kidnappers' car cut off after a while when the battery was drained. I could see the stars, a million of them.

After a long, drifting space of time, I felt a hand holding mine.

"Lizbeth?" Eli whispered.

"Yeah."

"I knew you'd come."

"Yeah."

"Paulina alive?"

"I don't think so."

"The others dead?"

"Yeah."

"Thanks."

"Welcome." Then we were silent. Until I thought to ask, "Where is your vest?"

"I think they burned it. We'll look. Later."

"You remember talking about the shadows, the last time you used that death magic?"

"Maybe," he said.

"That the one at the top was the sun, the

259

people in between the sun and the ground were the schemers, and we were the people on the ground."

"Yeah, pretentious."

"I don't know what that word means. But I don't believe I'm in anyone's shadow. That's all."

There was another silence.

"Looking at the stars?" he asked.

"Yeah."

"Nice."

"Uh-huh."

It was a long, long night. I would have liked to sleep. But I don't believe I did, at all. There were some things I should tell Eli, but maybe Paulina was alive, and I still hated her. But with great respect. I couldn't seem to make myself get up and move. Couldn't do any of the things that needed doing. The feeling was coming back in my shoulder, though it was still impossible to lift my hand. It was the weariness of this trip, the worry of every decision I'd made, the . . . everything.

"Maybe I'm dying," I said.

"At least we have company," Eli answered.

I didn't understand. "We do?"

"Each other," he said.

"That's good." And it was. "Tell me," I said. "Why do people keep trying to kill us?"

"Because not everyone wants the tsar to live," Eli said.

It simply hadn't occurred to me that not everyone in the HRE was as enthusiastic about Alexei I as Eli and Paulina.

I tried to figure this out, since Eli had fallen silent. "But Alexei's wife might have a boy," I said. "Even if he passes away in the meantime."

"It might be a girl," Eli said, sounding as tired as if he'd been up for a week. "The tsarina . . . is not popular. She wasn't brought up in the Russian way, or even the English way. She doesn't have a sense of duty. She's always on holiday. Doesn't take her position seriously."

"So who's the other contender?" That must be where this conversation was going.

"Alexei's uncle, Grand Duke Alexander."

This was really complicated, compared with our presidential race. Texoma elected a new head official every four years, and there were at least four parties, so it was a brawl, but an open brawl. "Is this Alexander married?" I asked.

I could see I'd struck gold.

"Yes," said Eli. "To an inappropriate woman, Sophia Feodorovna."

"Not a royal." That was the most inappropriate thing I could imagine.

"Correct. The grand duke's wife in Russia was a countess, and she was killed by the revolutionaries. His new wife is a common woman, a woman with whom he had three sons while they were unwed. Obviously, they were together for years before his true wife died. When Grand Duke Alexander escaped from the revolutionaries, this woman came with him. Alexander has a son by his first wife, and three by this Sophia."

They'd definitely won in the kid sweepstakes. This Alexander must not be any spring chicken. His older brother, Tsar Nicholas II, had died a couple of years ago after a bout of pneumonia; Nicholas's wife, Alexandra, had preceded him in death. So I figured Grand Duke Alexander would probably be in his sixties at least. Four sons!

"Are the sons healthy?"

"The oldest son, Vasily, fruit of the first marriage, is now in his thirties. And married to a Russian duchess. And he has several children, including a boy. His illegitimate brothers have very strong reasons to want Vasily in power. They are not good men."

"So that's why all this has happened. Because some people don't want Alexei's son, if he has one, to be ruler if Alexei dies."

"Yes. That's why all this has happened."

"If we get through this, you have to tell me why Oleg's blood is so necessary," I said.

I fell asleep.

CHAPTER TWELVE

While I slept, night lightened into dawn. Dawn into day. The glare of the sun was another kind of attack. I had to move or my skin would blister, or I'd die of thirst. My hand was free. I turned my head as much as I could. Eli was crawling over to Paulina.

It was time to live. I rolled to one side. If that sounds easy, it wasn't. I rested for a minute, panting, then rolled to my stomach. That was easier. I pushed with my hands and pulled my knees up under me, and that was another step. I gathered up some strength. I pushed again. Well, now I was on my knees only. Halfway standing. I groaned with the pain of movement, which shamed me. I forced my way to my feet. The landscape lurched. I took a couple of steps sideways, but I managed to stay upright, only through fear of having to get up again. I put one foot in front of another.

I made it to the tree where Paulina lay. Eli was sitting by her.

I wanted to sit down by him, but I wasn't sure I'd get up if I did.

I put my hand on his head to let him know I was there. He was staring at her.

"Well?" I got tired of waiting.

"She's dead."

"She gave us the chance we needed," I said, because it was the best thing I could say about Paulina. "I don't know if you were really awake for that."

He didn't say anything.

"We got to leave," I said, trying to sound gentle.

"How? Their car battery died."

"How do you think I got here? The car is a little ways away. I'll go get it," I said. "I'll drive it close."

"What about all the bodies?"

We don't have to do anything with the bodies. They'll be picked bare in two days. "All you care about is Paulina's, right? We can cover her with rocks." On second thought I added, "Maybe."

"I'll be better in a minute," he said.

I had no answer to that, so I made myself think of where I'd left the car. Once I did that, I could actually see it. I whined to myself. It looked so far. But I had to bring it over, no way around that. At least I didn't have to carry anything.

When I reached the Tourer—it was the only thing not worse for wear—I let myself drink as much as I wanted. I felt a lot more human after that. The driver's seat felt good after a night sprawled on the ground. I wasn't real sure I was driving like I ought to, but there was no one to collide with. I made it to the right place and parked the Tourer by the dead car. Well, the car of the dead kidnappers. I almost smiled.

When I got out, I found what was left of the two vests. Eli's was ripped, like they'd pulled it off of him, but it was still intact, all the pockets shut. The hem at the back was scorched, because his vest had been by the fire they'd built to burn Paulina's. Her vest was almost completely destroyed. I dragged Eli's over to him.

Eli had put *three rocks* on top of Paulina. He was struggling to place a fourth one. He was moving very slowly and his hands were trembling. I groaned inside myself when I estimated how long this was going to take.

"Eli, I don't think Paulina would care about being covered up," I said. "She understood the reality of . . ."

"Death," Eli said. He struggled with another rock. "The dead should be covered, to honor them. Paulina was a great wizard." He had that stubborn set to his mouth.

"Okay," I said, trying to sound like I thought that was reasonable. Trying not to sound like I was as tired as he was, just about.

"I'll finish it," Eli said, and then couldn't pick up another rock.

That meant *I* had to finish it.

I tried not to be angry. (What difference did it make? People were always so worried about what happened to the bodies. Why?) I handed Eli a canteen, bared my teeth at him, and set to work. I was real slow, simply because I couldn't go any faster. He was very glad to be reunited with his vest, scorched or not. He was able to help some, after he'd had a big drink.

We got it done.

I couldn't do anything with the kidnappers' dead car. At least it was slightly off the road, and anyone rounding the curve had a chance to see it. If I couldn't hide the car, there didn't seem to be much point in hiding the grigoris' bodies, assuming I had the strength.

I didn't.

Besides, I'd left bodies strewn between Segundo Mexia and here, all along the road to Ciudad Juárez.

I helped Eli stand. He made his way to the passenger door without a word. I thought of saying something more to him, but I didn't know what it would be. His face looked bare and bleak. He was hard hit, his body and his spirit.

I started driving. I didn't know what Russians said on sad occasions, and I didn't care. We had to get away from this spot. We were overdue for more bad luck. I wanted to get out of the area before it caught up with us. After I'd driven for an hour, my brain kicked in. One of us had to think, and it wouldn't be Eli, at least for a while more.

The kidnappers might have other people near.

At the least, someone was waiting for them to report, either in person or by telegraph or telephone. When that didn't happen, a search would begin. The bodies would be found. If we had bad luck—maybe more accurate to say if we had near-miss luck—then the other grigoris were on the spot in El Soldado . . . but if so, why hadn't they joined in the kidnapping? Okay, maybe they weren't close at all. That was great.

Unless they were waiting for us in Ciudad Juárez.

The bodies and the car would be found. Even if a lucky passerby stole the car, they'd hardly care about the bodies. Maybe I should have thought about Eli's objections to loose bodies with more attention.

Once the bodies were found, the search would focus on a tall male grigori and a short female gunnie.

For the moment there was daylight and a road and a tank of gas. I had to make the most of those things. I hoped I never forgot how bad it was to be without them. I went a little slower than I wanted, mindful I wasn't exactly myself—and neither was the Tourer, after my drive in the dark. Nothing seemed to be too banged or loosened to work, so far.

If we weren't ambushed and/or killed, we would reach Ciudad Juárez late this morning. And there we would find—maybe—the brother of Oleg Karkarov, and his daughter (or niece), too.

It was great to have everything pinned down, all right.

After a while I had to think of something to say to Eli. I knew he was suffering, and my own was recent enough to make it fresh in my mind. "What was Paulina to you?" I asked, and he startled. "Was she your teacher, or your lover, or . . . ?"

He looked surprised. "Paulina was my sister," he said.

"I didn't know. I'm really sorry, Eli." I felt really confused. The accents? Peter was her brother, too? "Are your parents still living?"

He looked even more confused than I was, for a second. "Not by the same parents," he explained. "She was my sister in the service of the emperor. She was already a . . . tested wizard when I came into training. So we lived in the same building for a time."

"With your mom and dad?"

"We don't stay with our parents after it's noticed we have power," he said.

"Why not?"

"We have to be trained," he explained. "We have to concentrate. There's a chance we could harm our families, by accident, or even on purpose . . . at least, the more volatile of the candidates."

I was almost too tired to be shocked, but not quite. "So you get taken away from your folks."

"Yes, put in the school in San Diego," he said. "That's where my brother Peter is now. At least . . . I think so."

"Real brother or magical brother?"

"Both. Peter turned out to have the talent, like me."

Every answer led to another question. "You have more brothers?"

"Two older half brothers, and two sisters who are younger."

"What do you do for the emperor?"

"We cast spells of protection and we defend. There is always a bodyguard detail with him, and we get detailed to the care of the grand duchesses, too, wherever they may be. Those of us who have the gift of healing, we're near the tsar. We are there when he receives the transfusions, to make sure it's painless and that his body accepts the blood of another of the chosen."

I'd heard of blood transfusions. I'd never gotten one, or seen one, and I was glad of that. "It can't be just any blood, you're saying. It has to be special blood." I'd always thought that blood was the same, no matter whom it came from. Now I was about to find out why that wasn't so. Finally.

"We've talked about Rasputin."

I nodded. "The holy man. Who wasn't exactly a

priest. He helped keep Alexei alive when Alexei had the bleeding sickness."

Eli said, "It wasn't just Rasputin's prayers that have kept Alexei alive, but his blood. It worked fine until Rasputin died, a month ago."

"I can't believe Rasputin lasted this long. That's a very long life." I spoke slowly, trying to understand. From Eli's expression this was really big information.

"We kept the starets, the holy man, alive by magic," Eli said. "Difficult magic. Dark magic." This memory looked like a very unhappy one.

"So, okay . . . you need more blood for Alexei, and maybe the baby to come, if it's a boy. You have to have blood like Rasputin's. But how do you know what to look for? Why do you think a child of Oleg Karkarov's has the right blood?"

"Rasputin was not a very moral holy man," Eli said. "He was married, and had children by his wife. But aside from his marriage . . ."

When I understood what Eli meant, I was shocked. "He had affairs with other women?"

Eli nodded, not meeting my eyes. "Even calling the encounters 'affairs' is elevating them."

The other shoe dropped. Took me long enough. "And so he had other children?"

Eli nodded again. "So we're tracking those children to see if their blood has the same properties."

"What happened to his kids with his wife?"

"Only one of them made it out of Russia with him. The rest were hunted down and executed."

"And how many bastards are there?"

"At least four."

"You've got 'em?"

"One of those died too early to beget any children himself, but the others lived longer. As you are well aware, Oleg Karkarov died last year. Rasputin's illegitimate daughter, Irina, died a year before that, of the influenza. Irina's male child is tubercular, her girl is a whore who has syphilis, so their blood is no good. Who knows what the tsar could contract from them? Another team is tracking a second Rasputin daughter in Poland. Paulina and I were sent to follow the trail of Oleg Karkarov. Since Oleg had some degree of magical ability, we had high hopes that his blood would be suitable. But of course . . ."

"You're hoping Sergei is his full brother."

"If he is, and the girl child is Sergei's, we would have a much better chance of keeping everyone alive. If Sergei has a different mother and the same father, his blood—and the child's—will work. But if Rasputin was not Sergei's father, they're useless."

I'd been right to keep my mouth shut. I liked my blood right where it was, in my own body. Unmixed with anyone else's. Time to move on in the conversation. "You got any ideas about how to find this Sergei Karkarov once we get to Juárez?"

"Paulina was better at searching spells," Eli said, sounding tired and way older than I knew he must be. "There are ways I can try."

I sighed, but I tried to keep it quiet. Eli dozed some, drank some more of the water we'd gotten at Ciudad Azul, and ate a scrap or two, which was about all we had left to eat. I wasn't hungry, and he needed it more. I hadn't lost someone really close to me.

CHAPTER THIRTEEN

Gradually Eli began to look better.

When the outskirts of Ciudad Juárez lined the road, and it became paved, I pulled over. "How much money you got?" I asked. Eli dug in his pockets. He'd been sane enough to get the money Paulina had had on her, too, though he'd looked disgusted with himself as he did. Like Paulina would need it.

I figured it would get us through a week of eating and lodging, if we were careful.

We. Wait. "Do you want me to just get lost?" I said.

He stared at me. "What do you mean?"

"I didn't keep Paulina alive," I said. "I can get home on my own." It wouldn't be easy. I stiffened my spine.

"How old are you?"

The question was right out of the blue. "Nineteen," I said.

He looked at me for a long, long time. "Lizbeth, I need you to stay with me," he said.

Maybe he wanted to keep me by his side to make sure I wouldn't betray him. Or maybe he really needed me to help him. Or maybe he'd figured out who I was. All of these ideas had pluses and minuses. And my age had nothing to do with it. I couldn't figure him out.

"Okay," I said. "How long do you think it'll take you to find Sergei?"

He closed his eyes. He was sending his tracking sense outward, or something like that, I guessed. "There are a lot of people here," he said. "Maybe I can find him in a few hours. May take another day. Or two."

That was better than I'd hoped. "Here are some choices," I began. I'd been thinking during our long, quiet drive. "We can dump the car—it'll be gone in hours—or we can sell it to a dealer. If we sell it, whoever's after you might see it in the lot and try to find out who sold it, where they went. Or we can sell it to some random person on the street. We won't get much, but something. Or we can try to hide it for a while and try to drive it back. Maybe we can find a garage to rent, something like that."

Eli said, "Which do you think is best? We have papers for the car." He dug them out of the glove compartment. The papers were made out to Esai González.

"This helps a lot," I said with relief. "Since we have a Mexican name on the papers, I think you could sell to a car dealer pretty easily. But you'd need to wear a disguise, or spell yourself to look different." I had hideous flashes of the thing that had looked like a pretty woman, the thing that had looked like Eli's brother Peter. "Or we could hire a go-between."

"Is your Spanish good enough to do it yourself? Can you be taken for a native?"

I was even more relieved to see that Eli was back on track. "No."

"Only if I keep my mouth shut."

Like I did this all the time. "I'll look around and ask questions," I said. "While you keep out of sight."

That was easier said than done. We drove into a busy area, not downtown Juárez, but maybe a bustling lower-class neighborhood. Eli waited with the car, parked out of sight behind the Espinoza Speedy Gas Station, after we got Señora Espinoza's permission and gave her some money. Eli stretched out his legs in the car and seemed ready to sleep some more when I left, leaving my guns behind as simply too conspicuous. Going by the women I'd noticed in the streets, an armed woman wearing pants would stand out enough to attract more attention than I wanted.

I wandered around the open-air market. I bought a skirt, a blue blouse, and a hair kerchief, bigger and cleaner than my filthy bandanna. I bargained for the items hard as I could, in the interest of fitting in. It seemed to work. No one challenged me in any way. No one seemed to realize I was on the run with a terrible wizard in quest of blood. No one tried to shoot me. I enjoyed that.

I went back to the car to change. I shucked

my pants and strapped a Colt to my left thigh. Uncomfortable, but being armed made me feel like myself. Then I put a knife in the conveniently deep right pocket of the skirt. I pulled off the shirt I'd worn for more hours than I cared to remember. There was a pump in the yard, and I ran some water to rinse myself off. It helped, a little. Then I pulled on the blouse. I turned to Eli in time to see him take a deep breath and look away.

"Can you tie this in back for me?" I waved the kerchief at him. "I want to look like I'm hiding a lot of hair."

Eli nodded. I handed him the black-and-blue square, folded in a right triangle. It felt funny, his fingers on my neck. "Take this with you," he said, handing me a rock. "Easier to handle than a weapon you have to draw from, ah, under your clothes. And just as potent."

"Why?" It was just a rock. It didn't sparkle or shine, it didn't feel different from any other rock I'd ever held. It was small, about the size of a marble.

"If you need to fight someone quickly and quietly, just throw it at them. For when you can't shoot because the noise would attract attention," Eli explained.

"Do I have to hit them with it?"

"That would be ideal, yes," he said with a faint smile. "At their feet would be good, too. Oh, and be as far away as you can."

I left Eli in charge of the car, which held my bag of weapons and our personal things. I started to order him not to move from the car, but I held my tongue. "Be back as soon as I can," I said. I was proud my voice came out so steady. Off I went to pick out a go-between from all the people moving up and down the streets.

Since I didn't know exactly what kind of person I was looking for, it took me longer than I wanted. There were plenty of idle people who had nothing to do, and all of them needed money. But most of these idlers would disappear without actually helping me, and some of them would try to kill me to take any other money I might have on me. A very few of them would go to the police.

Finally I spotted a thin man in his sixties. His clothes were just short of ragged. There were plenty of people in the same condition, but what stood out about this man was his straight back. He had dignity. And he was clean. He didn't have his hand out to beg. He had nothing to do but be in that spot.

"*Señor, por favor,*" I said, and he turned to face me. He had only one good eye. His left eye was covered with a patch made out of someone's patterned shirt.

"*Señorita,*" he said, nodding politely.

I told him a story about family disasters: My Mexican father had died suddenly, here. My

277

Texoman mother was ill, and I had to return to her to take care of my little brothers. I had to sell my father's car. But I was not wise in the ways of selling large vehicles, and I was a stranger in town. Without my father's guidance, I was afraid I'd be taken advantage of. I would be so grateful if he would assist me. I was afraid (more fear) the car dealer would cheat me if I was not accompanied by a man.

Whether or not José Reyas believed my whole story, he knew I was in trouble and frightened (and that was for damn sure). Señor Reyas agreed to help me for a percentage of the sales price of the car. We would have to go to a dealership where he was unknown, he pointed out, since he had to be Esai González.

"Then we will do that," I said in my careful Spanish, wondering how many car dealerships knew who Señor José Reyas was. "If you have some idea where such a place might be?"

After a moment's thought Señor Reyas nodded.

"Then I can meet you two blocks north of here in the automobile," I said.

"You can drive, señorita?" He looked taken aback.

I nodded. "My father taught me. My mother is too scatterbrained." I was sure glad my mother couldn't hear me say that.

"You are a very composed young woman," Señor Reyas said, not entirely with approval.

"Life is hard, señor," I said. Like he needed reminding. "So here is the percentage of the price of the car I will give you if we sell it successfully. . . ."

I returned to the gas station to retrieve the car, and found Eli sitting on a wooden chair in the shade in the little courtyard behind the garage. He had a cold soda to drink, and he'd picked up a broken piece of pottery and was turning it in his fingers. He seemed . . . distant, but calm. Wasn't expecting that. I told him what was happening. Seemed he was not in the mood for talk.

I unloaded our belongings from the car and left them at Eli's feet.

Though I was not completely sure Señor Reyas would show up at the designated spot, he did. He got into the car with some misgiving but gave me clear directions on how to get to the car dealer.

We didn't talk much on the way. I'd figured the older man for a conversational person, but I'd been wrong. When we got out of the Tourer, and Tomás of Hermosa's New and Used Vehicles came out of his little shack, I found out why Señor Reyas had been quiet. He'd been prepping for his amazing performance as Esai González.

The old man explained to Tomás—I never heard his proper last name—that since his accident (he gestured toward his eye patch), he'd had great difficulty driving the car. Even to come to the dealership, his lowly granddaughter had had to help him. Though Señor Esai González was very reluctant to part with the car, González's wife had persuaded him the money would be more useful now that he could not work at his chosen trade.

My new grandfather made it clear to Tomás that this was a preliminary visit only, so he could see how much money might be made. Señor González implied he had already visited several other dealerships.

The owner nodded furiously, said that made great sense, and the haggling commenced.

I think Señor Reyas, in his new identity, had a pretty good time. He had thrown himself into his new role. And he had an incentive to drive up the price as much as he could, which helped. During the negotiations, when a certain level was reached, my new friend turned to me with his good eye and raised an eyebrow. I nodded, keeping it a very small gesture. I approved the deal. Soon after that the car was sold. Trying not to smile with pleasure, Señor González and I walked away with beautiful Mexican cash.

When we had taken a seat in the corner of a cantina, we divided the money in as secret a manner as possible. After it was done, Señor Reyas said, "I thought you would kill me after the bargain was reached."

Yet he'd gone forward with the plan.

Sitting, the old man and I were almost the same height, so I could look into his eye. I couldn't think of anything to say. If I'd thought he'd run to the police or the enemy grigoris, or if I'd decided he'd sell the information about a half-gringo girl selling a car that didn't belong to her . . . I would have killed him.

"Go enjoy the money," I told Señor Reyas, and he left without a word. I had no idea what he'd do with his profit. Was there a Señora Reyas? Grandchildren? Did he even have a home? Whatever he chose to do, I hoped it brought a smile to his face.

CHAPTER FOURTEEN

It was a long walk to where I'd left Eli at the Espinoza Speedy Gas Station. I entered the little courtyard from the back way. I wasn't anxious to come under the eyes of Señora Espinoza again.

The seat under the tree was empty. The soda bottle sat on the table beside it. It was empty, too. Our bags were gone.

I waited a moment, hoping something would miraculously change. Eli would emerge from the men's room with all our bags, having been worried they would be stolen while he was inside. Eli would stroll in with everything over his arm, having walked down to a café. Eli would pop up from the middle of the ground or fall from a tree.

None of those things happened. Oh, *dammit*. If I hadn't been so tired, I would have kicked something. Instead I put a lid on my rage and pushed open the back door of the garage. I had to talk to Señora and Señor Espinoza. I hadn't liked the wife much, and I wasn't disposed to like both of them any more now.

I tried to arrange my face in an expression they might think was sweet. I may not have managed that.

The Espinozas were playing a game of checkers on a table in the main room of the gas station. Señora Espinoza was slovenly and surly, and her husband looked cast from the same mold. They pretended not to see me. I glanced through the big window overlooking the two pumps. There were no customers. I'd gotten the impression that business was poor. That's why I'd figured they wouldn't object to letting the car and Eli sit around in the tiny rear courtyard.

"My brother has gone," I said as mildly as I could manage. Of course they knew that already. Señora Espinoza made a good stab at looking amazed.

"He told us he had remembered where to find the cousin you are seeking," Señor Espinoza said, his awful, droopy mustache wiggling with every word.

I thought about that, staring at the man all the while.

Señor Espinoza began to look uneasy. "He left your little bags with us," he said. "With another token of his appreciation." Señora Espinoza pointed helpfully to the little area behind the señor's chair, and I saw our personal luggage—a knapsack in my case, a sort of valise in Eli's. Nothing else. I snatched up the bags and looped the straps across my body, thinking all the while.

The guns were gone. Eli had presumably taken that bag with him . . . unless the Espinozas had stolen it. At least I had the Colt and the knife. Oh, and Eli's protective rock.

I put my hand in my pocket. I was mulling over how much attention the señora's screams would draw before I was sure I'd gotten the truth out of her husband. I was not as fancy an interrogator as the late Paulina, but I could get the truth out of a slouch like Espinoza.

The garage owner seemed to understand where my thoughts were going.

"Your brother seemed in his right mind, and he is your elder, so we didn't question him," Señor Espinoza said, trying to sound righteously angry.

"My brother is *not* in his right mind," I snapped. "Which way did he go? Did you see him speak to anyone?"

"He came in here and said—in English, which we understand a little . . ."

His wife nodded frantically. Maybe she had caught a glimpse of the knife. I must have drawn it by accident.

"He said that he had had an alert? That he must follow, and he would return for you."

"How long ago was that?"

The couple looked at each other. Señora Espinoza said, "That was less than an hour ago." Her husband nodded.

I just about believed them, if only because Eli could have mopped the floor with the two of them in less time than it took to light a match. I didn't know how the Espinozas could have stopped Eli from leaving, or why they'd even imagine doing that, but I was angry with them anyway. If I hadn't come in all worried, they would have let me sit out on that patio waiting, and *waiting,* before they told me what had happened.

"Which way?" I asked, my voice angry enough to make them cringe.

Señora Espinoza pointed right. She didn't think about it, so that meant she was telling the truth . . . at least, I thought so.

"You will see me again," I told them. "You will see me again and you will not be happy about that if anything has happened to my brother." I was hissing by the time I finished.

I spun on my heel and walked out of the open door and into the glaring sun. I didn't look back, but I was willing to bet the Espinozas were staring after me, and I hoped they were scared out of their wits. Just not scared enough to talk to the police.

Fucking *Eli.* I walked in the direction he'd chosen, trying to think how I'd track him. In a city. He'd taken our canteens, the ones that still held water. Of course. I stopped at a pump to rent a cup from a tiny kid, and drank. I washed my face while I was there.

I spared a moment to be grateful I had the car sale money on me; at least I could get back home if Eli was dead. If I couldn't track him down, this would be the second job in a row where some of my clients had died. Except this time it would be all of them.

I had to stop thinking of any future. This was now, this was all there was. So far I'd walked in a straight line south from the garage. The farther I went into town, the more congested the streets became. There were cars and horses and burros and bicycles and people on foot, many people. And the grid plan of the newer neighborhoods collapsed into the random jumble of older areas. Though the same broad avenue continued, it passed through squares full of businesses, with stalls set up close to the traffic.

The cross streets narrowed into alleys that meandered in a confusing way. Glancing down them, I could see trash and homeless people crouched in corners they'd cleared.

I didn't see a single man or woman in uniform. No police.

There were street markets everywhere, stalls selling anything you might want, and little storefronts with shutters that would close at night. There were men playing music. Vendors shouted at me to look at whatever they had to sell. I paused, hoping I didn't look as lost as I felt.

Eli could have turned off into any of the cross streets. He could have wandered into any of the alleys. He could be winding through the maze of homes that were not more than huts. I could see them, a block or two away from this busy avenue. He'd been gone over an hour by now. His long legs could cover a lot of ground in an hour.

I was due for some luck. And I had it.

CHAPTER FIFTEEN

I spotted a familiar leather bag, mine. It was on the ground at the feet of a hat seller who had a small stall at a corner. The hat seller, a handsome, middle-aged woman, sported a tattoo on her forearm. From this distance it looked familiar.

With no other clue, I had to approach her. I waited until no one else was near before I said, "Señora, I am looking for the man who left this bag with you. Did he tell you I would come?"

She looked me up and down, and I couldn't tell how she felt about what she saw. "So what did he look like, this man?" she asked.

"He is tall and has a flat face, with long hair. And many tattoos, including one that looks much like yours."

"The magician did tell me a young woman would be coming for the bag, but I did not think it would be one such as you."

I had no idea what that meant. "I'm sorry to disappoint you," I said, wondering if she'd be more agreeable if I drew out my knife. "But I need to find him, real quick. And I need to take this bag with me."

"It is a heavy thing for a woman to carry," the hat seller commented in a snooty way.

Again I didn't know what that meant, exactly. Time to be direct. I got money out of my skirt pocket and handed it to her. "Thanks for keeping the bag," I said. "Where did he go?"

"He started off in that direction," she said, pointing to the southwest. "He went in the little alley there."

I nodded, picked up the bag, and strode off. The bag did feel heavier than usual. Maybe it was just the weight of her disapproval. I took a few steps before I thought, *If anything's unusual, I'd better have a look. Grigoris.*

It wasn't easy finding a spot I could be private enough to have a rummage, but I arrived at a stretch of empty alley. I squatted and unzipped the bag. Resting on top of my guns was a piece of pottery, part of a broken jar. I was sure it was the one Eli had had in his hand when he was sitting in the courtyard.

I was blank when I looked at it. Then I smelled the magic. Eli had laid a spell on the piece.

I could only figure that Señora Snooty would have gotten an unpleasant surprise if she'd opened the bag and tried to touch the contents. And that made me smile, for the first time in a long, long stretch.

I touched the pottery, and a pleasant warmth met my fingers. It knew me.

I looked up and met the eyes of a man who'd unzipped, about to take a whizz against the wall a yard away. He grinned in a very nasty way. He jerked with his fingers, telling me to hand him the bag. I shook my head. My hand closed around the knife in my pocket. I hesitated because he might yell, and I didn't want to bring down the barrio folks before I'd even found my missing employer.

Mr. Whizzer's fingers jerked again, and when I didn't move, he caressed his dick with them. What a choice: give up my worldly goods or get raped. I threw the piece of pottery at him without a single thought, and he let go of his dick long enough to catch it. He had quick reflexes; worse luck for him. His head jerked back on his neck in a very odd way, and his knees crumpled, and then he was facedown on the filthy surface of the alley, his whole body all twisted, and he was dead. No blood. No noise.

"Thanks, Eli," I said. I retrieved the cursed object from the dead man's hand and held it in my hand, not certain whether to keep it or not. Could it be used twice? Or was it spent, like a bomb that had already gone off? But I couldn't crouch there thinking, I needed to haul ass. Being found next to a dead man would not be a good thing. I remembered the gallows in Ciudad Azul, and I moved quicker than I'd thought I could.

As I walked, I felt the pottery grow warm in my hand.

Maybe if it recognized me, it would recognize Eli, too.

I had no idea how to make that happen, but it was as good an idea as any other. *Take me to him,* I told the broken thing, by way of encouragement. *You can do it.* And I started walking. I wondered if it would help to close my eyes, but I figured I'd just walk into a wall.

I started to turn left, just to see what would happen . . . feel what would happen. Wrongness happened. Like when I'd been driving the car after the kidnappers.

Okay, straight ahead, then.

Soon I was deep in the maze of alleys. My mother had shown me a picture of a labyrinth once, and this was the closest I'd ever come to seeing one.

None of these passages were straight for very long, and huts did not sit square to the line of walking surface, which was packed dirt and garbage. Every so often I'd happen upon a larger open place, a sort of square, where there'd be a water pump or a burn barrel. Even though these people surely lived close to the bone and used everything until it gave out, a lot of people meant a lot of trash. The cleaner areas were those around the burn barrels. The barrels stunk, but not as bad as the litter in the pathways. I was real glad I had boots on. The hem of the skirt was getting dusty, and worse.

I could feel my lips pull back in a snarl. I like to be clean. But I realized I had more serious troubles than my creeping, crawling feeling of filthiness. I was being followed.

The knife was out of my pocket and back in my hand. I'd kept the bag of guns unzipped so I could dip into it if I needed, and it seemed that was a good precaution.

Might be kids, intent on robbing me, or simply dogging the footsteps of a stranger who might be doing something interesting. Might be yet another man looking to take whatever he could get from me, like the one who'd died earlier. Might be someone who had ambushed Eli.

Might be Eli.

I turned a corner and took a few steps. Then I flattened myself against a windowless wall. I was surprised my shadow was a little girl, but I grabbed her anyway. She was silent, even with the knife to her throat, so she was no typical kid; though she sure smelled like the kids in this neighborhood.

"Talk," I said in Spanish. She glared at me. "Where is the grigori?" I asked her.

The girl did flinch when I said that. She knew what I was talking about. "Why did you take him?" I said, hoping to jar something loose from her tight little mouth.

"Sergei has him," she said. "He will kill him if you harm me."

"I will kill you if you don't take me to him."
I didn't enjoy threatening a child. I didn't want
to kill her. I gave her the fiercest glare I could
summon, because if she believed I'd do it, we'd
both get out of this unharmed.

Lucky for both of us, she understood I was
desperate. "I will take you," she said, all kinds of
angry, and scared underneath it. "Witch!"

I laughed. "*Soy un pistolera profesional*," I told
her, right in her face. *I am a professional shooter.*

This girl didn't quite believe in witches, but
she'd seen someone get shot. She gave a short
nod, to indicate she believed me.

"Walk ahead. Don't scream, don't run, don't
warn anyone."

Since she was leery of shooting, I dropped
the knife back into its sheath in my pocket and
reached into the bag to draw the other Colt. She
flinched. "Go," I said.

At first the girl kept glancing back over her
shoulder. Scared I'd shoot her in the back, I
guess. She got some ginger back in her after a
few minutes of not dying. She tensed as if she
was going to dart ahead. I couldn't have that.
I was holding a gun and a piece of a jar, and
carrying a heavy bag. I wouldn't catch her if she
ran.

I caught hold of the girl's shoulder, and I
squeezed her little bones. I meant business. She
whined, but she'd earned the pain. Though she

called me a few names, she kept her voice low. Good enough.

The girl tried to lead me astray, but I knew when she was turning in the wrong direction. Finally she gave up. The piece of pottery kept warm.

In five minutes we came to the right place. It was a little better than the shanties around it; it had been made all from one material, and there were chickens in a pen. I noticed hex signs hanging all around the pickets. The owner wanted to make sure no one stole the chickens. The girl shoved open the door and practically leaped inside. She shrieked, "*¡Otro extraño!*" *Another stranger!* Then she spoke in a torrent of Spanish so quick I couldn't understand her meaning.

But I was right behind her and found I was walking into a situation I also didn't understand.

Eli was sitting in a wooden chair facing the door. His hands were held up in a way that could mean he feared getting shot, or that he was about to hit someone with some magic.

To the right of the door, facing Eli, was the man who might be my uncle, Sergei Karkarov.

When I'd tracked down my father and shot him, I'd been surprised at how fair he was. I'd even said, "Oleg Karkarov?" Just to be sure.

I still remember the expression on Oleg's face when he turned and got a look at me. Because our faces were similar, the nose, the set of our eyes. I'd seen all that before I'd shot him dead.

Sergei was another kettle of fish. He was shorter than his brother, and his hair was a rusty brown. He was a lot less good-looking, too. He held a gun in his hand, an ancient revolver, and he spared me only one quick glance. Sergei saw Eli as a bigger threat.

I thought of what had happened to the man in the alley. Maybe Sergei was right.

"Who are you?" Sergei asked me in accented English. "I saw you shoot—"

"I'm your niece," I said very quickly in Spanish. If Eli hadn't already figured it out, I might buy a little time.

"No!" Sergei replied in Spanish, pretending to be shocked. "My brother had another bastard?"

The word didn't shock me. I'd been called that by other children often enough. I took one large step and stood between Eli and him.

"It's okay, Gunnie," Eli said from behind me, oozing calm. "You can stand behind me. This man and I are just talking."

I felt a puff of disappointment at not getting to kill another Karkarov, but I did as he'd suggested. I was careful not to turn my back on Sergei. The hut had one room and basic furniture: a little table, two small beds, a camp stove. "What happened?" I asked Eli once I was behind him.

"While you were gone, I picked up his scent," Eli said.

"And you didn't wait for me," I said, trying to sound calm, like Eli. Now that I'd found him alive, I really wanted to hit him in the head.

"I thought the track would get too faint," he said. "I knew you'd follow me."

"I saw my gun bag." Completely by chance.

"I asked the señora to keep it visible."

Or maybe not. "What are we doing here, Eli?"

"This man is Sergei Karkarov. He has told me he is the full brother of Oleg, but younger. But he is not as frank with me about whether the girl is his niece or his daughter, and who her mother might be."

The girl's eyes were going back and forth. I had no idea if she could speak any English or not. I thought it was real strange that the bastards of the same man, but with separate moms, would find each other and live together. If Oleg and Sergei had had the same mother, the whole situation made more sense. But nothing about this was exactly up my alley.

"Did you ask her?"

"Until now, I hadn't seen her."

"Yet she'd seen you. She was following me."

"Interesting." Eli sounded cold and confident. Good.

"*¿Cuál es su nombre?*" I asked my uncle. *What is her name?*

"*Su nombre es Felicia,*" he said.

"*¿Es la hija de Oleg?*" *Is she Oleg's daughter?*

And I was glad that, since I was behind Eli, my grigori couldn't see my expression when Sergei said in Spanish, "Why? Are you going to shoot her like you shot him?"

"This gentleman wants to talk to Felicia, if she is truly Oleg's daughter." I spoke in English because I wanted Eli to understand what I was saying now.

Sergei looked at me hard, trying to figure out the right answer. He was still holding the revolver at the ready.

And Eli's hands had not wavered. I didn't know how much he'd understood of the conversation, since there had been a lot of Spanish and a lot of tension, but he realized that the child's parentage was in question. "I need to talk about this girl's future," Eli said, to prod Sergei into an answer.

This weird standoff had to end. I was trying to weigh the problem a gunshot would cause us against the itch to kill Sergei. Or I could throw the rock at him . . . if only I knew what the consequences would be. Would it blow him up? Would we get caught in the boom?

Felicia was just inside the door, her back to it, looking from one of us to another with a lot of fear. The door behind Felicia opened, and I had a sliver of time to think, *A neighbor's come to check.*

But it was Paulina.

"Felicia, move," I said urgently, and she understood my alarm if not my words. She jumped to her left, glanced behind her, and screamed.

I just about did the same.

The thing that had been Paulina was stained with blood and dust, her gummy eyes staring out of a parched face, her fingers ripped and torn. My gun was up and ready. Sergei's revolver was trained on her, too, but I don't think he knew he'd pointed it at her. He was stumbling backward to get farther away, as much as he could in the small room.

Eli said uncertainly, "Paulina?" He didn't know if he'd buried her under the rocks while she was alive, or if this was a revenant.

But I knew. My gun was out instantly. I shot her straightaway. I shot her five times. It was hard to aim because of the girl and Sergei, but I got her each time. She fell to the floor.

Eli yelled, "No!" I don't know if he was telling me not to shoot (too late on that one), or if he was protesting Paulina's ghastly appearance.

The thing that used to be Paulina kept struggling to roll over so she could crawl to Eli. I didn't know if she wanted to hug him or kill him. I was betting she was aiming to kill him, since that seemed to be the theme of this trip.

Eli seemed stuck to his chair, so I circled it as I

reached under my skirt to draw out another pistol with a full clip. I stood between him and the thing. Since it was still twitching, I fired into its head. It quit moving. I'd settled it. I took a deep breath in, expelled it. Felt calmer.

The child, Felicia, was backed against a wall, her hands balled up and pushed against her mouth. Sergei was wide eyed and speechless, his mouth hanging open from shock.

Eli's eyes were wide open. Tears were rolling down his cheeks. He didn't seem aware of anything around him.

I was disappointed, because Eli had been showing some grit. I reminded myself he'd seen what he thought was his dead brother a couple of days ago, and he'd seen his dead partner rise from the dead just now. I should make him an allowance for that.

A man's voice called from outside, "Sergei! What's going on in there?"

I pointed at Sergei, who understood he had to pull himself together. He made a big effort. He cleared his throat a couple of times. "Nothing urgent," he called back. "We had an intruder. The problem is solved." It was the kind of neighborhood where no one called the police after they'd heard that.

To my relief, I could hear the voices grow fainter as the people scattered. They'd decided it was none of their business. They were right.

It was hard to figure out what to do next. Sergei and Felicia seemed pretty much fixed in position and quiet, so I knelt beside Eli's chair. "Look at me, grigori," I said, and I didn't sound like I cared that he was crying.

He did look.

"I'm real serious," I told him.

Eli nodded.

"That wasn't Paulina. That was the same kind of magic that made you believe you saw your brother, you know that's true. I thought Paulina was dead. You thought Paulina was dead. Because she was. We know what dead looks like. Even if we'd both been wrong and we'd left her alive in the desert, she could not have walked from her burial place to this house without help in the time since then. And who'd give her a ride, looking like that? You hearing me?"

"You saying that's a dead woman?" Felicia said in Spanish. She had a shrill little voice, and I didn't want to hear it right now, no matter what language she used.

"That's what I'm saying. Shut up." I had always heard sisters were annoying.

At least Eli was not crying anymore. But he was not speaking, either. I hoped he understood me, and I hoped he got back inside himself right now. Every bone in my body told me we needed to get the hell out of Juárez.

"You're the daughter," Eli said, as shocked as if the ceiling had fallen on his head. Or as if his dead partner had just walked into the room. Evidently, Eli spoke more Spanish than I'd given him credit for.

"Yes," I said.

"You shot your father."

"He raped my mother."

"You shot Oleg Karkarov. The man we've been looking for on this whole trip. And you never told us."

"Yes. Can we talk about this later? Someone's trying to kill us now."

Eli narrowed his eyes at me.

"Yeah, I know, that's always." I took Eli's hands and pulled. I got him standing upright. He took a few deep breaths.

Sergei exploded. He'd been so quiet. I'd hoped he'd stay that way. "You little bitch, bringing all this to my house! What do you really want with Felicia?"

Jesus, I wanted to shoot him. I just couldn't take any more.

Eli said over my head, "I ask you again, whose daughter is Felicia?"

"Depends on why you want to know."

I aimed my gun at him. "No, it doesn't. Talk." I wasn't negotiating anymore. I was going to start shooting again.

"She's mine," Sergei said.

301

I glanced at the girl as he spoke, and she looked surprised. Well, *hell.* "Is he telling the truth?" I asked Felicia. By that time, I wasn't sure what language I was speaking.

"Depends on why you want to know," she said. I was *so* willing to suspend my no-killing-kids rule.

Eli said, "If you are the child of Oleg, you can return with me to the Holy Russian Empire, and you will serve a greater purpose. You will have a good life in decent surroundings. But if you come with me, and I find out you are lying about your parentage, you will serve no purpose at all and you will be discarded."

That was almost as bad as shooting her, going by her reaction. Eli's tact had flown out the window. He was at the end of his rope, too.

"What does 'discarded' mean?" she asked Sergei in Spanish.

"Tossed aside," he replied in the same language.

Felicia chewed on her lip, while I pulled on Eli, trying to get him to the door. *Go, go, go,* my brain was chanting.

Eli was still knocked down with the shock of Paulina's appearance. (Or maybe with knowing I'd been lying to him from the beginning. Though why he would expect anything else, I couldn't figure. But I felt guilty.)

"Give my friend a drink," I said to Sergei, and he turned to get a bottle off a shelf. I could see when he considered hitting me with it, I could see him weighing the gun in my hand against his longer reach and his speed, and I could see him decide against attacking me. He opened the bottle and passed it over to Eli, who took a big swallow, then another.

After a moment Eli's legs worked. He was able to move with me pulling and supporting him. He was so heavy, so tall. I groaned but tried to keep it quiet.

"Go with us, or stay?" Eli asked Felicia. "You can choose. I will not force you. I should not have frightened you."

Felicia gave Sergei a glance that was all one big question.

"Whatever you wish," he said, a cruel burden to lay on someone so young.

"I will stay here," she said, making up her mind. She glared at us, all bravado. "Go to hell, you two gringos."

"Felicia," I said. "If you change your mind, meet us tomorrow at the train station. I think we'll try to catch a train out of here."

After a moment Felicia's head moved in a jerky nod. I realized the girl, my cousin or my sister, was terrified of the choices in front of her, no matter how angry she tried to seem.

We began to move awkwardly toward the door. I felt like a building was leaning against my shoulder. "It would sure help if you could walk on your own," I said, trying not to sound desperate. "But we'll figure out a way to get it done."

Eli stood free of me and took up his suitcase. He left Paulina's bag. I didn't know why he'd brought it this far, except maybe out of sheer cussedness. Not wanting Señora Espinoza to have Paulina's things. My little personal bag went over his shoulder. We were set to go. Then he staggered.

"Shit," I said. While he leaned against a wall, I reloaded both Colts. I gathered up my gun bag and put the long strap of it over my left shoulder so it'd hang to the right.

"Open the door," I told Felicia, and she leaped to do it. Finally she was willing to cooperate.

Putting my left shoulder under Eli's right armpit, my arm around his waist, we lurched forward, turning sideways in the doorframe to fit through.

The alleys were narrow and my burdens were heavy. I was as tired as I had ever been in my life. I wasn't happy about anything or with anyone. At least I hadn't had to clean up the remains of whatever had looked like Paulina. Maybe it had been Paulina, reanimated. Or maybe it had been a likeness. "Fuck it," I said, and Eli laughed like a coyote. "You're feisty," he said.

"I'm a gunnie. I have to be feisty."

"Where are we going?" Eli asked after a few

more yards of lurching. I was staggering a little myself.

"I don't know," I said, and that, too, was funny to my companion. I was glad someone was laughing. I wondered what he'd drunk. "What did your drink taste like?" I said.

"Like fire."

"Do you drink much alcohol?"

"I never have. We're not allowed." He laughed.

Things just got better and better, didn't they? "Eli," I said, having just enough spare wind to speak, "if we see any other grigoris, you have to kill them." It was late afternoon, so we had hours of daylight left. The only way we were going to hide was to find a house or hotel we could shut ourselves into. Eli was shocked, drunk, or a combination of the two.

"All right," Eli said, giving the top of my head a kiss. Jeez. "I will."

And he did.

They came around the next corner, looking for us.

They were as surprised as we were.

I shot the woman on the right—she was stout and old—and she went down with a gurgle of surprise, though it was a gutshot, so she was still alive. Eli withdrew the blood of the middle guy, a man with skin so black it was like coal. I shot the man on the left in the head, and whatever spell he'd had prepared went wide.

It was over in less than five seconds. I ended the woman as we stepped over the bodies. What was one more shot now? I could hear people moving around, and voices calling out, but the inhabitants of this corner of Juárez had retreated inside whatever door was nearest when they'd heard the first shot. They weren't coming out until they were sure the shooting was over.

We ran. It was awkward as hell, but we had to move fast. We were the most suspicious spectacle possible, we didn't belong here, and it would be amazing if we didn't have blood spattered on us. I didn't have time to check. We kept moving in the direction of broader streets and shops, the major thoroughfares.

Until I wondered why we were heading for the lights when we were really blood-spotted, dirty, and suspicious-looking. We couldn't stop now, but we had to talk about that as we moved forward.

"Eli," I said in as low a voice as I could manage. We slowed to a shambling walk. "We have to decide if we're going to try to find a hotel, or if we're just trying to find a park or something to spend the night outside."

"A hotel," he said instantly.

"Okay, great." That solved one problem, though I thought it was odd he was so firm. "Got any idea if we'll see more of your grigori buddies?"

"Maybe they're all dead. That was the biggest

team I've ever seen for any job." He didn't sound too certain, and I wasn't counting on us finally having some luck.

"All right, then, we'll keep moving," I said. We set off, sighting on the streetlights of the best part of town. Eli wasn't leaning on me as hard, but he wasn't letting go, either. It would be great if he could carry the bag of guns, too, but I wasn't going to ask him. He was doing so well.

"I don't know how come there's no crowd." Even if this was the kind of place where people hid from trouble, it was weird how empty the alleys were.

"I'm sending a stay-away message," he said. "But I'm getting weaker."

No wonder he was having such a hard time walking. Doing magic; being shocked several times over by attacks, deaths, deception; alcohol; and no sleep . . . "Keep up the good work," I said.

We were steering in a straight line, more or less. Surely a hotel had to be close. Maybe I could get a room without anyone seeing Eli. We could sleep and get clean and eat, all three things I wanted so badly.

But then we ran into the chief of the grigori hunting party. He was a stocky, bearded man in a dark suit, and his face was covered with ink. He was waiting for his crew to return triumphant, I guessed. Eli and I were the last two people he expected to see.

It was also lucky that he looked at me first, so he didn't recognize Eli for one important second. In that second I stabbed him. But as he was falling, he opened his hand, and something terrible happened to me. I felt a huge blow. I saw the ground getting closer. I didn't pass out completely, which was a pleasant surprise. Lately, I'd been unconscious way too often. But it would have been nice to be out of it for the next half hour or so. I was aware that a man in a grubby shirt was looking at me with the leer of someone who thought I was about to be taken advantage of, and I felt stairs under my feet, and I felt the huge relief of seeing a bed, being able to fall on it, having a soft surface under my back.

CHAPTER SIXTEEN

When I woke up for real, it was hours later. I could tell by the feel of the night.

It hadn't been only a happy dream. I really was on a bed in a large room. There was a ceiling fan, and it was rotating in a lazy circle. I was glad of the cool air moving over me. I glanced to the right, to see a dark window. It felt like past midnight.

Eli was lying beside me, sound asleep. The bed was so big we weren't even touching. His nose was pointed straight up at the ceiling. He was breathing so quietly that I put my hand on his chest to make sure it was rising and falling. His eyes opened and slewed toward me.

"You lived," he said with groggy relief.

"You kill that guy?"

"I finished what you started."

"What did you do with him?"

"Left him where he lay. No choice. We had to get out of there."

I thought this over. "I don't remember much after that. How did you get me here?" I asked, because I couldn't imagine.

"Hell if I know. I had bag straps hanging all over me, and I hooked my hands under your arms and just started dragging. I didn't stop for anything, and I couldn't focus on my magic anymore, and I think people were asking me questions. I just said I didn't speak Spanish, that we'd been attacked by a grigori for no reason. They were glad to believe that. Some of them offered to help me carry you. I said no thanks."

"Nice of them," I said, finding I wasn't sure if I was awake or dreaming.

"It was. But inconvenient. I told them we were close to home, and our mother would be very angry if we asked others for help. Eventually we were on a halfway-lit street, and the first hotel I came to—this one—I told them you were dead drunk and asked them if I could get a room where you could sleep it off. It's a pretty fancy place, but when I showed them the money, the bellboy and the desk clerk agreed to accept us, since they had an empty room. They took extra money in case you puked, but the desk guy helped me get you up the stairs. Then I got him to forget what we looked like. Magic, not money."

That was a lot of talk for Eli. "What did he do to me? The grigori?"

"A stunning spell. He didn't want to kill you, or maybe it was me he was aiming for. How did it feel?" he asked with professional interest.

"Giant hammer."

"Lucky it didn't strike you over your heart. It

would have stopped it beating, whether he meant to kill you or not."

"Yeah. I'm really lucky."

He moved a little. I could hear his hair dragging along his pillow. "I feel you are being sarcastic." He sounded almost playful.

"You're real smart."

"Very sarcastic."

"What do you intend to do?" I was tired of dreading the question.

"Intend to do? I intend to help you to get us out of Mexico. I hope I never come back here."

That hadn't been the question I was asking, but I would go with it. "But the bad stuff has been due to the people after you, and they could be anywhere."

"You're right. You're nearly always right," he said. He didn't sound happy about it.

"I should have told you about my father. I didn't like Paulina, and she didn't like me. She would have hauled me off to Holy Russia without a second thought. And taken all my blood."

"That's what you thought she would do." He didn't seem shocked or angry, though.

"I sure did."

"I think you're right." It was a big admission.

"So, what about you? You going to tell your wizard buddies about my blood?" I should have been ready to kill him, but instead I only felt tired.

"I am not Paulina. But I know my duty. You're sure you are the daughter of Oleg Karkarov?"

"I'm sure. That's why I killed him." It was oddly cozy, talking (finally) frankly to Eli in the quiet of the dim, twilit room. The ceiling fan was making the open curtains ripple.

"You shot your own father."

"He raped my mother and left her to raise me on her own."

"Did he ever know she was pregnant?" Eli said.

"Why would he care? He raped her. A ten-minute relationship."

Eli rolled to his side to look at me. "I don't know how to feel about you."

"I've saved your life about ten times." I was arguing my own case. But without a lot of passion. "I did lie to you." I would have shrugged, but lying down, that just felt strange.

"True."

"You've saved my life maybe three times? And you lied to me, too."

"Also true. Wait, how have I lied to you?" Eli had the gall to sound indignant.

"You knew there were people who didn't want you to find the blood the tsar needs, people who don't want him on the throne." I looked up at the fan, just able to make out the shape of the blades. The city was quieter, but it was not completely asleep. Somewhere blocks away, a band was making music. "A group that backs this Grand Duke Alexander. And they're passionate about thinking he'd be better for the job than Alexei, because he has a guaranteed backup in his legitimate son, who already has a male heir."

"It didn't seem necessary to draw you into our politics."

"Didn't seem necessary to draw you into my personal life."

"You have a point?" he asked. Not sharp, but curious.

"Yeah. I want to take off my clothes and kiss you."

"I have no problem with that. At all." And he began taking off his clothes first. "That's why I wanted to find a hotel."

"Give me a minute to feel clean." I wasn't going to kiss anyone feeling this grimy and nasty. Eli had already removed my boots and socks. I got up and struggled out of the damn skirt and blouse and my underwear.

"Look," Eli said, smiling, and pointed to his left. "Open that door."

I did, because I wanted to see what had made him smile. I looked back at him lying on the bed. "Oh, Eli . . . that's amazing." We had our own bathroom. No going out in the hall. There was a shower, a toilet, and a sink. Everything! I turned on the water after a careful examination of the handles, and in no time I was under a torrent of water. It was blissful, and I was clean in two minutes.

"Leave the water running," Eli called.

I stepped out and began toweling, and he came in naked to take my place under the water.

Eli, dressed, was flat-faced and hard and gawky. Eli naked was a god with broad shoulders, a neat patch of hair between his nipples and one around his dick, and muscular thighs and arms. He had a fine ass, too. I thought my mouth would water.

Three minutes later a damp Eli slid into the bed beside me, very ready.

I'd seen a nitwit use gasoline to set a fire, and I'd been impressed by the result. That was what touching Eli was like. Despite our battered condition and our wounds and our weariness, this was what we were supposed to be doing. He had a few rubbers, which just proved men were natural optimists when it came to opportunity.

Hey, I'm going down into Mexico with my big-sister grigori, and we're traveling through hick towns on a desperate secret mission. I may get killed. But who knows? I might also have a chance to have sex.

I'd had sex with two other men. This was nothing like that, like them. Galilee had told me the way sex should be: all in, shameless, demanding and giving. This was all that . . . and it was with Eli. The combination set me off like a shotgun. I have always been a quiet person, but I was not this night, and neither was Eli.

After an hour we were asleep before we'd pulled the cover up all the way. Eli woke me up a couple of hours later, and we did it again, slowly. I climbed on top; I am short, and it was like riding a horse, a bit. I had to bite my lips to keep quiet. He made a sound so primal I thought he'd sprout hair all over.

When we finally got moving around noon the next day, I was saddlesore but happy. And more relaxed than I'd been in . . . forever. Every time I looked at Eli, I thought of how he'd been in bed. How we'd been together.

It was sad that we had more important things to do. While Eli dressed, I thought about the day ahead of us, or what remained of it.

It was just barely possible my uncle and my tough little cousin would send someone after us for revenge, but I doubted it. Felicia was too little, Sergei was too afraid, and they were too poor. If I were them, I'd just be glad I was gone.

Sergei might decide he'd try to sell the girl to me, persuade her she'd have a great adventure in the Holy Russian Empire. That would be more in character. But Felicia seemed pretty damn stubborn. I wasn't worried about dealing with them, if we did.

Our real danger lay in the other camp of grigoris. If there were any left, and I hoped there weren't, they'd be searching Juárez for us now. Maybe, before we killed him, the head guy had already called for reinforcements. After all, the rate of attrition was high. And we hadn't traced them to Belinda Trotter, whose role in this I surely didn't understand.

Eli glanced at me out of the corner of his eye as he pulled on his pants. I thought he felt a little shy. That was kind of funny, because he'd seen me upside, downside, and from every angle.

"Did you know the circumstances of your birth all along?" Eli asked.

That was the last thing I'd expected to hear. "Pretty much, because other people were always pointing it out to me."

Eli looked shocked.

"Yeah, kind, huh? So I learned pretty early what 'bastard' meant, and even 'half-breed.' But my grandparents held their heads up, my mom became a teacher and held her head up, and I learned to hold my head up, too. And when I grew up, I took care of the problem."

Eli shook his head, his long hair sliding along his shoulders. It looked good, and I had to yank my mind back to the conversation. "Did you ever think about talking to him, asking him . . . anything? For example, if he'd known about you?"

"No," I said honestly. "I never did. My mom would have told me if she'd let him know she had a bun in the oven." If there was one person in the world I trusted, it was my mother.

"It is a wonder you could stand to do all this," he said, kind of waving his hand at the bed, "with a wizard. After that."

"I think it's pretty amazing myself. But at the moment it was what we needed to do. Right?"

"Yes, very much." Eli turned away to tie his boots, but he was smiling. He seemed more at ease. It came to me that Eli had felt uncomfortable because he'd been so personal with me . . . and yet he didn't know me very well. So he'd felt obliged to learn my life's history.

I'd thought he already knew most of it. It wasn't like there'd been a lot.

I didn't feel the same obligation to read the book of Eli. I had been learning Eli the whole trip. I didn't need to know his favorite color. I did need to know if I could trust him. Knowing what his dick looked like did not change that.

By the time we'd repacked, and I'd put on the skirt again—it looked surprisingly clean, and I'd traded the blood-speckled blouse for one of my shirts—we needed to eat. The desk clerk was surprised to see us walk out the door, since Eli had made him forget us. But he was a practical man, and distinctly relieved that we looked respectable—if mismatched. Eli told him we were keeping the room another night and paid up front.

And then Eli spelled him to forget what we looked like.

In the street we looked around carefully. Eli finally seemed as alert as I could ever wish. He even remembered to check the roofline. It was a relief to notice Eli was not the only tall, fair person in the vicinity. We were at the edge of as well-to-do an area as this city could boast. Here, at least, Ciudad Juárez had a sizeable mixed population of Anglos and Mexicans.

The sun hadn't yet reached scorch level, so people were still moving at a fairly brisk pace. There was an open-air restaurant on the next corner, canvas stretched between poles to form an awning, with the kitchen at the rear. We sat at a free table right by the kitchen so we'd be less visible. There was a gun in my lap, hidden by the table. I carried what could pass for a woman's handbag, and it was open, with my favorite knife hilt-up. The waiter appeared promptly, not blinking an eye at us, and we ordered everything we could think of. The orange juice was wonderful, and I got a second glass. We had eggs and toast and bacon. It was as peaceful a meal as any I'd eaten with Eli. It was also no place to talk about anything important. We concentrated on the food and on keeping a lookout. This must be what deer felt like, I thought, when they were drinking at a stream.

When our plates were clean, we were still alive.

Just in case someone had spotted us eating, I stepped out into the open first. I had to shove Eli back. Apparently, now that we were bed buddies, he felt he should take the risks. I shook my head, trying not to look angry. "My job," I said, and he let me take the lead.

We also got back to the hotel without dying.

It was going to be that kind of day. *Brushed my teeth, didn't die. Stepped outside, didn't get shot. Ate breakfast, didn't get poisoned. Got in our hotel, nobody waiting.*

We were in the hotel room, the door shut, as private as we were going to get, before I took a deep breath. Now that we were back at the scene of our mutual crime, Eli was having trouble starting the conversation. He didn't know whether to suggest another go-round, whether to pretend it hadn't happened, or whether to tell me how much he respected me. I was not so conflicted. I wanted to get out of this place.

"Do you want to try to buy another car or do you want to catch the train?" I asked.

Eli relaxed visibly. I don't know if he'd expected me to drop to a knee and propose, or what.

I wouldn't have minded having a day with only fun stuff to do. We could have sex (more). I could braid his hair. I could find a dress to wear that was actually pretty. I could wash my clothes. Eli could charge his magical batteries, or whatever grigoris did to refresh themselves. But that wasn't going to happen, because I didn't think we had the time. Getting out of Ciudad Juárez alive was more important.

CHAPTER SEVENTEEN

B uying another car would be better," Eli said slowly. He looked at me, waiting to see if I agreed. I tried to look encouraging. "On a train we'd be trapped," he said.

We'd be a little *more* trapped. "Okay," I said. "And when we get a car, where are we going?"

"North out of Mexico, any way we can," Eli said. No doubt about that at all. "The quickest way we can, that's not the obvious way. When we get to a telephone, I have to make a long phone call to my superior in the order. Then they'll send someone to escort me back to San Diego, probably my mentor, Dmitri Petrov." He brightened.

Because, obviously, he'll be safer with another grigori than with me. I felt all the muscles around my mouth get stiff. "Eli, you live in a different world than me," I said. He looked confused. "How do you know whoever they send won't be on the other side? How long do you think you'll live?"

Eli was shocked. My heart sank when I realized this had never occurred to him . . . though people in that same organization had been trying to kill him over and over for a week. "Master Petrov would never harm me," he said, but he didn't sound any real sure. "He loved Paulina. She was his first protégée." That, Eli was sure of.

"So all the grigoris we've killed, including the people they hired, starting with Josip while we were still in Segundo Mexia . . . they have nothing to do with your Master Petrov? Don't even know him?"

"Why . . . ?"

"Jesus, Eli, someone had to tell them you love your little brother. Someone had to say, 'Go take a gander at that kid. If you make the corpse look like Peter, Eli will take the bait.' "

Eli was looking at me, but he wasn't seeing me. "That makes sense," he said, and his voice made me sad. Older, grimmer.

"I'm sorry," I said, meaning it. Mostly. "This is hard for you. But you got to get this straight." I looked at his face and pondered.

Eli hadn't mentioned two important items. What he intended to do about my valuable blood . . . and when he intended to finish paying me. That wasn't on the top of my list of things to worry about—but it should have been.

I tried to imagine killing Eli and taking the money from the car sale. My problems would be solved. No one in Segundo Mexia would think twice if I said the grigoris had gone back to San Diego. In fact, hardly anyone would blink if I said I'd shot Paulina and Eli along the way to Ciudad Juárez. They'd be sure I'd had provocation.

That raised another question. Did anyone back at grigori headquarters, whatever it was called, know I'd gone on this trip with Eli and Paulina? The two might have reported in without me knowing it. In fact, that seemed real likely. I'd be pegged as the killer for sure. But there was no way to ask Eli, *By the way, does anyone know we're together?* without being pretty obvious.

I knew already that I couldn't kill Eli unless he was trying to kill me. I was wasting my time considering it. And that bothered me. I should have been determined to watch out for myself. Eli and I weren't tied to each other, like Tarken and I had been. We weren't bonded by family, or town, or profession. We didn't have the same religion or the same language, even. Plus, he was a grigori. The only person I'd ever deliberately hunted down and killed had been a grigori.

I wondered if Eli *could* kill me. He had the ability, but did he have the will? There was a lot I didn't know about him still.

Eli made a little throat-clearing sound, and I knew I'd been looking at him for a long time, thinking my thoughts, not satisfied with them. "Are you angry with me?" he said.

"Angry?" After a second I understood what he meant. "How could I be angry? That was the best sex I've ever had."

He grinned. "Yes, it was great." He looked kind of proud—totally guy.

To my disgust, I found that kind of cute. "We're going to get out of this," I said, almost at random. I wasn't sure we'd both get out alive, though. "I'm thinking of ways to do that."

We'd have to find another car dealer, but that was the smallest of our problems. If selling the previous car had been complicated, getting another one would be even more so. I tried to make up a story that would be credible to a car dealer if I went in by myself. Not too many single women in Mexico could buy any vehicle, and of those few, not many would. Cars and trucks were almost exclusively men's territory. It crossed my mind to track down Señor Reyas again . . . but then he'd know too much of our business, and I didn't want to have to kill him.

I explained all this to Eli, who was sitting in the cane chair while I sat on the edge of the bed. "I'm trying to think if you could do it," I said. "Not that you couldn't manage it, of course. I'm just worried about raising suspicion or being noticed."

"There were lots of other gringos around this morning," he said.

"At least you don't have the tattoos on your face," I said. "Can you disguise yourself? With magic?"

"I've never tried." Eli looked excited, like I'd thrown down a challenge. I stayed quiet while he thought and (I guess) rummaged around in his mental magic chest to find the tools necessary.

First he became a dog. I laughed my ass off. But that appearance didn't hold long. He became the woman he'd left the bag with the previous day. That lasted a little longer. Then he tried being the proprietor of the hotel in Mil Flores, Jim Comstock. That appearance he could stick with. It made me a little queasy, watching all this, and thinking that part of this man had been inside me. He could have turned it into something else.

I shook myself. It was no time to think of that. In fact, I should *never* think of that.

When Eli had held on to Jim Comstock's appearance for five minutes, I was sure we had something good. Though it made me feel awful antsy, sending Eli in to negotiate made sense. I rehearsed him about what the dealer would expect: extensive haggling, criticism of the car, and so on.

Eli nodded (he was himself for now). He'd listened intently, and he was no fool. For all I knew, they offered and counteroffered all the time in the HRE.

"What will you be doing while I'm getting the car?" Eli was pocketing the money we'd gotten from selling the Tourer.

That was a good question. "I'll walk through this neighborhood to see if I can spot any more grigoris. Could they possibly know me? Do they know, back at your headquarters or whatever you call it, that you've got a young female gunnie?" I kept every scrap of urgency out of my voice.

"No," he said. "I was the one who called them to tell them we were on our way to Juárez, that we had a lead, and we had hired a guide and bodyguard. I didn't specify further than that."

I was really, really relieved. "That makes it easier for me to keep an eye out," I said. "Since everyone who saw me with you . . ."

"Is dead."

"Just about." No way around that. Eli didn't look like he thought anything real suspicious about my remark.

When I really examined my skirt, flattening it out by the window, I found a bloodstain that had been hidden by the folds. It was unmistakable. Eli promptly went out to one of the little stalls and got me replacements for the whole outfit— including a new hat, so I wouldn't be covered with kerchiefs. The new skirt, which fell to the middle of my calves, was patterned in white and red, the blouse was sleeveless and white, and the hat was broad brimmed, natural straw color. He'd gotten sandals, too, which would help me blend in better. Everything fit well enough.

"Thank you," I said, after a quick glance in the small mirror.

"You look pretty," Eli said, almost shyly, and then he left on his errand.

I was out the door shortly after Eli, locking the door behind me and stopping at the front desk to tell the clerk that we didn't want the room cleaned. I had too many guns for the taste of most innkeepers, and we might get thrown out.

The clerk looked very confused. I had to remind myself that Eli kept making him forget us.

It felt good to get out and walk free, and it felt good to stop worrying for a few minutes. I didn't spot a single grigori, and I didn't feel the presence of any. On the other hand, I did see my friend Chauncey Donegan.

Last time I'd seen Chauncey, he'd told me he'd been guarding Mr. Harcourt and Mr. Penn.

I thought it was real odd that the two Britannians were nowhere to be seen.

I wasn't with my charge, either. But I had the feeling I'd gotten when my mother took me to the river when I was little. I'd waded out into the shallows, on the stones worn smooth with the passage of the water and slick with slime, and the next step I'd slid into a deep hole that had been hidden from sight.

Cee hadn't seen me yet, or maybe he hadn't recognized me in my skirt and sandals. I stepped into the open doorway of a jewelry shop that had just opened. I stared down at a turquoise necklace while the shop owner began to tell me how much handwork had gone into it, and how beautiful I'd be with it around my neck. I smiled and nodded, but I was thinking hard.

Running across Cee here again, that was a real strange coincidence. Meeting him earlier on this trip, that could happen to any two people in the same profession. It was even especially likely in Mexico, where affluent gringos often traveled with someone who knew how to shoot.

I was clean out of the ability to trust two coincidences in a row.

I turned down the necklace with regret and drifted away from Cee. The best way to get someone to not notice you is to not look at him. And the best way to do that was to be sure he was behind me. As I poked along, stopping to purchase a cheap shopping bag and buying a batch of tortillas to put in it, I thought over our encounter in the bar. Had the men he'd identified as his employers ever acknowledged him? No. But he'd told me they didn't hold him in high regard . . . maybe so I would not be surprised if they didn't nod or speak to him. Was Cee more clever than I'd ever given him credit for being?

That didn't seem likely, yet the evidence was before me.

When a hand clamped down on my shoulder, it was all I could do not to turn and stab. My hand was on my knife. But when I did glance over my shoulder, trying to look only as indignant as any other woman touched by a stranger, I saw Eli.

Who still looked like someone else, but I knew it was him. "¡*Hola*!" I said, and gave him a kiss. I knew Eli was taller than his illusion, but I had to kiss the mouth of the illusion, right? It was so weird. "*Mi corazón*," I said fondly, and wrapped my arms around what should have been his waist.

"I completed my mission. And someone's watching us?" Thank God Eli was smart.

"Yes, *mi hombre viril*," I murmured. "You remember the old friend I saw in the saloon where we had dinner?"

Eli nodded, smiling down at me.

"I spotted him just now, so he's on our trail. I don't know if those two Britannians were really his bosses, or if he just pointed them out to make his being in Mexico more believable."

"What had we better do?"

"We had better get back to our room as soon and as quietly as we can. Then we can talk."

Eli, wearing his illusion, and I, wearing a skirt and a big hat, made it back and hightailed it up to our room. Where we took off our clothes as fast as we could and had sex, bang-the-wall sex. He looked like him, and I looked like me.

"That was the best feeling I've ever had," he said with a gasp, rolling over onto his back.

"Yes," I said. I was in complete agreement. We lay for maybe five minutes in contented silence before dragging ourselves back to the real world and our real problems.

"What do you think will happen if no direct descendant of Rasputin can be found? Besides me, I mean. That is, do you think the blood Alexei needs has to be Rasputin's blood?"

"We certainly tried a lot of other peoples'," he said. His voice was very dry. "And none of it made the tsar recover except for Rasputin's. When we could see the monk was fading, we tried the blood of his oldest child, Daniel. It worked. And that gave us hope. But then Daniel died."

"What happened to him?"

"A terrible accident," Eli said without expression. "He was swimming by himself in the tsar's pool when his foot got caught in a drain and he drowned."

I shook my head. "Accidents will happen." Unless someone was there to prevent them.

"There was an investigation, which came up with nothing."

"And who headed that investigation?"

He hesitated. "Actually, my father."

"Wow. That's an important responsibility. Did your family come over with the previous tsar's?" Nicholas, Alexandra, and their children had been rescued in the nick of time by a team of White Russians and the English. Nicholas was first cousins with the English king. But Parliament had voted to keep Nicholas and his family from settling in England, so the royal family and all its retainers had started roaming in a little flotilla, until the offer came from the Hearst family to settle in California.

"Yes, my father . . . owned an estate next to the royal family's. In the country. He and Nicholas grew up together. My father is still alive."

"Your mom, too?"

"My mother is my father's second wife, and much younger than him. She became an attendant to the tsarina when they went into exile. She was on the same ship. Any other suitable ladies-in-waiting had been killed, or were too old or too young."

"Were you born then?"

"Yes. I was very young. I had two older brothers by my father's first marriage. Mother was carrying my little brother when we landed in America."

"And she's had two more children since she got to these shores. Girls."

He nodded proudly. "Yes, plenty of family. Do you have any sisters or brothers? By the man your mother has married now?"

I shook my head, my bristly hair brushing his shoulder. He rubbed my head like it was a good luck charm. "Not a one. Jackson has a brother, but no kids."

We sighed at the same time, because we had to get back to the real world, where none of our family history mattered because we didn't need to get to know each other . . . because we were both (probably) going to die soon.

I was surprised we'd lived this long, but it was waving a red flag at fate to say that out loud.

"Okay, then," I said, sitting up and swinging my legs over the side of the bed. "Where's the car?"

"It's parked behind the hotel, you can see it from the window," he said. "It's a black Proenza. It has only five thousand miles on it, at least that's what the odometer says, and the mechanic I hired to check it told me it was in reasonably good shape. I'm not sure what that means, but he said the brakes work and the tires are okay. I had to accept that."

I went to our window and looked down. There was a little parking courtyard behind the inn. There were four cars parked there, a shiny black Proenza among them.

"You got a mechanic to check it out," I said, hoping I didn't sound amazed. I'd never thought of doing that. Of course, I'd never bought a car before, and all the people I knew who'd bought vehicles had been mechanics, more or less.

"Sure," Eli said, trying just as hard not to sound surprised.

Galilee had once told me she knew an early boyfriend wasn't going to work out because there was a difference between them as wide as a river. There was more like an ocean between

Eli and me. At least our parents both served their communities, my mother by teaching and his father by helping the tsar.

I'd been staring at Eli, and he was beginning to look uneasy. I had to talk fast. "That was a good idea. So the Proenza runs, it's downstairs waiting for us, and how much money do we have left?"

Eli sat up, too, and bent over to get his trousers from the floor. I tried not to think too much about the long line of his back, to say nothing of his butt. He rummaged in his trouser pocket and pulled out a much smaller wad of money, which he handed over to me.

I felt like his mom. I counted it, trying not to make a big show of doing that. But I had to know if the cash could fund our trip out of Mexico. I breathed out, long and slow. "This should cover us," I said. "For the distance we got to go." I tried not to think of the many things that could happen to eat up that money.

"I haven't paid you," Eli said, holding his shirt in his hand. I could tell from the way he looked at it that he was thinking that if he talked about money while he was putting on his clothes, it would feel awfully like asking a prostitute how much he owed her.

"At this point I'll be glad to get out of Mexico alive," I said. "If we manage to do that, I trust you for my pay." More or less. But I had to say it. I handed him the cash.

Eli looked a little embarrassed and a little gratified. He didn't have simple emotions except when he was naked with me.

"But I'm going to give you some expense money. You'll need it in hand, in case I'm not near when you need to make a purchase," Eli said, sounding very reasonable. He divided the money and set some bills on the night table for me, putting the rest in his pants pocket. "So what do we do now? Start out of town?" He felt he could dress now, so I did, too.

"Maybe I should find out what Chauncey is up to. I don't know if we can drive out of the area without someone noticing, now that I've seen him prowling. If he's watching, maybe other people are, too. Cee knows for sure I'm with you. Maybe he doesn't know Paulina is dead." There were too many things I did not know. I was trying to steer a course that would take everything into account, and that was impossible. "The thing is, I wouldn't have thought he was smart enough to have acted so innocent when I saw him, and now to seem so deep into the plot . . ." Imagining Chauncey caring about Russian politics almost made me laugh.

"Maybe he's just doing it for the money," Eli said.

"Exactly like me," I said. "I got a deep interest in this whole thing now, but I took the job for the money. Also, I had to find out what you and

Paulina were up to, naturally. And if I had a sister."

Eli's accent got stronger as he said, "I hope now we can be honest with each other."

"I hope so, too," I said, but I didn't have any surety that would be so.

I thought while I pulled on the new skirt and blouse. I didn't mind the sandals so much, or the hat. But after a couple of days I was getting tired of skirts flapping around my legs. I opened the room door, and I heard a familiar voice floating up the stairs. I raised my hand and Eli stopped to listen, too.

"You got a young gringo gal here, maybe twenty, with real short black hair and a lot of guns? My boss asked me to track her down to offer her a job, and I ain't had any luck."

"No, sir," said the desk clerk politely. "We have no one here like that."

"She might be with a tall woman and a man, older than her. Some of them tattooed Holy Russians?"

"I haven't seen people of that description," the clerk said just as politely.

"Lucky I blurred his memory," Eli said into my ear.

If we ever got naked together again, I was going to do something really special for Eli.

CHAPTER EIGHTEEN

We waited until Cee had left—and then a bit more—before we went down. The clerk pointedly nodded to us without looking directly at us, and Eli slid a coin across the counter to the young man, which appeared to startle and confuse him. I pulled my straw hat over my hair, tied the damn kerchief around my neck (which looked and felt much better), and prepared to step into the street.

"He went to the right," the clerk murmured almost as if he were talking to himself, and we went to the left without saying a word. When I glanced at Eli, who was a step behind me, I saw I was actually accompanied by Jim Comstock again. It gave me a little shock, and I glared at him.

"Let me know when you're going to do that," I said, and then I steered us back to one of the open-air markets and got a very thin shawl to drape around me, the kind that's not meant to keep you warm. It was just for pretty. Off went the hat, folded under my belt, and I covered my hair with the shawl and tossed the ends around my neck. It was red and green, and I was looking almost as colorful as the other young women on the street.

Eli said, "It becomes you, Lizbeth."

I smiled up at him and took his arm. We didn't look like an employer and his gunnie, for sure, especially now that he was Jim Comstock. We looked like an older man and his young companion, who was well paid and not abused . . . and, therefore, happy.

We wandered and shopped for a little, to see if anyone was paying attention to us. I was always on the alert. It paid off. We saw a grigori, a very old woman, walking through the driveway that led to the back courtyard of our little hotel. She had a cane and her hair was white, but if you peered under the brim of her hat (which was very like mine), you could see the faded tattoos.

"Shit," said Eli. "It's Klementina."

"She's . . . ?"

"She's the head of my order," he said. "And she's the one who sent me on this mission."

"So she might be here to rescue you?" I sounded doubtful, and that was how I felt.

"Klementina might be here to help me and Paulina," he said, but sounded even more doubtful than I had. "But she's not exactly a rescuer. She believes a good wizard should be able to rescue himself."

She would be awfully disappointed in the wizards we'd killed in the past week.

"Klementina preferred Paulina to me, by a large margin."

I tried to figure out what he was really telling me. "You don't want to approach her?"

"I wonder why she went to the parking space behind the hotel," he said, instead of giving a direct answer. And I figured that was an answer in and of itself.

So we returned to the hotel, and the clerk was luckily turned away from us, putting notes in the key boxes. Maybe it wasn't luck. Maybe he was making a conscious effort to not see us. Or maybe it was Eli's spell. We ran up the stairs as quietly as we could, and were in our room and at the window.

Klementina was looking at all the cars. From the way she bent over, I decided she was actually smelling them. Her hands were moving. She was trying to find out if a grigori had been in one of them.

Because there was really nothing to say, I calculated angles. "Shall I shoot her?"

Eli looked at me as if I had suggested shooting God. "She might be looking for me to . . ."

"Help you? Right, so why aren't you running out there yelling, 'Klementina, I'm so glad to see you'?"

"You are a sour person," Eli said. Now he looked like Eli again, and himself was being pretty judgmental, though there was a little smile on his face.

"Yeah, that's my job," I said. "I just want to

stay alive, and we have only each other to depend on."

"I am sad," Eli said, his face expressing that sorrow. I could tell he was expressing a new and deep truth, and it had made him a different person. "I see traitors everywhere, and I don't know who is for me and who is against me."

I said, "I just assume everyone is against me." Except for the few people I trusted, who all lived in Segundo Mexia. But three of those people had died less than a month ago. "And if you tell me what a terrible world I live in, I'll punch you. We do live in a dangerous world, all of us."

I raised the Winchester and experimented with the shot. "I can take her."

Still Eli hesitated. "What if it's not really her?" he said. "Or what if she knows we're here watching her, which is quite possible, and she is waiting for us to reveal how we are going to proceed?"

"All that might be true," I said. "Make up your mind."

"Hide," he said. In the next instant he opened the window and leaned out, while I flattened myself on the floor. "Revered mother," he called.

"Ah, good to see you. You have saved me from having to wait for you to come, in this hot sun." The voice definitely belonged to an older woman, but there was no tremor, no hesitation.

This Klementina had all her wits, and maybe more than her fair share.

"She's on her way up," Eli said. "It's really Klementina."

"How do you know?" I sat up and dusted off my skirt. This hotel was not as well kept as the one in Mil Flores.

"She used the word 'hot,' " he said.

"Code word?"

"Yes."

"No one else could know it?"

Eli shook his head. He seemed certain.

"And you don't think there's a chance that the word 'hot' would be easy to use in Mexico, even if she didn't know it was the code word?"

And then there was a knock at the room door, and no more time to think about what danger we were in.

Eli moved to open the door, and Klementina strode in. No other word for it. She glared at me, and I realized she was very sharp. Well, shit.

"And you are?" the older woman said.

Up close she looked much older, her face seamed and cracked like dry dirt in the desert. But Klementina's eyes were a bright brown, and her hair was wiry and thick.

"I'm the gunnie. Lizbeth Rose." I was too tense to be frightened, which was an advantage.

"And did you want to shoot me, young woman?"

"So much."

"What stopped you?"

"Eli says you are who you say you are. Though I'm not sure that's a good thing."

Klementina laughed. "And you call him Eli, eh?"

"What should I call him?" I didn't understand this question, or comment, at all.

"Where is Paulina?" Klementina asked, turning to Eli, as if one thought led to another.

"She's dead. She died in the desert when we were abducted, and they made her rise again to attack me."

This seemed to be a real shock to Klementina. Her mouth tightened, her whole face shut down. It was possible she might be willing herself not to cry.

"You must tell me everything," Klementina said, and she sat on the chair. Eli sat opposite her on the edge of the bed. I stood by the window to one side, where I wouldn't be easily seen. One of us had to keep watch.

Eli told the story of the last few days well. From Josip the Tatar, who'd tried to kill them in my cabin, to the clue we'd picked up in Cactus Flats, through the expedition and all the attacks since then. He concluded with the terrible previous day. Then he told Klementina how many times I'd saved their lives, until I hadn't. Saved Paulina's.

"I tried," I said, unable to stop myself. I almost added, *She might have lived if she hadn't been so intent on saving Eli,* but there was no point in talking about that.

"I'm sure you did," Klementina said, with no meaning in her voice at all.

"That wasn't her yesterday," I said, still full of anger. I hadn't liked Paulina, but someone had used her body in a horrible way. She would have hated that, I thought. Or she might have shrugged indifferently. I never knew her well enough to say, and now she would always be a puzzle to me.

"That was a zombie of Paulina," the older woman said, mostly to Eli. "It really was her body, since you say it kept her appearance after you killed it again. The simulacrum of your brother was a clever use of magic. The zombie of Paulina was an even stronger use of magic. You have a powerful enemy."

I glanced at Eli, who looked as though he was biting his tongue not to say, *I know all that.*

"Don't you mean, '*We* have a powerful enemy'?" I said. "Aren't you the head of his clan, or whatever you call it? So his enemies should be yours."

The sharp eyes fixed on me again, but I was not sorry I'd spoken. If Eli had such a mass of other magic people behind him, it was time for them to show up and help. I couldn't do this alone, and neither could Eli.

"You are very aggressive," Klementina had the gall to tell me.

"Yeah, I've been trying to keep him alive for a week," I said. "And it's been killing, killing, killing. And almost being killed."

"And you think I should put up or shut up?" Klementina thought using that saying was very funny, and she produced a rusty laugh. Neither Eli nor I smiled.

I kept my mouth shut. It was time to hear from Eli. "I need help," he said. "Paulina was a great wizard, very tough and more experienced, but now she is dead. We have strong opponents within our own profession, and it makes my heart hurt. And it makes me very angry. Gunnie and I are trying to get out of here, get home again."

"Why will you be returning, if you don't have what you set out to seek?"

Klementina might as well have slapped Eli. "It's not available," he said. "The girl says she is not the daughter of Oleg Karkarov. Have any of the other searchers found a direct descendant?"

Klementina looked surprised, just for a moment. I expected her to ask Eli a question, and from his face, so did he. But the old woman just nodded.

"It's not her," I said, and in the interest of silence I pulled out my knife and stabbed her, under her ribs and up.

Eli was so shocked his protest was just a sound

pushed through a choked throat, reedy and high like a bird's cry.

Klementina's eyes bored into me, and I felt the hate in her. But I had hit her first, and hardest, and her eyes dulled.

That's why I like guns so much more than knives. I was too close to her.

I pulled out the knife and stepped back and waited to see what happened. I am pretty sure that only the fact that we'd had sex kept Eli from attacking me. He looked from the body to me, over and over, as if that would undo what I'd done. She'd crumpled sideways to the floor, and I flipped her so the wound was up—I didn't want the blood to stain the wood. I yanked a washrag off the rack by the sink and pulled up her shirt, then pulled it back down again so it would hold the washrag in place over the incision. Not that she'd bleed much more.

Eli squatted beside me and seized my shoulder, turning me to face him. I really hate being made to do anything, and I yanked myself out from his grasp. He didn't seem to notice. "Why did you do that?" His voice was shaking.

"Not her," I told him. "She didn't know there were other teams of grigoris looking for other descendants. She only knew about Paulina and you."

Eli looked at me, the shock clinging to his face, until gradually he began to absorb what I'd said.

"How do you do it?" he said, shaking his head. "How do you kill so easily?"

"Easy?" Now I was the one who was taken aback. "You think this is easy? No, no, no. It's quick. But it's not easy."

"Do you pay for this? Inside yourself?"

"Eli, how do you feel when you take a life?"

Eli didn't answer in words, but he nodded after a moment.

"I'm not lesser than you," I said.

But this is what I'm good at. This is my job. And I have standards.

Eli still didn't seem to be sure I'd done the right thing, but whether right or wrong, the thing was done. "They'll come looking for her," he said. "Whether or not she really was Klementina."

"If she was such a great wizard, why didn't she stop me?"

That seemed to hit Eli right between the eyes. "Why not?" he said very quietly, as if to himself. "Indeed."

And there was a knock outside. We hadn't even heard footsteps. I was getting too involved with Eli's feelings to do my job. I drew out my gun and pointed it at the door. Eli stood, took a deep breath, and readied his hands.

We both stepped out of a direct line with the door. The body on the floor had not changed its form. A little doubt began to niggle at me. What if this really had been Klementina? But I pushed that little doubt down in the hold where it should be.

"Who is it?" Eli's voice was so quiet I almost asked him to repeat his words.

But our new caller heard him just fine. "It's Klementina, you idiot," she said.

Eli said a word I'd never heard him say before. He stepped to the door, grasped the knob and turned it, and stepped back, out of the line again.

And Klementina, in the doorway, looked down at her dead self.

"What an interesting situation," she said. "Who killed me?"

"I did. Do I need to do it again?"

Klementina glanced at me. "I certainly hope not. You seem to have done a good job the first time. Who are you, young woman?"

I didn't speak. Eli needed to step in and do some work on this situation.

"Klementina, what's your code word?" Eli said.

"Hot. But it's a bad choice for April in Mexico."

There was a long moment where anything could happen.

"Who's on the other team?" I asked.

The woman gave me a look that would have withered an apple. "As if I would tell you," she said scornfully.

"Tell *me*," Eli said.

For the first time the woman seemed to notice that Eli's hands were at the ready. "As if you could defeat me," she said, a little wonder in her voice.

"Tell me." He was not going to back down.

Her gray brows drew together. "You're serious."

Eli did not speak.

She looked down at the body. Then she came into the room and shut the door behind her. "All right, I guess you have reason. Benjamin the Brit, Anna, Andrei, Evgenia, Peregrine, Belinda . . ."

Paulina had been proof that there were English wizards in the Holy Russian Empire, driven there by the scorn and mockery of their countrymen, but I hadn't known there were so many.

"Belinda?" I said. "Would that be Belinda Trotter?"

Klementina looked at me curiously. "She might go by that name. She's a middle-aged woman, as nondescript as they come. Wears frumpy clothes." She sat on the chair, the same one she'd been sitting on before I killed her. I shivered. "Why do you ask?" the old woman said.

"This one"—and Eli nodded at the body—"didn't know that. Didn't know any of those names."

"So you killed her." The real Klementina looked directly at me.

"There have been people all along the way who weren't who they looked like," I said. "And I killed them, too. Though Eli and Paulina did their share." I didn't know what to make of this woman, but I knew she was scary.

"Of course they did," Klementina said, but she wasn't thinking about the death-dealing excellence of her junior grigoris. She was still thinking about me, and I didn't like it at all. Maybe I'd kill this Klementina, too. Killing the same person twice would be a real milestone. I dug my nails into my hand. My brain felt itchy, like this woman was trying to get inside my skull and rummage around. I wasn't going to let that happen. I gave her stare for stare.

Eli put his big hand on the old wizard's thin shoulder. "Klementina," he said, his voice hard. "Leave her be."

"Oh, have you found a sweetie?" she said, her voice dripping distaste.

"She's saved my life over and over," Eli said. "When it would have been far easier for her to save herself and let us die."

The old wizard turned her eyes on him. "But my Paulina, my star, she did die." Maybe that was what Eli had intended, to turn Klementina's focus on himself. If so, I was grateful. The relief of being free of her gaze was like cool water on a dry throat.

"Tell me about Paulina," Klementina said. Ordered. She was telling Eli, so I got to stay out of it. I was on my feet, but it was an effort. That old bitch packed a punch without even reaching out a hand.

This was the second time Eli had related our adventures to Klementina, and it was easy to think of something else. I kept watch, standing carefully to one side of the window.

Right in the middle of Eli's story, I saw Chauncey in the courtyard below.

It was weirdly like seeing the false Klementina only a short time before. I waved my hand, and Eli's voice came to a stop.

"What is it, girl?" Klementina snapped.

"Is this really my friend Chauncey, or is it someone else in his body?" If anyone could tell me, this old woman could.

A backward glance told me she was mindful of that compliment. She rose and came to the window, and I made plenty of room for her. I did not want to touch her. When I stepped back, I was against Eli's front, and I inched away to stand free. I was working.

Klementina said, "I can't tell."

I felt angry. And unhappy.

"But that means I do know who's behind this whole sabotage," Klementina went on.

That sounded promising. Knowing who the enemy was . . . that was a great step forward.

"Who?" Eli didn't sound like he'd been in suspense. And that was a big step backward. He sounded terrified.

"Your father," Klementina said.

I could have smacked him with the butt of my

gun, but I did not let my face change, because I knew the older wizard would see that. Eli was the only ally I had. I'd thought of him as a real young oak tree; he was a reed. But look what I'd done to him, led him on a wild-goose chase when I could have told him my father was dead and gone, and I was his best hope.

And look where that had gotten me. Look at all the bodies that had piled up.

I did not turn to look at Eli. When he spoke, he said, "I was afraid of that. But I could not believe he would sacrifice me. Gunnie, make me a promise."

"What's that?" I was trying to follow this, but I was stunned.

"If you ever see my father, kill him for me."

"Sure thing," I said.

"He thinks his goals are for the good of the country," Klementina said, strictly to Eli. Her voice wasn't consoling, but her words were. Maybe.

"He's a traitor," Eli said, and there was no give-and-take in this. "He owes fealty to the tsar. Anything else is treason."

"This is big news," I said without any excitement or pleasure. "But it doesn't solve the problem we have now at this instant, which is that a man I know is down there trying to find me and kill me or Eli, if we assume he's following the pattern of the past few days.

Chauncey's got a kid, and I'd just as soon not have to kill him. Can he go back to his right mind?"

Klementina gave him another, longer look from the window. This time she had her eyes closed. "No. The damage to his brain is considerable." Klementina didn't have any give, either.

Well, hell. "All right," I said, leaving with Jackhammer and a knife.

"Where are you going?" Klementina asked as I shut the door behind me.

"She's going to kill him," Eli said, though I had to imagine the last two words, because I was moving quickly. I went up the steep attic stairs—not far from our room—unlocked the door at the top, and climbed onto the flat roof. The next building was jumping distance, and almost level with the hotel, so I leaped over. It was easy, even with the skirt. I went to the far corner of the building, which gave me a different shooting angle. Hopefully, it would not look like Chauncey had been killed from the roof of the little hotel. While I was aiming, a woman in her sixties emerged through a trapdoor, stepping out onto the roof, dragging a basketful of wash. I should have noticed the clotheslines. I could have blocked the door somehow.

"What are you doing?" the woman asked with more curiosity than alarm.

"I'm sorry," I said. I hit her with the rifle butt. She went down like someone had cut her strings.

I shook so much after that I had to wait a moment before I could take up my rifle. I blanked my mind out. It took a big effort, but I managed long enough to aim and fire.

And then what was left of my friend Chauncey was gone.

I do not remember going back across the roof and down the stairs to the second floor and going to our room. The two wizards were at the window, looking down into the courtyard. The body of the Klementina stand-in had changed to that of a woman, maybe thirty, with raven-dark hair. She was still dead. I squatted to check.

"You need to do something with this," I said. I stood, just looking at Klementina.

"What's wrong with her?" Klementina just sounded grumpy.

"That was her friend she just shot," Eli said, but he knew there was something more.

Anyway, it was done, and it had had to be done, and I'd done it. *Hitting the woman in the head was better than killing her,* I told myself.

"We have to get rid of this body," Eli said.

"Do you have any suggestions about that?" Klementina said.

Eli glanced at me for ideas, but I didn't say anything. The body had looked like

Klementina, so it should be her problem, especially since she was supposed to be so all-fired amazing. Reluctantly I said, "Turn it into a sneak thief."

"I've never transformed a dead person," she said as casually as I'd say I'd never eaten grapes. "Transformation is Eli's father's specialty, not mine."

"What's your dad's name?" I said, looking at Eli.

"Vladimir Savarov," he said, looking off to the side.

"Prince Vladimir Savarov," Klementina said, grinning at me. "Eli is Prince Ilya."

I held on to my temper with a desperate grip, but my fingers slipped.

"Screw you all. I'm outta here," I said, and picked up my stuff and headed to the door. Just to show I had no hard feelings, I gave Klementina the gunnies' good-bye. "Easy death," I told the old grigori.

It was a great sound, that door shutting behind me.

The skirt was dragging around my legs and after I draped the shawl over my head, it limited my side vision. I could hardly wait to wear my own clothes again.

Now I had a whole heap of new problems. I had to figure out how I was going to get home. I had some money, courtesy of Eli—excuse me, Prince

Ilya. I had more than enough for a train ticket. I'd seen a few train signs in my wanderings, so I knew the station wasn't far.

At least the problems I faced now were my own. For me to solve.

CHAPTER NINETEEN

It was possible Eli would try to catch up with me, but I figured he'd be too proud with Klementina watching him. After all, he was the son of a prince. I could feel my face pucker up. I was disgusted, angry. What a slum dweller I must have seemed to him. What a convenience. And I had been that close to trusting him.

I got as far away from the hotel as I could, walking as quickly as I could walk, laden as I was with guns and the skirt and my small bag of clothes. I turned some corners sharply and waited to see if anyone else was following me, any of *Prince Ilya's* many enemies.

I was calming down. I felt uneasy, as though I'd betrayed my employer. My grand gesture of sweeping out had felt good at the moment, but every step I took made me more convinced I had only given way to my momentary pique. I should not have left Eli. But after all, he had the great Klementina to protect him, and he was good in combat himself.

He just couldn't shoot, and sometimes that was what you had to do.

I felt a strong urge to become somebody else. I stopped at a secondhand clothes stall and bought a different skirt and blouse, and when I ate a light lunch in a restaurant, I changed in its ladies' room, transferring everything in the pockets. I wadded up the hat and shawl and stuffed them into my bag, and I resumed the kerchief over my hair. When I came out, I looked different, but I did look like most of the young women I'd seen in this area. Paler, for sure, and my hair was still too short under the kerchief, but otherwise I blended.

They found me anyway.

I'd counted my money in the bathroom, out of sight of prying eyes, and I was sure I had enough to get to Sweetwater in Texoma. From there I could walk home. It would take me several days, but that seemed like nothing compared with the vision of my relief when I was out of this mess, a prospect so golden that it lured me forward.

I set out for the train station at a brisk pace. I had about a mile to go when I realized I'd picked up a follower. When I got a look at her, I saw a girl, younger than me, no visible tattoos, but wearing a city-type dress and low-heeled shoes. I wondered if we'd killed off all the mature grigoris, the strongest ones. I hoped so.

Since she was blond and dressed like a foreigner, the girl attracted a lot of attention on the street. A couple of men were trailing her, and they weren't being subtle about it. I didn't want her to get raped, and I didn't want to kill her . . . but I would if I had to.

I changed my course, took every dodge I could think of, switched back and forth between the hat and the shawl, and I simply could not shake the bitch. I didn't know how good a wizard she was going to be, but she was a skilled tracker. Then, after ten more minutes of walking in the wrong direction, of getting tired and hot, I realized Blond Girl was only the lightning rod. There was another follower, a boy who could pass for Mexican. He was wearing the right clothes. He was as young as she was.

He had a gun, too. I could see the outline of it under his shirt.

Time to work. I set about it with a grim resolve. I was so tired of this city and its crowds. Everywhere someone was watching. And surely, one of those people would be law-abiding enough, or angry enough, to call the police. I couldn't have that. Jail would kill me. Galilee had been in once, and she'd described it to me in a lot of detail. Jailers didn't like gunnies at all, and I could be sure that was true here in Mexico as well as in Texoma. Walking faster, I headed for a place in the distance, an open space with no roofs. I hoped that meant no witnesses.

When I got there, still ahead of the trackers by only a little, I discovered I'd worked my way into a section of the city that held the stockyards. And that was by the railroad, naturally. The fear of the animals was as heavy in the air as the odor of shit. There was lots of bellowing from the cattle, combined with the sounds of trains being shunted from one track to the next. Men shouted in the distance, but I couldn't see a living soul.

Perfect.

I went around the corner of one pen, ducked behind a bin of hay, and waited.

Sure enough, the girl reached me first. I had her before she could get her hands up, and she gasped behind my hand. "Don't bite," I said, in case she'd thought of it. I showed her my gun. "If you do, I'll tap your skull."

Her eyes were wide, but not with fear. I know what that looks like. I turned just in time to see the boy coming up behind me, his gun raised to give me the skull tap I'd promised her. I swung her around, the gun descended, and she was out. He jumped back with a cry of outrage, and I had my knife out, ready for a fight. Instead he turned to run. I tackled him and held the knife to his throat.

"Who do you work for?" I stuck him with the point of the knife, just enough for him to feel the prick of the steel and feel the blood trickle.

"I—I—no one! I'm just a thief!" The Russian accent told me that was a lie, even if I hadn't known the truth already.

"How did you find me?"

"You looked like you had a bit of money on you," he said, insulting me by hanging on to the story.

I jabbed him with more force, and he yelped. "This is the last time I'm asking you. Who do you work for?"

"Klementina," he said.

"Liar." He'd given that up too easy. Klementina was way scarier than me. Of course, she wasn't here with a knife.

"How did you know?" He believed I could tell he was lying, maybe by magic.

"Who?" I said, making him bleed a third time. I hated being this close, smelling his fear just like the animals', watching the trickle of red.

"Our prince," he said, and I killed him.

I got out of there fast. The girl was still unconscious, and I did not know whether or not she would live. But I could hardly stay there with her. She'd have to wizard her way out of her situation.

I walked quickly, glancing down to make sure I was not bloodstained. I was clear of blotches, though I was dusty from lying on top of the boy in the dirt. That wasn't critical. There were plenty of people who needed to wash, in these streets. I shook my skirt.

I figured out my route to the station. I could actually hear the noise of an incoming train. I was so close. I was leaving Eli (Prince Ilya, I reminded myself) with his new champion, Klementina, so I should have had a clear conscience. I had done my job, all the way down the line. I could simply buy a ticket and get on the train—which I'd only once done—and go in the right direction. Sooner or later I'd be back to the life I knew and understood.

I should have had a clear conscience. But I did not.

I looked around me very carefully when I got to the edge of the large paved plaza outside the station. And immediately the situation got complicated again. In the middle, right out in the open, I spotted my niece—or my sister, or the unrelated girl child. Felicia was looking from side to side, and she was very nervous, her hands clenched into tiny fists, her shoulders rigid.

Now that I was getting a look at the child in the daylight, she was short and grubby—like just about everyone I could see, really—and her black hair was dusty and needed washing and trimming. Felicia was darker skinned than I was, and wearing worn sandals, and was painfully skinny. I watched her from the shadow of an awning for a minute or two. The girl might as well have hung a sign around her neck that said she was waiting for someone, someone she thought might not come.

Very reluctantly I stepped into her line of sight, and her whole face came alive with relief. She hurried directly to me. I watched behind her, and no one else turned in my direction. Felicia threw her arms around me, pinning my skirt to my hips, and said "Sister!" in a loud voice.

"Hello, squirt!" I tried to sound teasing, happy, like I'd heard other adults sound with kids.

"They're coming after you," she said, very quietly, in English.

"I've already met a couple of 'em," I said. "Others here?"

"This awful old woman and your boyfriend, they're one street away."

"I think they won't hurt us. Others?"

"Yeah. Two grigoris, men, both grown up. They're following the old woman and the boyfriend."

"You did good, finding me to tell me." Felicia let go and looked up at me, beaming. "You are my sister," I said, "aren't you?" For no sure reason, I felt it was true.

"I don't know."

"Where is Sergei?"

"Dead," she said, her face an awful blank. "That thing killed him."

"Paulina? The zombie woman?"

"Yes. When he went to pull her body out of the house, her hand grabbed his leg, and she bit him."

"What did you do?"

"I cut off her head with a shovel, and Uncle Sergei, he told me to leave before he changed into one of them."

"And he turned?"

"I don't know. I got out of there. I locked the door behind me, like he said."

She could follow instructions, which was a good thing.

"All right," I said, though it absolutely wasn't. "Felicia, we're going to see how far we can get on the train. How long until it leaves going east?"

Felicia glanced up at the sun. "In less than an hour," she said.

"Here we go, then." I took her hand. "Let's pretend we're good sisters now," I said. "I'm letting you buy the tickets because you're so little and cute."

Felicia smiled up at me like I was a vision of the Virgin Mary. "Come on, then . . . wait. What's your name?"

I laughed a little then, because my sister didn't know my name. "I'm Lizbeth Rose," I said. I eyed her closely, but she hadn't heard of me.

"So here we go," she said, trying to keep the smile on her face.

"Here we go," I agreed. "How old are you, Felicia?"

"I'm ten," she said. "I think."

"Did you know your mom?"

"I kind of remember her. She was half Mexican, half Holy Russian."

"Was she a grigori?"

"Not like Oleg or Sergei," Felicia said. "Like your boyfriend."

This "boyfriend" thing grated on me, but this wasn't the time to talk about it. "So she had power?"

"She did," Felicia said. "She was incredible."

I wondered if the girl had any real memories of her mother. "How did she pass away?"

"She caught the fever. He wouldn't take her to the hospital. She died."

"Not much doctors can do for the flu."

"No. But they didn't get to try."

She was old for ten. "So you just stayed on?"

"He was my dad. One of them was. And there were women. Some of them were nice."

And some weren't. Well, hell. "Listen to me now. Whatever I say, go along with it. I don't have time to explain everything ahead of time. I want you to be safe. You do the talking for us," I whispered as we stepped up to the ticket window.

"Where are we going?" she asked, staying more on the subject than I was.

"To Sweetwater. That's in Texoma. See how much it is for four tickets."

Felicia put on a perky smile that almost made her cute. She began talking to the older man behind the grille in rapid Spanish, tossing her head back at me, laughing. She asked a question. He looked behind him at the train schedule, gave her a price.

She turned to me. Very slowly, in Spanish, she said, "It's fifty pesos for the four of us."

I felt in my pocket and withdrew the money. I'd put it in separate rolls of bills, so it was easy to count out fifty. I had very little left. I nodded at the ticket seller, who gave me a serious bow back. I gave the money to Felicia, who handed it in to the older man. He passed over four tickets. We turned away.

And here came damned Klementina and Eli. I did my best to look surprised and pleased, which startled both of them. Quite a bit.

"Auntie!" I said, and embraced the old grigori. She hated every second of my touching her. I enjoyed that. "I took out two teenagers over by the stockades," I said into her ear. "There are more following you, two grown men. Felicia and I bought four tickets for the train going east."

"Who the hell is this child?"

"Someone you should treat with great care," I said, making sure Felicia and Eli could hear me. "She is the daughter of the late Oleg Karkarov."

That hit home. Felicia looked up at me, her little face unreadable. I returned her eye contact with some force. I wanted her to stay alive. Klementina and Eli could protect her. If they believed she was the key to saving Alexei's life, they would do anything to get her to the Holy Russian Empire in safety.

Eli said, "Is this the truth? She was lying to us yesterday?"

"Yes," I said. "She was afraid of being taken from her home."

"How has that changed?" He was definitely suspicious.

"Sergei was murdered after we left."

"By whom?"

"Paulina." I had been hoping he wouldn't ask, but of course that was stupid.

Eli was staring at me, but he wasn't seeing me. "We killed her," he said finally.

"Not enough," I told him. "Just . . . not enough." And there really wasn't time to talk about this.

The departing train left with a great deal of noise, and the next train came into the station, shrieking and spreading gusts of hot air and dust in every direction.

"You have to get on this train," I told Klementina. "As soon as you can."

"What are you going to do?"

"I'm going to hold them off until the train leaves."

"Are you trying to be noble, like Ilya? These are trained wizards, and they will kill you."

"They haven't yet. Could be I'll get them before they get me."

"Very well," the old woman said. "I want a crack at them first."

"Be my guest." I smiled at her.

Eli was about to protest—he'd been listening to us with increasing fury. "I can fight," he said.

"Of course you can," I said. And I meant it. "But I can't get this girl to the HRE. That's why you hired me, so you could do this for . . . your cause."

As I looked up at Eli, his face hardened. He let out a deep breath. "Easy death, Lizbeth," he said, stretching out a hand to Felicia. She dropped mine and took his without hesitation. Twisty little thing. I thought about giving her a kiss, but that was silly. And her forehead was dirty.

"They are letting passengers on now," Klementina said, her voice harsh. "Go, then."

"They'll be here," Felicia said urgently, and tugged on Eli. She glanced over at me. With her free hand she pointed at an alleyway.

At that moment I didn't doubt she was my half sister. She had some magic in her, more than me. I believed her mother had had the power. The grigoris weren't in sight, but she knew they were about to come out of a side street onto the station plaza.

I handed Eli two tickets, stuck one in my own skirt pocket, handed one to Klementina, who glanced at it and stuffed it into her blouse. "Just in case," I said to her. I turned to Eli and Felicia. "Go," I said, jerking my head toward the train. "Now. Don't make me waste this."

I dropped my bag on the platform, pulled out

the Winchester. I liberated the Colt strapped to my leg, and pulled out the other one. I put on my little-boy gun belt so I could draw them fast. Every other firearm in the bag was ready.

I could hear people begin to exclaim, but I paid no attention.

I didn't look after Eli and Felicia. They'd get on the train. That was the point, the point of this whole damn trip, though I hadn't known that when I'd signed on for it.

Klementina strode a few yards to stand in the exact center of the paved area. She looked tiny and aged, but hardly frail. She looked exactly like an old witch, and she looked scary as hell. The plaza had been busy, with the shops all around and customers and train passengers walking rapidly with purpose. Now that began to change.

No one exactly shrieked and ran when Klementina took her position, but the people crossing the plaza gave her a wide berth, and the ordinary foot traffic began to slow and hesitate. After observing Klementina's Alamo-like stand and my guns, those boarding the train hurried to get on. Anyone with business they could postpone began to move away from the train plaza and head back into the neighborhood. It was easy for the most ignorant passerby to see that trouble was coming, coming real fast.

The train made its long hoot. It was ready to pull out.

"Alternate," Klementina called.

"Me first," I said, because I knew it would irritate her. And then the first wizard stepped out of the alley, and I shot him in the head, worked the lever. I put another one in his body to make sure.

The next one, a short, stumpy woman, ran out of a shop on the other side of the plaza, and Klementina got her with a terrible spell that almost decapitated the woman. I had fired at the woman twice, to distract her.

There was running and screaming. I like to work quietly, but this had never been a quiet job and it would not have a quiet ending. Where was the second man? Felicia had said two men were following Eli and Klementina.

The train was moving, with that chuffing noise. But not as fast as I wanted it to move. I fired a shot into the opening of the alley, just to slow down whoever was coming. I hit some stonework, and the chips flew, prompting a yell of anger.

Got a woman next, a fortyish redhead, who dashed out of the alley with blood on her cheek. She was furious and tough as nails until she went down with a bullet to the left shoulder. Worked the lever. Her right shoulder would have been better, but she turned.

Klementina paralyzed the man who leaped out at her (finally, the second man), but he got a partial hit, I could see out of the corner of my eye. Could not spare a moment for Klementina, who was on the ground but not dead.

Another man went down, and the Winchester was out. I dropped it and raised my Colts. Two-handed firing. Didn't do it often, but this time I had to keep up a barrage and it had to hit the target more often than not.

Finally, running at me with her hands outstretched, that damn Belinda Trotter, and I fired at her with all I had. Suddenly realized it was not really her, because there was no shadow. The real Belinda was directly behind her illusion, and when I saw *that* shadow, I hit her center mass three times. She went down hard, sprawled on the hot paving stones, and there was an abrupt silence.

I wheeled in a circle, looking for someone else to shoot. But there was no one standing.

The train had gone.

The police would be here any second.

Klementina was not yet dead. As I looked, her hand twitched. I went over to her, knelt. I realized I wasn't sure I could get up again. Tired.

"Here," she said, and made a hand motion and uttered some words.

"What?" I felt gray suddenly, gray and thin.

"No one can . . . ," and she died.

Well. All right. I stood—it seemed to take a terrible amount of effort—and looked around me.

There were other bodies strewn around, including a civilian or two. At least three of the bodies had died in ways I could never explain. Klementina had been creative.

Shit, shit, shit. I hadn't planned on living through this, and now I had to try to get out of it, when all I wanted was to sit down in the middle of the plaza and just . . . rest. In the sun. With no shadows on me. Yet here I was, a shadow myself.

Standing around being shadowy wasn't doing me a damn bit of good. I gathered all my arms and my bags and I went west.

For maybe twenty minutes I struggled to get away from the area. The gunfire and the screaming had motivated a number of Juárez citizens to seek the possible safety of their homes, but others were beginning to come out of them, creeping in the direction of the plaza to see what had happened.

Though I could barely drag one foot from behind and place it in front of the other, I kept moving, trying to walk steadily, to look like I was simply making my slow way home, or to work, or someplace else equally boring. I'd been hurt, not too bad. I could feel the place on my middle that seemed to be burned. Burns are lots more unpleasant when they get hot and sweated on.

I leaned against a wall for a minute, outside a cantina. The proprietor was standing against the wall, looking toward the plaza. His hands were folded. He looked right through me.

I expected him to gasp at the sight of me, or yell at me to step away from his wall, but he did nothing. And finally I realized that he actually could not see me. Klementina had given me one last present. I had felt invisible because she had made me invisible, so I could escape.

The front of my skirt had a scorch mark on it. Well, best solution for that was to take off the damn skirt. I would find out for sure whether or not anyone could see me, right here, right now. With no ceremony, I stripped it off and pulled on my jeans, changed the blouse for one of my shirts, folded the shawl and put on the hat, all in the space of seconds.

The man didn't so much as blink. I watched a bead of sweat creep down his forehead, wondered what he'd do if I blotted it with my discarded blouse. I didn't do that. I figured he'd been messed with enough for today, even if he didn't know it.

I felt somehow lighter in my real clothes. I was able to move more quietly, even with the bag of guns, which occasionally clicked against one another despite the skirt and blouse wadded in there.

When I came to a public pump, I was still invisible, and I filled my canteen after the child custodian looked away. No point in screwing him over, too. I took a long swallow before I resumed walking.

People would look around in confusion as I passed them, thinking they heard something but unable to detect what it was.

While I walked, just to keep myself alert, I wondered what would happen if the spell never wore off. After all, my mother wouldn't like it if I were invisible forever. When I thought that, I began laughing, and it wasn't the kind of laugh I liked to hear coming from my own throat. It sounded kind of crazy. I was really tired.

I kept on walking. No one called the police. No one pointed and screamed *She's the one!* or *Look at that blood!* And I began to realize I really wasn't going to get caught, thanks to Klementina's gift.

CHAPTER TWENTY

I was going to have to work out a way to get home. I could not return to the train station to board a train. I would be recognized and arrested. I didn't know when the spell would wear off. I didn't see how I could board a train while I was invisible. I took up space, and the trains were crowded, I'd heard.

And I had almost no money, due to my foresight and planning in buying tickets for all my good buddies, who were on their way to safety now. Or dead. While I . . . And then I realized I was saying Klementina was better off than me, so I shut myself up. Although it was true that Felicia was probably on her way to a life of ease, if she could get used to being bled occasionally, she was also heading off to a life among grigoris, and that would be an almost intolerable condition, as far as I was concerned. I'd never used that word in my head before, because people in Texoma have a lot to endure, and they do it. Calling something intolerable is drastic.

I had to make some kind of plan. What did I need right now?

I needed ointment for the burn over my ribs. I needed to wash. I needed clean clothes. I needed to dump the damn skirt. I'd lost track of how many I had in the bag. I needed to eat and drink and sleep.

Even if I could have afforded a hotel room, I was too bloody to rent one, assuming I could be seen. Now that I was calmer, I could see my skin was spattered. I like guns because they ensure your enemies die far from you, but the enemies had gotten really close today, and Klementina had killed some in messy ways.

Okay, that was the first thing to do. Find water and bathe. If possible, wash my bloody clothes.

I found a horse trough. It was in a stable in a suburb, and there were actual horses, who thought my behavior really odd. Maybe they didn't care for the smell of blood, or maybe they couldn't see me. How would I know, with horses? They backed off from the trough, and though a man walked by, I was able to see him in time to hold absolutely still while he was within sight. It would have been very uncomfortable if he'd noticed the water in the trough moving and investigated how that could be.

I wasn't sure how well I was doing with the tiny sliver of soap I was carrying in my bag, but I got myself as clean as I could. I cleaned the burn very carefully, trying to keep my fingers light over the painful surface. I washed the blood out of the skirts and the blouses I'd accumulated. I wanted to throw them away, but I might need to sell or trade them. I air-dried in three minutes, and then I resumed my jeans. Luckily, the burn was above the waistline. I felt much more like myself after that, and I collected all my things and found a spot in the corner of the barn. I would wait until my things were all dry, repack, and start out again.

I fell asleep.

When I woke, there was a short, dark man fiddling with a bridle under a lantern. I didn't move, hardly breathed. I had no idea what my state of visibility might be, a really strange state of being.

After a while he said, "Señorita, I have left some food for you. Please be gone in the morning." And he walked out of the stable with the lantern.

That was my stroke of luck. Now I knew two things: I was visible again (and that was a huge good thing; I hadn't realized how odd it made me feel, not knowing if I could be seen or not). And even better, he'd left me food. For nothing.

Somehow, as I groped my way to where he'd been working and found a plate with beans and rice and tortillas on it, I thought I might live to see home again.

I ate and was full. I slept for another while, maybe a couple of hours, and then I started out. I was afraid of oversleeping, and I wanted to be sure I did what he'd asked. Walking in the dark was not easy or pleasant, but when is anything?

I managed to get at least a couple of miles away before I gave up. I sat down to wait out the night. When dawn broke, I could see I was in the nothing that lay all around Juárez, and I began walking, facing the rising sun.

I had to think about something.

First I thought about Eli.

Once I got over him being the son of a prince, I couldn't figure out why I'd been so angry or why that had made any difference. After all, we'd lied to each other equally. And he hadn't acted like the son of a prince, though I wasn't sure what that behavior would look like. At least, he hadn't been all lordly or snooty. And he hadn't looked down on me any more than Paulina had, and she'd definitely not been a princess.

No wonder Paulina had had such an attitude about Eli. She'd made an effort to defer to or at least confer with him, when her natural inclination was to dominate. Respectful, when she would have enjoyed scorning him.

Eli had always treated Paulina with respect, too. I figured he had admired her skill, if not her winning personality.

So I didn't hate Eli quite as much after a day or two. Because we'd had some hours together when I had seen the real Eli, and he'd been a lot of fun.

It's no news that most men who want you will act completely different once they've had you.

376

This is a true thing. But Eli hadn't. He'd been the same person.

These thoughts didn't get me any food or water. But I felt like a more reasonable person, more grown up.

I would have given a lot to have a map. I was out in what I thought of as a semidesert. By the third day my situation was pretty desperate. If I was near a town, I could live. If I wasn't, the prospect was iffy at best.

There wasn't a town, but there was a little settlement, huddling around a well. Not exactly in the middle of nowhere, but just off-center. My arrival was the biggest thing that had happened to these families in weeks. A stranger! And a lone woman! Both things they didn't often see. They gathered around that evening and asked me a million questions. It wasn't hard to make up a bad-luck story, because I had one. I just didn't tell them the true one.

I had a mother in Texoma. I'd come south to meet my father for the first time. (They gasped at that. An unknown father! They'd never heard of such a terrible thing.) By the time I'd arrived, my father had died, and I'd had to stay with my uncle. He'd beaten me, burned my skin with a match, and told me I had to marry a man who was many times my age, with grown sons and daughters, a man to whom my uncle owed money.

So I'd decided to return to my mother, carrying

the guns my father had left me, his only legacy. My mother was sending her brother to meet me halfway. I expected to encounter him any day. (That seemed like a good safety measure.)

In the meantime, I would like to sell a gun. Could I have food and water and a place to sleep while I rested up a bit, and then be on my way? And was there any ointment for a burn?

After a lot of consultation, that was fine with them. They didn't want trouble, and a woman with a lot of guns might be trouble. On the other hand, the town bachelor proposed within two hours. With great regret I turned him down, because I hadn't had a chance to consult with my mother and uncle.

"Yes," said his aunt with approval and some relief. "Every traditional girl should consult with her family before she enters into a marriage."

At the end of two days of sleeping and eating, I bid them good-bye. We were best friends by then, just about, and I left them a pistol and ammunition. They were delighted. They would rather have had one of the rifles, but I pointed out that the rifles were my dowry. A very old woman helped me clean the burn, hissing in sympathy when she saw it, and she gave me some kind of liquid from a proper bottle, which might have come from a real pharmacy. It hurt enough to work well, I figured.

I set off very early the third morning, hoping

to get a good distance before the sun killed me. I had water and food, and they'd told me that in two days I would come to the village of Hortensio . . . of course, unless I missed it entirely.

If it hadn't been for the dog, I would have. I saw a dog trotting all by itself, and it had a purpose. A lone dog was not with a pack, of course, and that meant it was going somewhere where there was food and water. It was heading northeast, so I followed it. I had to pick up my pace to keep it in sight. This dog was really covering ground. I was sweating, and I had to fight the urge to sit down, just for a minute. I knew I would not catch up if I did that.

Hortensio was mean.

I was on guard from the moment I saw a man kick the dog. That dog had gotten me to a place where I could find water and food, and I didn't take kindly to it being kicked. Neither did the dog, which growled at the kicker. Who then shot the dog dead.

So I had both Colts out when two men decided to rape me right in the middle of the village, despite the protests of several women. I didn't know if the women were upset because they didn't think I should be raped, or because they didn't think their very own men should have sex with someone else. After all, I might be diseased. Or a demon. A lot of the yelling was beyond my Spanish, and I was ready to kill them all by the time a woman with a withered arm told them I had the mark of a sorceress upon me, and anyone who harmed me would regret it a whole lot. Forever.

I didn't know if it was true that Klementina had put some kind of mark on me that only people with magic could see, and at the moment I didn't care. For all I knew, the withered-arm woman didn't want me to shoot the men or didn't want the men to harm me for her very own reasons. She was clearly the village wisewoman.

After some tense moments a little boy was delegated to approach me and take my canteens and refill them. I was terrified he would not come back with them, that they'd drive me off into the wasteland with no water or food, but he returned and laid the canteens, full, at my feet. And one of the women contributed some kind of meat jerky and a couple of tamales. I literally backed out of Hortensio while the village people were having another huge argument, deliberately started by the withered-arm woman. She jerked her head at the path I should take after she'd yelled for a minute at one of the men. Whatever she'd said, she'd hit a nerve.

She was very clever, and I found myself wishing I'd learned her name.

That day I shot and killed a rabbit, and I ate it and the tamale. I saved the dried meat for the next day.

Two awful days later I knew where I was. I saw Ciudad Azul atop its hill. I got only close enough to find a stream, where I finally got to wash myself and my clothes. When I didn't look too much like a scarecrow—as far as I could tell—I used some of my precious money to buy some food from a vendor, and I sat down to eat it on a bench in the plaza. I was comfortable in the mild air because my burn was finally getting better. I ate every tiny crumb of food. As soon as I was through, I shook the dust of the town off my feet and got out of there.

After I left the outskirts of Ciudad Azul, hoping I never went back, I got a ride from a family crammed into an ancient vehicle, which was the most wonderful luck I'd ever had. They were on their way north to visit relatives, and they worked me into the car somehow. I was glad I'd taken the time to clean up in Ciudad Azul, because otherwise they would have been stunk out of the car. There were three adults and three children in this ancient Ford, and they asked me about a million questions because they didn't have anything else to do.

I stuck to the story I'd created in the nameless settlement, and they oohed and aahed like they were watching a film or a play. By the time they let me out, we were all good friends, and they wished me well and wanted me to write them to tell them what happened after.

By this time my Spanish was better, and I was so exhausted I could hardly imagine another day on the road.

But I had to. I had to imagine several days.

When I walked into Segundo Mexia from the south, I weighed so little my jeans would hardly stay up. I was as tan as I would ever get. I had blessed the stupid hat I'd gotten in Juárez over and over. I'd traded both the skirts for bits of food. I still had my guns, having carried them the whole damn way.

My mother cried. The only other time I'd seen her cry was when one of her students died of a spider bite. Even Jackson looked somewhat relieved. I could tell my mom wanted to keep me near her, but I wasn't putting any strain on her and Jackson, and after so long by myself, I liked that state even better. So after a big meal and a lot of catching up on the Segundo Mexia news, I set off to my own place.

Chrissie let out a yell when I passed her cabin. "You're alive, you're back! Hey, I let them in because they said you'd want it!"

I could only stand and stare at her. "What?" I was in no mood to be delayed.

"You'll see," she said, grinning. That is my least favorite thing, not being told something I want to know, because surprises are not something I'm fond of.

But I was so anxious I strode up the remaining

bit of hill, unlocked my cabin, and opened the door.

I had a refrigerator. I stepped back outside, to see the electric wires running to my roof. I went back in. The refrigerator was small and white and perfect, and it hummed. The refrigerator. And my bed was new and bigger. And I had an easy chair.

I decided to get pissed off. "He better pay me anyway," I said out loud. "This is not what I would have done with my pay." Because I couldn't have. I could not have paid for the electricity to the hill to be beefed up so much. I could not have imagined buying a refrigerator, of all things, though I'd wanted one very much. I could not have imagined having anything besides the bench and stool on either side of my table. And I could never have chosen the beautiful new gun belt lying across the table. The pay I was owed was in an envelope beside it.

And there was a note. I had a little trouble reading the spiky handwriting, but I worked on it for a few minutes. Eli had written: *I saw how you looked at the refrigerator in the bar in Cactus Flats, on our first trip together. I hope you enjoy it. I would not have lived through our adventure without you. I don't know if I will see you again, but I hope I do.*

I didn't know how to act. I pulled the door shut behind me and sat on the edge of the bed. I stared at everything. I'd come home, but it didn't look like home. I tried to get angry about it, but the truth was that my home looked a lot better. And this wasn't payoff for the sex. This was gratitude that he was still alive, and that his mission was done.

I had a lot of feelings, and I wasn't used to that.

Finally I put the gun bag down on the floor, and realizing I didn't have to carry it anymore made me cry. I pulled off my boots, my socks, my everything, and I got in the shower, which was also working. This was everything I'd longed for all those hot, dusty miles, when I'd suffered and sweated and thought about home. The kindness and meanness, the blood and hate and friendliness, the dying and the dead.

"It was the grigori," Chrissie told me the next day. I'd slept almost around the clock. She'd peeked in at me a couple of times, she told me, because she'd wanted to make sure I hadn't died and gone to heaven from the magnitude of the gift.

"He was here?" That was hard to picture, Eli back here, without Paulina.

She nodded, her pale hair swinging with her head. I could see she was pregnant again. "He come back after about, I dunno, two weeks after you left? We thought that meant you were dead. But then he went to talk to everyone in town, including Jackson, about the electricity, and after that things started happening like you wouldn't believe. We're all hooked up out here, and it's wonderful. Thank you!"

"Not my doing," I said, and she knew that was true, so she nodded.

"And then the men from Seewall's in Corbin brought the refrigerator and the bed and the chair." She glanced down at her cabin, where her oldest, Dellford, and his brother, Rayford, were playing a game with rocks and sticks.

"All at once." I couldn't think of anything else to say.

"Yeah, all at once, so it was good you left your key with me, because I could let them in, and they had it all done in lickety-split. What you gonna keep in the refrigerator?"

I had no idea. I shook my head. I was sitting outside my cabin on the little bench, working the stiff leather of the new gun belt, making it pliable, and wondering how my Colts were going to look holstered in it.

I glanced up when I sensed movement. There was a gunnie coming up the hill. "Get out of here, Chrissie," I said, and she looked where I was looking. She was gone in a flash.

Of course I had a gun with me, and I was on my feet with it before he'd gone another yard.

"I'm a friend," he called, real easy, and proved it by drawing and shooting. He was faster than anyone I'd ever seen. He would have gotten me if Chrissie's Dellford hadn't chosen that moment to throw a rock at him. Either by chance or by God, the rock hit his right arm, his shooting arm, and the bullet missed me by a hair. My bullet did not miss him. But it didn't kill him, either. He proved he was as versatile as I was by drawing with his left and shooting me that way. If I'd been where I'd been standing a second before, he'd have gotten me, but I'd dived for the ground, and the bullet went over my head, while mine plowed into his leg.

And he was down. Hit twice. Not dead.

"What the hell did you do that for?" I asked when I'd gotten up.

He just smiled. "Paid to do so," he said. "Plus, I didn't think no girl could shoot the way you do. Pride goeth before a fall."

"Who sent you?"

"Father of a man who gave you a refrigerator."

"Son of a bitch. That prince."

He nodded. "God have mercy on my soul," he said, and he died, bled out.

By the time Eli's dad showed up at the Antelope, which was a month later, I'd prepared for him. I figured someone who could hold a grudge and spend money on it like he had was not going to let the matter lie.

I'd had a consultation with Jackson and with the staff of the Antelope and with my mother. We'd all reached an agreement. So I knew the minute Prince Vladimir arrived in Segundo Mexia, calling himself something like Alex Budurov, but that didn't match the initials on his fancy luggage. Eli's dad arrived with two servants, that's the only thing I can call them. Both men, both cheerful killers. I knew that the minute I saw 'em, which was from a safe distance. I was standing in Trader Army's, watching them lounge down the street. They were smiling, and they were contemptuous of everything they saw, and it was going to be a pleasure to kill them.

Trader Army said, "How come you got to do this, again?"

"He got me to promise I'd kill his dad if I ever saw him," I said. Not for the first time.

"And you have to stick to it."

"Normally, I'd just take it with a grain of salt. Did he mean it? Maybe not. He was pretty mad at the moment. But this asshole has tried to kill me six ways from Sunday, and I think I'll make good on my promise."

"What you going to do about the hired help?"

"Oh, I got a plan."

It wasn't much of one, but it was a plan.

I walked into the Antelope that evening when the prince was sitting down to dinner. His henchmen were at a separate table. There was one other guest in the hotel, a gnarled little woman with a withered arm. She was eating with her one good hand, eyeing the prince and his men as though they were scorpions.

It had been hellish, tracking the Hortensio shaman down. I didn't exactly have clear memories of directions I'd taken during my long march through the desert.

The prince, it was clear, did not enjoy being in the same room with the withered-arm woman. She did not look like she had ever shared a space with royalty. She did not look like she'd ever worn a pair of shoes, for that matter. However, she was eating neatly, and she was intent on her food.

When I came in, I was disguised. I was wearing a green dress I'd borrowed. My hair had been busy growing. I had curls all over my head. I wasn't quite as brown as I'd been after crossing back into Texoma . . . or as peeling and red.

I hadn't put on the weight I'd lost, though. Maybe my fat had gotten burned off.

So while I was sure Eli's father had heard a description of me, that didn't match the woman he saw in front of him. As grigoris do, he pretty much ignored me. His employees looked up, gave me hard eyes, dismissed me.

If I had started shooting then, it all would have been over quick. But I could see the face of one of the cooks peering through the glass in the swinging door to the kitchen. They weren't supposed to be there.

I crossed the room to the kitchen door and went in. The cook, the server, and the dishwasher had overstayed their welcome.

"Sorry," whispered Don, the cook, as he threw off his apron. They ducked out the back door.

I had to refocus myself.

This was the man who had tried so hard to kill his own son, to kill me, too. He had killed Paulina and Klementina and sent many grigoris and gunnies against me, and I had killed them all.

I wondered how Eli would feel about me killing his father. But even if he were on the spot and voted no, I would do it.

Just in case I was killed before I could wipe Prince Vladimir out, I had Jacinta of the withered arm as backup. Turns out, what Jacinta wanted more than anything in the world was a mule. And she was willing to help me out to get it.

I had one of the Colts in my purse. I had another in the kitchen already. There was another pistol, Tarken's, in the dining room waiting for me. I'd determined the shooting order. Common sense said to kill the gunnies first and the prince last. But I'd thought about it over and over, and the prince needed to go out.

Gun in hand, I pushed open the door to the dining room, to see someone else had entered while I prepared.

It took me a second to recognize Eli's brother Peter, whom I'd last seen lying dead on a hotel room floor; Peter, who'd come back to life so spectacularly to try to choke me to death. That had been an image of Peter, but this was the real thing. He had a gun, too. But it was pointed at his father.

Peter opened his mouth to start talking. No! Never talk! Shoot!

To get in there ahead of him, I threw the small rock that Eli had given me so many weeks ago in Mexico, the one he'd said would help me. I had transferred it from pocket to pocket, every day when I dressed.

I hit Prince Vladimir square in the middle of the chest. His arms flew out, as if he'd been going to cast a spell, and he tried desperately to breathe, his face all twisted with the effort of sucking in air . . . which didn't agree to enter his lungs. He slumped forward, his hands clawing at his throat. Peter turned to me with his mouth still open and his gun rising.

The two gunnies pushed up from their seats, both with their pistols in their hands, one turning to me, one turning to Peter. Deciding without thought, I shot the one aiming at Peter, and I paid the price for that. At the impact of the bullet, I staggered back a little, but I kept my aim and got the second gunnie in the head. A .45 will take out a lot of head.

I was so angry. "You little asshole," I said to Peter with great sincerity. Then I hit the floor.

Eli was sitting by my bed. I'd known he was there. I was never unconscious, though I'd wished I was, until the doctor put me under. I'd never had an operation before, never been in a hospital, and I hated every minute of it. A different bed, strange smells, people coming in when they wanted to without asking permission, people touching me when they decided to. The anesthetic made me nauseated, which is just what you want after you have a bullet taken out of your side.

Now, two days after, I was real sore and real cranky, and yet here was Eli.

"This is too familiar," he said.

"It's the job," I said. "If you shoot at people, they shoot at you."

Eli'd gotten a new tattoo. I could see it on the back of his hand. It was still red. "What for?" I said, pointing at it.

Eli glanced down. "Protection against bullets," he said. "We'll see if it works."

"That gets widespread, I'll be out of business."

Eli smiled, but only a little. "You planned all this."

"I did. I knew he'd come."

"But Peter got in the way."

"He did."

"He's sorry now."

"He ought to be. He's okay?" The boy had been standing the last I'd seen of him, but I'd had my own fish to fry after a certain point, and I had not been in the condition to watch him.

"Yeah, but I'm bawling him out at least once every day."

"Well . . . good. Idiot kid."

"He's not that much younger than you." Eli's eyebrows made a point.

"Idiot kid, like I said. Hey, thanks for the refrigerator."

"*De nada.* Well, it wasn't nothing. It was a lot of arranging, what with the electricity and everything." This time Eli really smiled at me. That was better.

"The whole neighborhood thanks you. That was lots of money to spend. . . ." I let my voice trail off, because I didn't know what to say next.

"Glad to be alive to spend it," Eli said. "Now my oldest brother will have the pleasure of asking me why I sold off one of the family heirlooms."

"Your dad didn't know?"

"I told him I needed to make a thank-offering for my life, and he agreed that was the pious thing to do. He never asked me who I was going to thank. I think, somehow, he had the wrong idea the money would go to the church. And though he didn't know I understood who had tried to kill me, he did understand that the less we discussed it, the better."

"So you're okay with . . ."

"You killing my father?" Eli looked down at me, and I could not read his expression. "I am. I'd made you promise, after all. He tried to kill me, he would have let his gunnies shoot Peter, and he was a traitor, though he called me one."

"So what happened with the grand duke?"

"He knelt before Alexei and pledged his oath in front of the court. In return for his life and the lives of his family."

"Did you believe him?"

"No. He'll have a reckoning."

From Eli's face, that would not be long in happening.

"Do you want to know about Klementina?" I said. "Because you all had left."

"Tell me. I know she didn't survive the train station. I put feelers out to the police to find out what bodies they had taken from the scene, and hers was among them. Yours . . . wasn't."

I felt a little awkward, as though I'd committed a social mistake in not letting him know I was alive. But I hadn't had any way to do that; I hadn't had the money and I hadn't been close to a telegraph office. "Klementina saved me," I began, and told him the story of the train station and my journey. "So in the end I came home, to find out I had a refrigerator. Oh, has the baby come yet? Alexei's?"

"A boy. Healthy, so far."

"So that's good, I guess. What about Felicia?"

Eli smiled. "She's a pistol like her sister. In a different way."

I tried to think how to put it, and then I just asked. "How's she with the bloodletting?"

"We found one other descendant, a boy who's

sixteen, and she has watched the transfusion process with him as the donor. We don't want her to be frightened or furious. She is furious a lot."

I found something else to talk about, because it kind of hurt to talk about Felicia. "Your mom? How's she?" Being a new widow, whose husband had tried to kill her son.

"She's coping with the situation. He was not always good to her, and she loves us."

I'd run out of things to ask, though I had more questions. But maybe it was better not to ask them? I was out of my depth. I sighed and turned my head to look out the window. At least I had a window, though it opened onto a boring street, where the most exciting thing that happened was a mother walking by with her baby in her arms.

"My father came to Segundo Mexia to kill you," Eli said.

"Sure." That was plain and clear.

"And you'd expected that."

"Sure."

"Why?" I could tell Eli was a little delicate about asking that.

"Killers got to kill," I said, shrugging. "I made him mad, though I'm not sure how he found out about that; about me, I mean." I waited for Eli to tell me.

"That would be Peter," Eli said, looking away. "That would be my fault. I thought Peter was ready to hear the truth, but he wasn't. He went off like a stick of dynamite. He's more volatile than me."

I was assuming that meant Peter flew off the handle real quick. "So he had some kind of showdown with your dad?"

"Yes, and in the conversation Peter mentioned you, and to my father that was enough. He felt you'd thwarted him and his ambition, and he decided to teach you a lesson. And that would have an effect on me and Peter, of course. Show us our places."

"He came all the way here to get vengeance." That was some expensive grudge holding.

"Yes. Exactly."

"And I guess your brother followed him?"

Eli nodded. "Yes, Peter saw the receipts for the tickets, understood what they meant, and set off to follow Father, leaving me a note."

Peter was clearly rash and a man of action, even at his young age. I kind of admired that.

"So you followed."

"A trail of Savarovs, leading across the continent," Eli said, trying to sound light.

As soon as we finished this conversation, he would leave. "How are your brothers with this? The ones by another mom?"

"I don't know." For the first time he looked guarded. "I think they are on my side, the tsar's side, but I can't be sure. Speaking of unknowable . . . who was that woman?"

"Jacinta, with the withered arm? She's a witch woman who kept some men from raping me. She's really something, huh?"

"She handled one of my father's gunmen, who didn't die right away," he said. "She said something about you throwing a rock at my father?"

"It was the one you gave me," I said. "I kept ahold of it." After a little silence I said, "Did you give Jacinta the mule I promised her?"

"She has knowledge of things," Eli said. "I asked her to come to San Diego with me."

"What has she said?"

"She only wants the mule."

I laughed, and it hurt, but it was worth it. Eli laughed with me.

"Mom tells me you got your dad's body shipped out."

"Yes, I got it embalmed. We have to have some kind of service. And his servingmen, they were buried in the gunnies' corner of the cemetery in Segundo Mexia."

Mom had told me that. I found I was getting tired, but I didn't want Eli to go. I knew I'd never see him again. I didn't know how I felt about him, but did it make any difference? He'd be gone, and that would be bad.

Eli stood up. "I have to catch a train," he said. "At least this time I won't have Felicia with me. She nearly drove me crazy on the way to San

Diego. Never been on a train, never had a real bath, never eaten any of the food. She loved all of it."

I felt a swell of pride, though I had small right to feel that way. "You know you have to keep an eye on her," I said, by way of warning.

"What do you mean?"

"I thought later about what she said. That Paulina wasn't dead? But had bitten Sergei?"

"Yes." Eli was still sad about Paulina, which didn't surprise me. And it seemed to me that he felt guilty, though I couldn't imagine what he thought he was guilty of. He said, "She died trying to save my life."

So that was it. "So you should live to deserve that," I told him. I couldn't think of how else to say it. Eli looked surprised, and then maybe thoughtful, so I let it be. "Here's the point I want to get back to," I said. "This is all what Felicia says."

Eli looked inquiring. The eyebrows again.

"She's the only word we've got for that." Explanation finished.

But not enough for Eli. "What do you mean?" He looked almost amused. "Do you think *Felicia* bit her uncle?"

I shifted my shoulders a little. "Let's try again. My point is, we don't know what happened to him. Maybe what Felicia says is gospel. Maybe she panicked and shut him in with Paulina and locked the door from the outside. Maybe she . . . I don't know. But only one person showed up at the train station, and that was my sister, Felicia."

"I'll remember that," Eli said after a long and thoughtful pause.

"Well. Good-bye," I said, and closed my eyes. I didn't hear anything. I opened them. He was still there.

"It was great," Eli said, looking directly at me. "You're unforgettable."

Then he left.

By the time I returned home, two days later, the bullet holes in the Antelope dining room were all patched up. The gunnies had been buried. Prince Vladimir's body had gotten to whatever funeral service Eli and his brothers and sisters had cobbled together. It was all over.

I was frail for a while. This was a square hit with a bullet, and you pay for those. No matter where the hit may pierce. I took to taking long walks into the country around Segundo Mexia. I rented a horse, and I rode, too. I could afford to rest up, for the first time in my life.

My mother spotted a few white hairs on her head, and she had a fit. Jackson laughed. Mom decided to blame me and Jackson agreed with her.

After three or four months I got a letter from Felicia, written in English. It was in this lovely handwriting, and I could tell it had been rewritten at someone else's direction. Maybe Eli's, maybe a teacher's.

> *Dear Lizbeth,*
> *It is very grand here. I have four dresses and no pants. I wear different shoes every day. Already once I have given blood to the tsar, may his name be blessed. A privilege I have not earned, but my cousin Franklin got sick, so it was my turn. I was very brave. It made the tsar feel much better. I go to school every day and now you can see I read and write. I am the only Mexican here. It would be nice if you could come to see me.*
> *Your sister,*
> *Felicia Karkarov*

I smiled sometimes when I read it, and other times I frowned. It seemed silly and almost outrageous to think of making that long journey, a journey that would cost me a lot of money. I had the money at the moment, but I had to live, and I still didn't have a job with another crew. I'd heard there was one forming up in nearby Celeste, by a newcomer named George Ramsey. Maybe I'd go see him.

I was getting that restless feeling, and I was tired of admiring my refrigerator.

Books are
produced in the
United States
using U.S.-based
materials

Paper is
sourced using
environmentally
responsible
foresting methods
and the
paper is acid-free

Books are
produced using
top-of-the-line
digital binding
processes

Center Point Large Print
600 Brooks Road / PO Box 1
Thorndike, ME 04986-0001 USA

(207) 568-3717

US & Canada:
1 800 929-9108
www.centerpointlargeprint.com